MYTH & MAGIC

QUEER FAIRY TALES

edited by

RADCLY*f*FE and STACIA SEAMAN

A Division of Bold Strokes Books

2014

MYTH & MAGIC: QUEER FAIRY TALES
© 2014 BY BOLD STROKES BOOKS. ALL RIGHTS RESERVED.

ISBN 13: 978-1-62639-225-0

THIS TRADE PAPERBACK ORIGINAL IS PUBLISHED BY
BOLD STROKES BOOKS, INC.
P.O. BOX 249
VALLEY FALLS, NY 12185

FIRST EDITION: DECEMBER 2014

THIS IS A WORK OF FICTION. NAMES, CHARACTERS, PLACES, AND INCIDENTS ARE THE PRODUCT OF THE AUTHOR'S IMAGINATION OR ARE USED FICTITIOUSLY. ANY RESEMBLANCE TO ACTUAL PERSONS, LIVING OR DEAD, BUSINESS ESTABLISHMENTS, EVENTS, OR LOCALES IS ENTIRELY COINCIDENTAL.

THIS BOOK, OR PARTS THEREOF, MAY NOT BE REPRODUCED IN ANY FORM WITHOUT PERMISSION.

The Vain Prince previously published in 2010 by the *Ganymede Journal*, Issue 6 (Winter 2010) and *Ganymede Stories* 1 (December 2010). Both publications are out of print.

CREDITS
EDITORS: RADCLYFFE AND STACIA SEAMAN
PRODUCTION DESIGN: STACIA SEAMAN
COVER DESIGN BY GABRIELLE PENDERGRAST

Contents

THE VAIN PRINCE Andrew J. Peters	3
BEANSTALK Clifford Henderson	31
SWF SEEKS FGM Allison Wonderland	49
A HERO IN HOT PINK BOOTS J. Leigh Bailey	57
RED Andi Marquette	73
THE BEANSTALK REVISITED Rob Rosen	91
HEARTLESS Veronica Wilde	101
THE IVY AND THE ROSE Juliann Rich	111
GOLDIE AND THE THREE BEARS Sasha Payne	129
FINAL ESCAPE Stacia Seaman	143

SNEEWITTCHEN (SNOW WHITE) 　E.J. Gahagan	151
THE RED SHOES 　Alex Stitt	167
THE PRINCESS AND THE FROG 　Barbara Davies	181
THE SNOW KING 　Rhidian Brenig Jones	197
RIDING RED 　Victoria Oldham	215
BAD GIRLS 　Jane Fletcher and Joey Bass	225
ABOUT THE EDITORS	229

Myth and Magic

Andrew J. Peters writes fantasy and re-told legend. He is the author of *The Seventh Pleiade* and the Werecat series. A former Lambda Literary Foundation fellow, Andrew has written short fiction for many publications. He lives in New York City with his husband and their cat Chloë.

This story is based on "The Frog Prince" and the opera *Turandot*.

The Vain Prince
Andrew J. Peters

In the land of Evermore, beauty had a name, and that name was Adalbert.

He was the only son of King Heinrich and Queen Lutecia, who were widely known to have been matched to link the kingdom's two most prominent families, and in whispered gossip, to mind toothsome curiosities about the King. Nonetheless, on the day of Adalbert's birth, his father and his mother linked arms and stood at the towering palace balcony overlooking the grand courtyard to present their swaddled child to their subjects.

It was said that on that day, the sweet melody of songbirds carried across Evermore's vales and bluffs. Fallow fields turned green, and toadstools in the forest's dankest reaches surrendered their slimy heads and blossomed petals like shiny buttercups and hollyhocks. Squires, ladies, woodsmen, and dairymaids from every hamlet in the kingdom filled the palace grounds, and plum-faced, blond-haired Adalbert looked out at them, his deep blue eyes twinkling as though to say: "Yes, here I am."

The boy grew hardy in his childhood, nurtured by his mother and indulged, more accurately, by his father. At four years old, Adalbert complained that noise from the palace servants disturbed his naps. Heinrich had the stone floors carpeted and the sandals of Adalbert's attendants upholstered with downy cushions.

At six years old, Adalbert requested a pet porpoise. Heinrich ordered the palace moat dredged and refilled with seawater and sent his navy to bring back six dozen of the healthiest specimens from the Everblue Sea.

At ten years old, Adalbert openly wondered at dinner why he had never been asked to commandeer a mounted brigade. The next day, Heinrich assembled every cavalry and pikeman in his service so that Adalbert could direct mock battles in the palace's grand courtyard.

Under such an influence, a child is apt to develop a rather rich sense of self-importance, and such was the case with young Adalbert. He went through nursemaids weekly, daily in some cases, owing to his rigid specifications for his care.

He insisted on being addressed as "His Exquisiteness" at all times. Adalbert loudly protested deviations from his routine of morning baths in cow's milk, heated by wood-stoked cauldron to the proper temperature; and outfit changes preceding each of his meals (he never wore the same trousers twice); and foot and neck massages following any activity involving physical exertion from croquet matches to cribbage. He was frequently distracted by the sight of himself in his shiny bronze goblet and the glistening marble walls of the palace parlor, and he was known to spend long hours in smiling self-admiration.

Such behavior barely registered to Heinrich. His son was his pride and joy, after all. But as Adalbert grew into adolescence, Heinrich noticed, with growing worry, that his son had become apathetic, if not hostile, to the company of others.

One day, Heinrich returned to the palace to find Adalbert's riding partner stripped and tied up to a scaffold, the boy's punishment, Adalbert explained, for trotting too vigorously and splattering mud on his caparison. Heinrich decided it was time for a talk.

"A young man needs a companion," Heinrich told Adalbert.

"What for?" Adalbert twitched and scowled in protest of his father's shadow blocking the light for his midday sunning on the palace's southerly terrace.

"For companionship, surely," Heinrich said. He stepped to the other side of Adalbert's divan with his broad shadow in tow.

"I've nursemaids and servants to take care of me," Adalbert replied, the matter settled.

"Yes, but a companion is different."

Adalbert stared at his father, genuinely confounded.

Heinrich tried to explain. "Wouldn't you like to fall in love someday? And to have someone fall in love with you?"

Adalbert brandished a dimpled smile. "I've you and Mommy to love me."

"Of course. And we do love you very much, Adalbert. But your parents will not be here forever. A young man starts his own family. With a woman, or a man."

Heinrich's last words hung in the air for a moment. He knew his son well enough to understand his leanings. It is a very particular kind of boy who wears a felt hat and scarf to dinner, after all. Meanwhile, Adalbert looked no more enchanted by the conversation.

"I don't see the point in it," he said. "Look at you and Mommy. You hardly see each other. You sleep in separate bedrooms."

At this, the King shifted his weight. He knew that Adalbert would someday reach an age when he would perceive the truth about his parents' relationship. But it was all the more reason for Heinrich to press the matter with his son. He could abide his own mistakes, but he would never forgive himself if Adalbert repeated them.

"And so you shall have more than me and Mommy," Heinrich said. "A true soul mate. Romance. *Sensuality*. These are life's greatest joys."

Adalbert pouted. "What's the rush? I like my life the way it is. I'm too young for sugary conventions."

But Heinrich had already seized on a tack. "Young and virtuous you are, Adalbert. Savor your springtide years, and for your twenty-first birthday, we'll celebrate your arrival to manhood with the grandest occasion the kingdom has ever seen. There'll be harp players, acrobats, a tournament of jousts. Whatever spectacle you desire. And at the end of it all, we'll enact a contest. Let any willful bachelor in the kingdom make an appeal for your heart. You'll have thousands of suitors competing for you, and you can choose whichever one to stay with you in the palace for the rest of your years."

Heinrich beamed encouragingly. Adalbert kept his own counsel when it came to boyhood crushes, but Heinrich knew his son could not resist such a deluxe opportunity to command attention.

Adalbert sneered at first. Then a flash of his dazzling blue eyes betrayed a certain curiosity. Self-centered as he was, he was not immune to the stirrings of pubescence. A stolen glance at the tight fit of the palace herald's hosiery. A lingering gaze at the stable hand unburdened of his shirt while pitching out the mews. One spring day's fascination with two fantail pigeons building a nest in a flowering cherry tree out by the palace orchards. They were far-flung pieces of a puzzle that did not quite fit together for Adalbert. But he looked up at his father and heaved a sigh.

It was decided. On his twenty-first birthday, Adalbert would choose a mate.

❖

As King Heinrich promised, Adalbert's twenty-first birthday party was an unparalleled event. Every rafter in the palace was strung with flowering garlands. Every chamber resonated with the harmonies of string-players. Every fountain was filled with bubbling wine. The walls were painted over with murals of the guest of honor, now tall and strapping in his ripened perfection, and freshly embroidered tapestries with his smiling image were rolled out across the floor. There were roasts of suckling pigs, breads and jams, fan dancers, pantomimes, and all the things young Adalbert enjoyed. The better for Adalbert to see the entertainment, in the center of the ballroom, a platform was installed, rotating at a leisurely turn by the workings of a silent gear.

The contest drew men from every corner of the kingdom eager to try their luck with Evermore's most handsome son. Adalbert's peevish reputation preceded him, but for those less encouraged by a lifetime of Adalbert, the promise of free room and board at the palace provided the necessary enticement. There were square-jawed legionnaires, fresh-faced sailors, dapper sons of dignitaries, and hopeful journeymen of every trade, all groomed and dressed in their formal best. At the appointed time, Heinrich gathered them all into the ballroom, shooed the ladies and the gawkers away, and announced for the contest to begin.

One by one, the bachelors were called up to the platform. Adalbert looked them over from head to toe. He was at no loss for variety, but his deliberations were brief and final.

"Too tall."

"Too short."

"Too light."

"Too dark."

"Too fine of hair."

"Too coarse of beard."

And so on.

Each bachelor slunk away, deflated. The ballroom was half-empty in less than an hour's time, and Adalbert started to reduce his judgments to wide-mouthed yawns. Heinrich pulled his son aside for a private conversation.

"Surely there must be one among these men who pleases you?" Heinrich said.

Adalbert rolled his eyes. "I haven't seen him yet."

"You've every eligible bachelor in the kingdom here."

"A sorry lot they are."

Heinrich eyed his son sternly. "Adalbert, you're being too picky."

"This is *my* contest. *I* choose who'll be my mate. And so far, every one I've seen has been plain or downright gruesome."

"These are fine men, Adalbert. You cannot judge them entirely on looks. Finding true love requires courtship, charm and conversation. Compatibility. Not just in the physical sense. Give these men a chance."

Adalbert huffed. "It all sounds dreadfully boring."

Heinrich put a hand on his hip—an unkingly gesture, perhaps, but his patience was wearing thin. "Should you like to spend the rest of your years alone?" he asked his son.

Adalbert glared. "I should much rather live out the rest of my days by myself than with any of these goons you've invited to my party."

Heinrich studied his son, and in that moment, a veil was lifted. He no longer saw a perfect little boy, innocent of heart. In fact, when he envisioned his son in five years, ten years, twenty years' time, the picture was monstrous. Heinrich pointed his gaze away. "Very well," he said. "Continue with your contest. I'm tired of all this. When you've finished making a mockery of all your guests, send a page to my room."

Adalbert returned to his throne on the platform, and the event continued in the same manner as it had started. An eager swain presented himself. Adalbert dallied for a breath, and then he pronounced the suitor unfit. It was all quite tiresome, Adalbert thought, and painfully unfair that he should face an endless procession of inadequate candidates considering he had so much to offer.

The next to approach the platform was a tall man, entirely covered in cloak and hood. He held out in his gloved hand a fuzzy stalk with many tiny florets. Adalbert eyed the offering peculiarly. "What is this?" he asked.

"Bluebonnet, Your Grace," the stranger replied. "It is the only thing that grows in the kingdom that has the color of your eyes."

Adalbert considered. "Looks like an awfully common thing. It's not the sort of weed that sprouts out of manure in a shepherd's pasture, is it?"

"Certainly not, Your Grace. Bluebonnet only flourishes on the hilltop. If it pleases you, I'll tell you the story of this flower's retrieval."

Adalbert nodded.

"While I was traveling through the countryside, I came to a mountain pass and whispered your name thrice, the better to navigate its treacherous trenches and falling rocks. When I emerged from the gulley, no worse for wear, I came to a rolling glade blossoming with blue wildflowers. I climbed to its upper part where the sun beat down the strongest and the air was most refreshing. There I spotted this sprig. I rooted it from the earth to give it to you." The stranger bent down on one knee, bowed his head, and raised the flower toward Adalbert.

Adalbert leaned forward and took the sprig. He stared at the shadowy man, intrigued if not yet disarmed. "Why is it that you do not reveal yourself?" he asked.

"I am a humble man, Your Grace," the stranger said. "The sight of you brings me great delight but sadly a most unfortunate discoloration of my cheeks. I do not wish to offend."

Adalbert grinned. "I think you're being coy. Your tongue is quite adept. Why deprive us of your other parts?"

The stranger hesitated. "As you wish, your Grace." His hands reached for the brim of his hood, and he pulled it back. Slowly, he raised his head.

Adalbert's blue eyes widened. Standing before him was a hideous creature. It was crook-nosed with a patchy face blighted by boils. It had a spindly, oily head of hair and bristles sprouting from its oversized ears. In short, a troll.

Adalbert's shock transformed into hysterics. "This is the man who presents himself to be my mate? Please—the hood. You'll scare the varnish off the ceiling."

The ballroom pealed with laughter. The Troll dropped his head. "I've traveled many miles to see you," he said.

"You needn't explain," Adalbert said. "The wear and tear shows on your face. Or is that a permanent condition?"

The Troll looked up and scowled.

"Now that's a pretty look," Adalbert said. "I fear we were doing much better with your eyes pointed on the floor." He waved his hand. "Now move along, Troll-ie. I'm certain there's a muddy trestle sorely missing your company."

The Troll pointed a gloved finger at the prince. "You'll regret treating me this way," he said. His finger twirled in the air in some sort of arcane gesture.

Adalbert scoffed. Then he waved over a pair of guards. "It is you who shall regret disturbing my party," he told the Troll.

The two armored men took the Troll from the room. Everyone

was silent. It was common knowledge that trolls did not like being insulted, and they had a repertoire of tricks for those who crossed them. The bachelors and court attendants passed spooked looks at Adalbert.

Adalbert glared back at them. He didn't believe in troll magic. He knew of spite, but that rarely created the desired effect in his experience. He held up the bluebonnet clover to take a sniff. It shriveled, and its petals dropped to the floor.

❖

The next morning, Adalbert found the porpoises floating belly up in the moat. When the gamekeeper pulled them out, there was not a scratch on a single one of them. Adalbert brushed it off. Porpoises didn't live forever. It was an unfortunate coincidence.

The following day, a chill wind blustered in from the north. By noon, there was frost on the cherry trees in the orchard, and their shriveled fruits fell from their branches. That evening, the cows died of hypothermia. Bundled in his bed, Adalbert gazed out to his terrace and saw that there was snow accumulating. Adalbert snorted and ordered his manservant to stoke up the fireplace.

The wintry storm passed, but then the rivers and lakes dried up. Peasants packed up their mule carts for better terrain. Soldiers deserted the King's service, and the court bursar absconded with all the gold in the treasury. Rumors spread that raiders were creeping toward Evermore's borders to plunder whatever was left. Adalbert lay on his bed staring at the desiccated stalk of bluebonnet in his hand. He didn't stir when his father stammered into his room.

"We're leaving Evermore," Heinrich said. "Take what you can carry. There's a carriage and an ox left. We'll head to port and sail away."

Heinrich moved about the room making a hasty appraisal of his son's decoratives and furnishings. He stopped when he noticed that Adalbert had not budged from his self-pitying position. "It's a full day's travel to the coast, and there's raiders coming," Heinrich said. "You better get a move on."

Adalbert let out a trebling sigh.

Heinrich stood over his son. "There's no time for dallying, Adalbert. Everything's gone. We'll start anew overseas. Your mother has relatives in Furthermore to help us get settled. Now let's go."

"I don't want to," Adalbert said.

"You haven't any choice. We'll all be pitted to stakes when the raiders come."

"I don't feel like going anywhere."

A furnace of heat rose to Heinrich's face. He drew a deep breath. "I'm going to help your mother collect her things. We'll be leaving in less than an hour's time." He clopped out of the room.

Adalbert lay back in his bed. He didn't want to do anything but stare at his wilted flower. It was all the Troll's fault. He was too dejected to move. He figured he'd conserve his energy until his father came back to push him along.

There was a lot of commotion carrying into Adalbert's bedchamber. He turned onto his stomach and pulled a pillow over his head to drown it out. Adalbert heard his father's voice, hurried footsteps down the stairs, a woman's scream, and a lot of shouting back and forth. He eyed his bedroom door peculiarly. Then Adalbert stepped out to his balcony.

He saw an army of raggedy men fording the moat and teaming through the palace gates. There was no defense. Adalbert looked to the horizon. Far down the path leading to the coast, he saw his parents' carriage. His father hung out of the back side of the transport, waving and calling out for him. But it was too late.

❖

The few court attendants who had remained in the palace quickly surrendered, and the raiders took over the palace. The foreign men didn't pit Adalbert to a stake, but they did have the King's dungeon keeper lock him up in the cellar. They had decided Adalbert might come of some use for ransom should the King decide to return to Evermore.

Adalbert found himself in a dark, windowless cell. Many days passed, and the only light he ever saw was the dungeon keeper's torch when he stopped by to deliver his daily ration of a cup of water and two bowls of gruel. There were two straw cots and a trench in one corner where the cell's former residents had relieved themselves. Adalbert spent the long hours hunched over at one cot, trying to make out the silhouette of the flowerless stalk he held in his hand. He thought it would be his only companion for the rest of his life. Until one day.

A muffled cough punctured the silence.

Adalbert shuddered. He searched around the pitch-black room. He thought for a moment he had descended into some kind of delirium and his head had begun to invent sounds. Then the cough came again, strong and near.

"Who is that?" Adalbert said. The source of the noise seemed to be across the room, at the opposite side of his cell. Adalbert strained his eyes. He knew a cot was there, but he could not see it. A gravelly voice spoke.

"It's the Duke of Lessermore. Seems a terrible mistake has been made. Neither one of us was supposed to be assigned to this room. They'll be coming to bring us up to the King's suite any minute."

Adalbert narrowed his brow at the man's sarcasm. "How long have you been there?"

"Who can answer such a question? Tell me, sir: how long has it been since *you* were locked up in this eternal night? Perhaps you're better than me at counting the number of times our warden's torch appeared on the other side of the gates. I gave up long ago."

Adalbert fidgeted at the thought of being watched all this time in the darkness. He tried to recall the sight of the other bed. He'd been certain it was empty. It was just covered over with a bunchy blanket. Adalbert had chosen the other cot because it looked less used.

"What crime did you commit to put you here?" he asked.

The stranger chuckled. "You've a knack for asking churlish questions. Better to ask the one who decided to sentence me to this pit of hell. I say my only trespass was love."

Adalbert clucked. "That sounds like a tall tale. Who'd lock you up on account of love?"

There was a long pause. Adalbert wondered if he'd been too brash. Strange as it was to have a conversation with a disembodied voice, it was his only contact since he'd been locked up in his cell. He stared across the room, willing his companion to say something. At last, the stranger spoke.

"I've a tale, yes. Not one of height, but one of length. I'll tell it unless you've a scarcity of leisure."

"Yes," Adalbert said. "I'd like to hear it."

And so the stranger began his story.

I was born a bastard. My mother was poor. She took what work she could get in our woodland hamlet. She darned socks, spun silk, and fancied herself an innkeeper when the King's servicemen passed through the village. I figure my father was a foot soldier who stayed the night, had his lump of millet in the morning, and went on his way. I saw many men come and go growing up, and I wasn't the first or the last souvenir from one of my mother's guests. We were a house full of fatherless boys and girls.

My mother couldn't afford to keep one child, let alone the seven of us. So she settled on a plan. As soon as one of us could stand up on two feet, she sent him into the forest to collect wild turnips. If he could find his way home, he'd get hot soup for supper. Most of my brothers and sisters, I never saw again. I kept coming back.

When I was old enough to be of some use beyond digging up root vegetables, my mother sold me off to a mage. He was a peevish sprite who lived in a cavern, deep in the woods. He didn't much like company, but he needed an apprentice. He taught me how to find magical herbs and berries for his potions. I'd become a fine fetcher by then. He only thrashed me once for bringing back the wrong ingredients. He kept me bound by an eternal spell so I could not venture beyond the forest. But it wasn't bad work. I didn't know much better than being indentured. Until one morning when he sent me on an errand for nettle sting.

Nettle sting likes the damper parts of the forest, so I headed there. It wasn't long till I spotted the spiny devil sprouting up on the margins of a creek. I fixed to carefully uproot it and put it in my bag. Then I heard someone coming through the brush. My master wasn't keen on leading visitors back to his place, so I hid behind a tree. I peeked out and saw a woodsman.

Handsome he was. Broad-shouldered from his work, and he didn't look much older than me. He was circling around a chestnut tree, eyeing its branches. I watched him get to it with his axe. I noticed he'd set down a satchel a little ways off. I crept toward it and took a look inside.

It was his lunch: bread, cheese, an apple—a pretty good find considering I was heading home to a supper of boiled pokeweed. I decided I'd play a trick. I pocketed the food, scooped some fallen chestnuts into his bag, and snuck away.

I returned to the same spot the next day. Sure enough, the woodsman came back for more of that chestnut wood. I carefully turned over his sack and found another lunch of bread and cheese. There was also some gooseberry jam. I took the stuff, and this time, I'd brought better barter. I left him some mushrooms and leeks, tied up his sack, and headed off.

Over the next few days, we continued our game. Blood sausage for porridge. Smoked fish for pheasant eggs. Barley ale for birch tea. Every night after I was done with my master's chores, I stayed up late planning new exchanges. I got more gutsy by the end of the week and stole out of the sprite's lair while he slept. I caught a hare in the dawn's light and cooked it in an open fire in the woods. Later that day, I hid in the spot by the chestnut trees waiting for the woodsman. He came walking through the brush as usual, looked around for timber, and settled on his quarry for the day. He set his satchel down and took up his axe. Then he stopped and twitched his nose.

"I don't like rabbit," he said.

I scrunched up behind the tree.

"Where are you, forest spirit?" he said. "I've brought you a *fine meal of mutton chop and wine. It's time you showed yourself to me."*

I didn't budge. I listened to him rustling through the leaves. The damned hare in my bag was my mark. I heard him on the other side of the tree.

"Come out, forest spirit. Or do I have to lop off this trunk to get to you?" he said.

I drew a deep breath, straightened out, and ambled around the tree. My face burnt hot. As many times as I'd imagined one day meeting the woodsman, I was struck dumb and my feet swayed beneath me.

The woodsman stepped toward me with a devilish smile. He put his hand on the nape of my neck and pulled me close, and our lips met.

That kiss unlocked something in me. Desires that had been buried deep in my head were suddenly set free as possible. From as many times as I had imagined being with a man, I knew all of the motions.

We shucked each other's clothes, and I stooped in front of him. My mouth truckled greedily to coax the seed from between his legs. He halted me gently and he raised me from the ground, and he led me to a spot beside a tree trunk. I hunched and bared my buttocks so he could claim my bowels. It was far more brutal and exquisite than I had ever dreamed. And when he was done, he lay down on a mossy patch beside the creek, and he bid me to do the same to him. We were like rutting stags, discovering for the first time how well two men's bodies fit together.

Adalbert interrupted. "You did all that and you'd only just met?"

"Where'd you grow up?" the stranger said. "Under a rock?"

Adalbert sneered. "It sounds to me like he forced himself on you."

"No," the stranger replied. He paused thoughtfully. "Everything that happened that afternoon was entirely agreed upon."

Pictures streamed through Adalbert's head, the kind he had at night thinking about the stable hand dropping by his bedroom unexpectedly. Adalbert blushed. He had a lot of questions about how things worked. Could something like *that* really fit inside *there*? Adalbert brushed it off.

"I think you're very brazen," he told the stranger.

"Like a goat."

Adalbert sat up on his bed and tented his knees to cover up the stiffness in his pants.

"May I go on now with the story?" the stranger said.

"Go ahead."

The next few days passed like a dream. The woodsman and I met each morning. Sometimes we played over that wondrous day when he had caught me hiding. Other times we got straight to business. Afterward, we'd take a swim in the creek, share a meal, and talk.

The woodsman told me he'd been raised by his grandmother after his mother fell ill. He'd recently moved out on his own and was collecting chestnut for a new bridge out by the river. He liked his work but found it lonely. I listened intently to everything he said. When he asked me questions, I veered away from my situation. I told him I had a boss who sent me out for errands, but I didn't mention that I was bound to him and could never leave the forest. Nestled in the woodsman's arms, it was easy to pretend that finding each other straightened out life's complexities. My mage had a commission ridding a wealthy squire of a witch's curse—a very difficult procedure, so I had my freedom for a time.

The woodsman brought me presents. I knew he wasn't a rich man, but the things he gave me were more precious than anything gold could buy. He carved figurines from wood—a deer, an eagle, and my favorite of all, a rendering of the two of us, bowed down with our foreheads touching. There wasn't much I could give him in return, but he told me that my company was enough. I'd never imagined meeting someone like him. I never thought that love and kindness were ever meant for me.

One day, the woodsman asked me to come live with him at his cottage. That was when I knew I had to confess the truth. I told him about the sprite. If he found out about the woodsman, he'd punish me or punish us both, for all I knew. The woodsman and I kept quiet company for a while. I could see thoughts stirring behind my lover's distracted gaze, but I saved questions for another day.

The stranger's voice trailed off. Adalbert stared across the black cell expectantly. "And?" he said.

"You'll have the rest of the story some other time," the stranger said. His voice had turned hoarse. "I'm not well and tired of telling. You seem not to have noticed but those two bowls of gruel aren't your breakfast and supper. It's one bowl each."

Adalbert huffed. "But you can't stop the story there. Tell me what happened with the woodsman. You haven't even gotten to the reason you were put here in the dungeon."

"Another day," the stranger said. "I need rest. Now shut up and let me sleep."

❖

When Adalbert next saw the flicker of the dungeon master's torch, he tried to follow its faint glimmer onto the opposite side of his cell. He could see the cot but nothing more than a murky silhouette covered in a blanket. The dungeon master slid a water cup and two bowls of gruel through the grating at the floor. Adalbert took one bowl to his cot and came back to bring the other to his companion.

The trail of torchlight faded away in the distance. Adalbert took half steps through the darkness.

"Time to eat already, is it?" the stranger said.

"Yes. I'm bringing you your gruel."

"Leave it on the floor. You're close enough. I like my privacy."

Adalbert set the gruel down and shuffled back to his cot. He found his own bowl. Though his stomach growled, he held off from eating. He listened to his companion lift the bowl from the stone floor. With his ears focused very sharply, he heard some slurping sounds and a swallow.

"It's bad manners to stare," the stranger said.

"How do you know I'm staring?"

"I've a keen set of eyes. That's what happens when you're stuck in the dark."

Adalbert grinned. "I don't believe you. I could be doing anything right now—looking up at the ceiling, sticking out my tongue, picking my nose…"

"You're not doing any of that. You're staring."

Adalbert clicked with an idea. "What am I doing now?" he asked. He pointed his finger across the cell.

"You're pointing."

Adalbert tried again. "What am I doing now?"

"You're pulling out your ears like a donkey."

"What about now?"

"You've got your hands folded in prayer, and you're batting your lashes."

Adalbert laughed.

"Having fun?" the stranger said. "Stick around here long enough and you'll be able to see every time I scratch my balls."

Adalbert sat cross-legged on his cot and took a few slurps of his gruel. "Feeling better?" he asked.

The stranger grunted a vague assent.

"Ready to tell me about the woodsman and the mage?"

There was no reply.

"I couldn't stop thinking about it," Adalbert said. "Your story kept me up ever since you finished."

The cell was silent. Adalbert turned worried. Truthfully, he didn't like being alone. Especially in the dark. He found his mind drifting, his whole self drifting it seemed, and he was constantly fighting back the panicky thought that he had disappeared from the world entirely. "Please sir, I'd like to hear some more," he said.

After some moments, the stranger's voice came again. "All right. I'll tell you. But this part is not so cheery."

I kept meeting up with the woodsman for two glorious seasons. Through autumn, we'd wrestle in the fallen leaves after he finished his work. Through winter, we'd warm each other beneath a giant pine while the snow blanketed the forest. But when the creeks thawed and the trees started budding, my master finished his commission. It became more difficult for me to get away. I think he was starting to get suspicious because he didn't want me leaving his den unless it was to fetch water or catch pigeons for supper. I tried to stretch out my errands as long as I could to steal a few moments with my love. Then the mean sprite sent me out with time spells that brought me back to his lair if I didn't return promptly.

It was excruciating. I was trapped in the cave, knowing that my love was waiting for me. I fumbled through my chores. Weeks passed without seeing my love. I wondered how long the woodsman would wait for me. At darker times, I imagined him finding another man who didn't come with such complications.

The sprite made me sleep on some straw by his bed, so it was no easier getting away at night. But I had watched him work, and I had figured out how he made a sleeping potion. I prepared our supper, so one night I slyly drafted a batch in a teacup and mixed it in with his cabbage soup.

The concoction worked. The imp teetered back in his chair and passed out. I didn't know how long the potion would last, but I hurried out into the forest.

When I found the woodsman by the chestnut trees, I could tell he had been crying. It tore at me how much I had hurt him by my absence. There was no fooling around that time. We just held each other tight. It was almost worse than not seeing each other at all.

The woodsman begged me to run away with him. I told him I couldn't risk the mage hurting him in revenge. The woodsman told me he would die all the same from our separation.

We talked it out. We'd have to kill the imp. We didn't know exactly how to do it, but we figured not many things could live through fire. We decided that the next night I'd mix up another sleeping potion for my master's supper, but this time I'd cast the little beast into the hearth before leaving. The woodsman clipped off a lock of his hair and gave it to me for good luck. He said he'd be waiting for me at gloaming outside the sprite's den.

I returned home and found my master still tipped over in his chair. I thought my fortune had already taken a good turn. Then I heard his drowsy breathing. I brought him up to his bed, hoping he'd chalk up the night to the effects of being overworked. I slept with the woodsman's lock of hair pressed against my cheek.

My master was up before me in the morning. He was down in his workshop and didn't mention anything when I brought him his tea and porridge. It was a hell of a jittery day. I broke three vials of attar straightening up the apothecary and knocked over two urns sweeping out the antechamber. My master cursed and pelted my head with an onion. It made the task ahead of me a little easier. Plus it gave me an idea.

I told the sprite I'd prepare his favorite meal for supper to make up for the damage I'd done. Slugs with creamed onions. The idea seemed to settle his mood. He went into his workshop to look over some correspondence.

I took to the kitchen, got the teacup, and mixed together the sleeping draught. I started supper on the cauldron and went up to the bedroom to change out of my shirt. I'd sweated through the armpits. Fighting to pull a fresh shirt over my head, it hit me. Sometime in my nervous daze, I'd lost track of the woodsman's snippet of hair.

I rifled through the bedroom for it, but there wasn't much time. The stench from the kitchen told me that my master's supper was simmering and ready. I hurried back to serve it. I decanted the teacup into my master's bowl.

He was at his chair when I brought it over to the dining table. Sitting in the middle of his place setting was the lock of hair.

I stumbled and dropped the bowl on the floor. The sprite looked at me with a cruel grin.

"Been keeping company you have," he said. "This looks to be a trinket from a lover. I've enough here to fix up a curse to make his thumbs drop off or twist his intestines into a knot."

I pleaded with him not to do it. I begged him to punish me

instead. I promised that I'd never see the woodsman again, my most painful oath, but I was desperate to save my love from harm.

The sprite scratched his tiny chin. "I've a better idea that'll teach you a lesson. Let us see just how strong this woodsman cares for you. I've a charm that'll make you a sight of horror in your true love's eyes. But when he sees you, if he's game for giving you a kiss, the charm will break." He grinned and threw his head back with a cackle. "I wouldn't get my hopes up, duckie. This charm's never been broken before."

He reached up his wand, and I saw a flash of light.

The stranger choked on a cough. Adalbert sat up on his haunches. He listened to his companion recover from the fit. But the stranger didn't speak. Adalbert gazed through the pitch air.

"You can't stop there. What happened next?"

The stranger cleared his throat. "I've had enough storytelling for today. I told you, I'm not well."

"But there can't be much left. What did the woodsman do when he saw you? How'd you get away from the mage? You haven't said anything about how you ended up in the dungeon."

The stranger's reply came back faintly. "There's more. For another day. Or night, I should say."

Adalbert poked a finger into his bowl. He'd been so rapt in the story, he hadn't eaten all of his gruel. His stomach lurched hungrily. He licked his finger. Then Adalbert climbed down from his cot, took a few steps, and slid his bowl along the floor toward the other side of the cell.

❖

The stranger didn't speak for a long time. Adalbert tried to coax him at intervals.

"Talking makes the time go by faster, don't you think?" he said.

No answer.

"I've thought a lot about it. The woodsman breaks the charm, doesn't he?"

Dead silence.

"I've a story too. It's about porpoises. You want to hear it?"

Nothing worked. Adalbert gave up and fell back on bleak thoughts. He wondered how long it was possible to survive on one bowl of gruel a day. He worried whether he could catch whatever was afflicting his cellmate. Adalbert thought about his father and mother. They could've been killed trying to escape to Furthermore. Or maybe they had made it there and forgotten all about him.

Adalbert went over again and again how he had ended up in the dungeon. Thoughts twisted and turned in his head. It wasn't fair for the Troll to place a curse on him. But none of the bad things in his life would've happened if he hadn't made fun of the Troll. Adalbert remembered his bluebonnet and felt around his bed to find it. He reclined on his back and clutched it to his chest as though he was laid out for funeral.

His cellmate broke out with a hacking cough. When the dungeon keeper brought the daily ration, Adalbert took a sip from the water cup, wet his hand with some gruel, licked it off, and brought everything over to the other cot.

He sat back in his bed and waited for sounds. There was nothing for a long while. Then Adalbert heard the scrape of the bowl coming off the floor, a swallow of food, and a gurgle of water.

Adalbert repeated the routine the next few times the dungeon keeper came by. When he collected the bowls to return, he saw that his companion was eating less and less. He could feel the man's fever when he stepped near to his cot. Adalbert stared from his bed, trying to measure the space of the stranger's breaths or a change of temperature in the room. He jolted when he heard the man speak.

"Have you time to hear the rest of the story?"

Adalbert nodded his head.

"Then settle in for the end."

I couldn't truly say what happened when the sprite struck me with his wand. I felt different, but when I touched my face and looked down at my hands, nothing seemed different. I checked myself in a mirror. I scrutinized every side. It was the same young man's face I'd always seen. I could only hope that my master had been trying to trick my mind.

My love was waiting outside the lair. For the first time, I dallied before going to meet him. I washed and rewashed my face. I changed my shirt again, and then I put on musk in case my master's curse involved foul smells, though there were none I could detect. I paced the room considering the possibilities and wondering if I was better off hiding forever. All the while, the sprite taunted me.

"Stop being a coward and go see your lover."

I looked to the door. I drew a breath and strode toward it.

It was a mild spring night. I remember how peaceful it was. Crickets chirped. There was a soft breeze. It made me think of summer and the nights I'd snuck out of the den to forage a lunch for the woodsman. I could sense him there. He was under a shadowy tree, and I was veiled beneath the lip of the cave. There was a moonlit glade between us.

"Is it you?" the woodsman spoke. He stepped into the clearing. He stared curiously at the entrance to the cave. I wanted to rush out and embrace him, but I couldn't move. The woodsman crept toward me tentatively. I decided to save us both some time. I stepped under the moonlight.

"My love," I said. "It's me."

The woodsman doubled back. He grasped his axe and held it at the level of his shoulder.

"What have you done with him?" he demanded. "Where is my love?"

"It's me," I said again.

"What trickery is this?" he said. "You've his voice but nothing else. Have you eaten him? Is it by some vile act he speaks from inside you?"

His face was wildly frightened. I inched toward him, hands drawn up in front of my chest. Then his eyes flashed murderously.

"I'll kill you and I'll cut him out!"

He lurched toward me with his axe. I ran into the forest as fast as I could. He was on my heels, and I knew if I slowed down a jot, he'd have time to swing his weapon down on me. He chased after me for a long stretch. Then I heard him panting with fatigue.

He stopped. I hid myself in the brush some yards away. I watched him drop down to his knees. He was breathless, and his face was screwed up in a way that made me shiver. He cried. He screamed. He looked up to the sky, and then he buried his face in his hands.

A calm passed over him. He took the blade of his axe and slit his throat.

I ran out and held him as he bled. The woodsman sputtered out his last breath. He had no parting words for me. I stared into his glassy eyes and searched for some glimmer of the terror he had seen. What disgusting sight could have driven him to such desperation? I only saw the reflection of myself I had always known.

I howled for my love. The chattering crickets turned silent. The woods were still. The only thing left was my grief. I carried the woodsman to the chestnut grove, dug out a plot, and buried him.

There was a long silence. Adalbert held himself quietly. The sight of the dying woodsman was fixed in his head, as real as if he had witnessed it himself. Adalbert wondered if the stranger was crying. But the room was dead still.

Finally, a hollow voice traveled from the stranger's cot.

"Some days later, my heartbreak turned to bitterness, and I overturned a scalding bowl of soup on my master's head. I seized the moment of surprise to pluck off his wings.

"There is a way to kill a sprite."

He cleared his throat with some effort.

"I left his cavern and set off on my own. I was free, but there wasn't any joy in it. I'd lost my love. Even on the brightest morning, when my heart thawed for a moment and I considered I might fall in love again, there were facts to face. I'd never know if the sprite's curse was broken. I'd killed one lover, and I didn't know if I could bear it happening again. I hid myself in the thickest part of the wood and scurried away from the sound of travelers. Sometimes I'd watch them from the cover of brush and listen to the news they'd bring. But I never showed myself. My fear kept me bound to living in the shadows and believing I would always be an unspeakable thing. I'd never experience another kind look or a fond touch. I'd be a monster for the rest of my years."

The stranger stopped there. Adalbert listened keenly. He scooted to the edge of his cot, and then he stood. Adalbert reasoned if the man was crying, maybe it was too faint to hear. He wanted to reassure him. He stepped through the dark space toward the stranger's cot.

A desperate shout halted Adalbert. "Come no farther. I told you: I crave privacy."

The stranger sputtered and coughed to regain his breath.

Adalbert turned around and got back in his bed.

❖

Two meals passed, and the stranger wouldn't eat. Adalbert stayed up waiting for the sound of his cellmate taking up his bowl of gruel, but it never came. He heard the man's wheezy breaths every now and then. Adalbert fought off his drowsiness for fear of waking up to a silent room. The man had to eat. Adalbert got up and walked through the darkness to the other side of the room.

He wished the man's grumpy voice would tell him to go away, but there was no protest. Adalbert judged his steps and stooped to the floor to move about on his hands and knees so he wouldn't overturn the gruel bowls. He found one, took it, and then reached his hand and felt the cot. It was still warm. Adalbert carefully hoisted himself up while balancing the bowl in one hand. He took a seat beside the man.

The stranger fussed a bit. Adalbert found his arm covered up in the blanket, and he held it still. That seemed to calm him.

Adalbert felt around for the man's lips. They were sweaty and hot. He brought the bowl near and angled it so the man could take a drink.

The man sputtered on the gruel. Adalbert reached around to

lift the man's head so the meal would go down easier. Adalbert felt him swallowing. He tipped the bowl against the man's lips again. Adalbert did it a few more times, always lifting the man's head to help him swallow, and then he did the same with the water cup.

When everything was finished, Adalbert looked back to his side of the cell. He lay down next to the man instead. There was more fussing, but Adalbert reached his arm over the man's chest, and he didn't fight it after a while. It was warmer this way, Adalbert thought. Cozy like snuggling up on a winter's night. The man coughed. Adalbert pretended to cough, a little mischievous. He could feel the man shaking his head, weary of his humor.

For the next meal, it was a struggle to get the man to eat. Adalbert used a corner of his sleeve to dab up the spit-up gruel from the man's face. Then he hit on an idea. He ripped off part of the sheet from his cot, wet it with some of the water, and washed the man's face.

Adalbert whispered in the man's ear, "Beautiful."

Then the stranger just wouldn't eat at all. Adalbert tried until he became worried that the man didn't have the strength to spit up the gruel before choking. Adalbert set down the bowl and clung to the man. He imagined that by holding the stranger tight he could transmit his own warmth and vitality into the man's faltering body. It was hard not falling asleep, but Adalbert pinched himself awake every time he felt light and dizzy.

The man's breathing became so shallow, Adalbert could barely feel it against his cheek. Adalbert poked the man in the ribs. He didn't budge.

Adalbert climbed over him. He turned the man on his side, draped his arm over the man's shoulder, and looked out into the darkness. He imagined the two of them gazing out at a forest blanketed with snow.

At the next meal time, Adalbert was still curled up with the stranger. He didn't notice the dungeon keeper's torch until it was just outside the cell's gate. Adalbert squinted toward the light. The guard stopped and angled his torch. He chuckled thickly at the sight of the two men on the cot.

"Am I disturbing you lovebirds?" the guard said. He looked at Adalbert. "Never thought you'd take a fancy to the man you put away for your twenty-first birthday."

Adalbert froze over. The dungeon keeper slid the gruel and water beneath the grating and walked away. Adalbert followed the trail of light all the way down the corridor until it disappeared. He could have looked earlier, but only then did his eyes turn to the stranger. He couldn't see the man an inch away from his face.

Adalbert sat up. His mind raced. He should have figured out sooner that all this time he'd been keeping company with the Troll. Adalbert took inventory of his emotions. He wasn't revolted. He was surprised that he didn't feel deceived. In fact, the only bitterness in his heart was toward himself. The man was dying.

But he wouldn't die alone. Adalbert knew what he had to do.

The problem was how to do it now that the cell was devoid of light. Adalbert hunched over his cellmate. He could feel the man's cheeks against his face, but he could not see him. Adalbert remembered the mage's curse: He needed to behold his love in order to break the spell. He wondered how long he'd have to wait until the dungeon keeper came back with his torch.

Adalbert got up, stumbled through the darkness, and banged against the gates. He shouted until his throat burned. No one answered. Then Adalbert worried about the man. He couldn't hear a stir coming from the cot. He needed to check on him. But first, Adalbert made his way to his side of the cell and retrieved the bluebonnet.

Adalbert settled back in the bed, found the man's hand, and pressed the flower stalk into his grip. The man's hold was loose but the stalk stayed put. Adalbert linked his arms around the man's shoulders and embraced him.

Sometime later, the man began to tremble. Adalbert tried to hold him still, but whatever had possessed him was strong and defiant. Eventually, the man settled into a calm. That was even scarier. Adalbert hovered over him to feel or hear the sound of breathing. Over many hours, Adalbert couldn't sort out the man's breaths from his own. Adalbert's pounding heartbeat blunted any sound. He stared toward the gates and visualized the glow of the dungeon keeper's torch.

A flicker pierced the darkness.

Adalbert sat up. He watched the light stretch down the corridor, lapping at the gates of the cell. It entered the cell a foot. Then another. Then another. Then it reached the edge of the cot. Adalbert put his arm behind the man's shoulder to prop him up.

The torchlight shone into the room. Adalbert looked at his bedmate. He saw the Troll, gory-faced and pale. Adalbert's mouth pinched into a smile. He bent down and kissed the Troll on the lips.

❖

Adalbert broke two curses that day. With his kiss, he dispelled the magic that had doomed the mage's apprentice to forever be a sight of horror in his lover's eyes. Adalbert saw the kind, young man he'd pictured so vividly combing through the forest with his sack.

But another transformation happened that took longer for Adalbert to reconcile. The cot, the cell, and the entire dungeon disappeared, and Adalbert found himself in the bright ballroom of the palace, surrounded by a crowd of his countrymen and court attendants. On the platform throne, Adalbert saw Heinrich and Lutecia, back in their regal costumes, just like before the storm, the drought, and the raiders had come to Evermore.

Heinrich stepped down from his throne and threw his arms around his son. Adalbert stared at him queerly. Heinrich winked.

"I needed to do something so that you wouldn't be alone for the rest of your life," Heinrich explained. "It was a bit of Troll magic that sent you to the dungeon where you could find your true love. We've all been waiting for you."

Adalbert's head spun. It had all been a trick to teach him a lesson. He scowled at his father, but it was hard to keep a sour face. The room was filled with laughter and cheers.

The mage's apprentice stood beside Adalbert. He was holding the stalk of bluebonnet, and it was fully restored in bright, shiny colors. Adalbert smiled. His love reached out and took his hand. They both leaned forward so that their foreheads touched, and then they kissed, long and deeply. Heinrich led a rousing cheer.

And Adalbert and the mage's apprentice lived happily ever after.

Clifford Henderson (cliffordhenderson.net) is the author of three award-winning novels. Her fourth, *Rest Home Runaways*, was released in August 2014. When not writing, Clifford and her partner of twenty years run the Fun Institute, a school of improv and solo performance.

This story is based on "Jack and the Beanstalk."

Beanstalk
Clifford Henderson

Once upon the future, in a town called Utonia, there was a strikingly handsome, but seriously unhappy, young woman named Jackie. It was unusual for Utonians to be unhappy because most of them were very happy, or if not very happy, at least relatively content. And why wouldn't they be? Utonia was a beautiful town. It rested between two plump mountains and had soil so fertile, it was said if you weren't careful the seed in your pocket might take root. So everyone was well fed and strong and generally stayed that way until they dropped dead, at which point there was much crying and singing and gratefulness for having known the deceased. But mostly the people were happy and even when they weren't they moved through their unhappiness quickly, never thinking to hang on to grudges or grievances.

You might wonder why Jackie was so unhappy. After all, she had a strong body and a wonderful mop of curly, bronze hair, green eyes that shone like peridot cabochons, and a mind quick as light. What's more, she lived and worked in an elegant, arty little studio, which she paid for with the sales of her stunning 3-D landscapes, each one its own liquid crystal display that changed with the seasons. But while others thought her landscapes dazzling and extravagant, the edges of these masterpieces depressed her, made her feel hemmed in. At the start of each new landscape she would brace herself for its eventual disappointment.

The Utonians did not know what to make of her predilection for gloominess, but then Utonians, on the whole, were a little unclear about unhappiness—what caused it and such—but they were great believers in the power of love. They didn't much care who loved whom, some women loved women, some loved men; some men loved men, some women, it was all the same to them. Indeed, parents noted their children's gender preferences in the same light as they might note their eye and hair color. Love was simply love and it was good. Consequently, some speculated that Jackie's unhappiness was caused by a lack of love. Others disputed it. She'd had lovers before, after all, some of the most beautiful women in Utonia. Shouldn't that have cured her? In the end, none could come up with a definite cause. None, that is, except for the crone, Marta, who lived by herself in a hovel made of bones, clay, and hide. She was an ornery spit of a woman who, it was understood, was happiest when left alone with her garden of cabbages, beans, and carrots. She was also the only one old enough to remember how things used to be. And she understood exactly the cause of Jackie's unhappiness.

It was no surprise then that when Jackie was walking to the gallery one day, her most recent landscape tucked under her arm, she bumped right into Marta, because solutions are forever seeking out problems. Sadly, it takes a quick wit and cleverness to knit the two together, and while quite clever, Jackie was not clever enough to recognize her deliverance.

"Watch where you're going!" Marta said.

Startled, Jackie looked up from a smattering of withered bougainvillea petals on the ground. "Oh, Marta! I didn't see you."

"Of course you didn't. You were too busy staring at your feet."

"I was looking at these petals. I—"

"I know what you were doing, girl."

Jackie, like all Utonians, was slightly frightened by Marta. The stench of less-happy times hovered around her, an ominous fog of what *could* be if one weren't mindful.

"Poor, poor me," the crone taunted. "That's what you were thinking, wasn't it? Poor, poor me. That's what keeps you from looking where you are going."

"Well, I…" But Jackie could not find it inside herself to admit that what Marta said was true, that she *was* feeling particularly low. While the world she lived in did not have "edges" the way her landscapes did, it felt as if it did. Utonia was too small, too predictable, too conventional. Where was the challenge?

"What's that under your arm?" Marta asked, pointing to the landscape.

"One of my landscapes. I'm taking it to the gallery."

"Let me have a look at it."

Jackie held it out for Marta's inspection. The landscape was one of her Foggy Morning series, an 18" x 24" rendering of a willow tree by a stream.

Frowning, Marta turned her head from side to side as if to get a better angle, then said, "Flip it upside down." Which Jackie did, although she felt insulted that the old woman was treating her artwork as if it were the ugliest thing she'd ever seen. After viewing it upside down and then right side up again, Marta said, "I'll take it!" and snatched it from Jackie's grasp.

Jackie did not want to sell it to the crone, figuring it would be tossed and forgotten among her notorious collection of bones and skins, but there was no arguing with Marta, so she agreed to the sale, but before she had a chance to name her price, Marta handed her a large speckled bean.

"What's this?" Jackie said.

"Payment," Marta said.

"But it's a bean. What am I supposed to do with a bean?"

"If you have any sense at all, you'll plant it." With that Marta began hobbling up to her hovel on the hill, robbing Jackie of the chance to quarrel.

Not that she would have. Quarreling with Marta simply wasn't done. The many tales of her turning people into worms and lizards made it inadvisable. Jackie didn't need the money anyway. Her landscapes made her a comfortable living. She only placed them into the gallery to keep them from collecting cobwebs. So, dispirited, but not much more than usual, Jackie slogged back to her studio. Once there, she had just enough energy to curse Marta's meager payment and toss the stupid pink and black bean between two prickly thistles in the weedy plot in front of her house. She then dragged her sorry self inside and flopped down on the daybed, her final thought before nodding off that she might get lucky and actually die in her sleep from boredom.

The next morning she slept in, not realizing how late it was because her studio, oddly, was still dark. Lying on her daybed, rubbing out a crick in her neck, she heard an eerie humming coming from outside. Yawning, she stumbled over to the window and was shocked to see a huge, fibrous stalk with plate-sized, heart-shaped leaves coiling up and up, like a corkscrew, from between the two thistles in her weedy plot. As she was staring, her mouth agape, a scarlet flower bloomed from the stalk. Then another. And another. One on top of the next. *What the hell?* she thought. Then she remembered Marta's bean. Clearly, it had been no ordinary bean. It was bewitched! She should have known.

She slipped on her slacks and tee, slid on a pair of sandals, and charged outside, her curiosity piqued. The beanstalk spiraled upward past the house, past the trees, and was just breaking into the clouds—piercing the edges of her world! Marta had made her wish come true!

Jackie grabbed a hold of the beanstalk, wedged her foot into the axil where leaf met stalk, and tested to see if the stem would hold her weight. It did! She tried the next one up. This too held her weight. Impulsively, she began climbing, stopping only to catch her breath. The growing stalk aided in propelling her upward like an escalator. She couldn't wait to see what lay ahead, knew it must be wonderful. Why else would Marta have given her the bean? Happier than she'd felt in years, she began to sing a childhood ditty as she climbed, never once looking back at Utonia, now little more than a speck in the distance.

When she reached the clouds she started having reservations. It was cold for one thing, and disorienting, the puffy whiteness making her lose her equilibrium—both physically and mentally. *What if Marta doesn't have my best interests in mind? What if Marta is sending me to a place from which I can't return—to rid Utonia of my gloominess?* But she couldn't stop now—not so close to learning what was beyond the edges. So, like a little goat, she continued on.

Having made it through the clouds, she was rewarded to find the stalk curling up through a tunnel of solid earth toward a patch of blue sky. She scrabbled up through the wormy earth and hauled herself up onto the land into a wonderfully warm, sunny day and a long dirt road that appeared to lead to some sort of distant city. She could just make out a jagged skyline of enormous, erect buildings, each one taller than the next.

Jackie did not stop to think what kind of a self-important place would encourage such ostentatious architecture. Oh no. She imagined it to be better than any she'd ever seen, the buildings filled with beings much more technically advanced than Utonians, much more complicated and interesting. What a ninny she'd been for doubting Marta! Clearly, the crone had only her best interests in mind.

She trotted toward the city, passing through grassy hills dotted with oversized cows and sheep. She passed farms and ranches, the houses and barns perpendicular and huge, in strange contrast to the soft, undulating landscape.

She spotted a shepherd trying to coax a wayward sheep out of a gulch. A pimply teenager, he was close to twelve feet tall!

"Hello!" Jackie yelled.

He looked up from his charge, gave Jackie the once-over, and yelled, "What's wrong with you?"

This took her aback. "Wrong?"

"You're so small."

She laughed. "Oh. That. Where I come from we're all this size. Or thereabout."

"Is your husband tiny too?"

"My husband?"

"Yeah. You know, the guy you're joined to."

"Actually, I don't have a husband."

"Sorry to hear that," he said, shaking his head. "At your age."

She chose to ignore his rudeness. "What's this city up ahead?"

"Pureland. Where every man is happy and every dream fulfilled."

Excited, she said, "Thanks!" and continued on her way, unmindful of the bitter tone with which he'd uttered these last words.

Soon other people joined her on the road, peasants mostly, filing out of their giant farmhouses and heading toward the city, all of them dressed in what looked to be their finest clothes, all of them walking with a steadfast urgency. They were huge, some of them as tall as sixteen feet, but unlike in Utonia, where there was no dress code, where a person wore what she or he felt best reflected his or her personality—skirt, sarong, slacks, tunic, gown, or suit—the women here all wore coarse ankle-length dresses; the men, simple slacks and tunics. Most would not look at her. Those who did, did so with pity. She spotted a boy, about her size, struggling along behind his parents on painful-looking stilts. He glanced at her briefly then looked away, clearly ashamed to be associated with someone of her diminutive stature. But she didn't give much thought to the Purelanders' obvious discomfort with her size, reasoning that if any of them set foot in Utonia, people would stare too. Besides, up ahead a phalanx of young giantesses decked out in flowers and long white dresses paraded with great importance. Clearly the crowd was heading to some kind of special event. It had now grown so large it was more or less pushing her along.

They arrived in what appeared to be a suburb of the gleaming city. Giant houses with giant lawns and giant birdbaths and decorative gnomes lined the road with military precision. But it was the people streaming out of these houses that fascinated Jackie. Not only were they huge like the peasants, but they were also dripping wealth.

The giant women clung to their giant men's arms like pocketbooks, their faces masked in self-righteousness. They wore opulent ankle-length dresses so snug they were forced to take tiny steps—two or three high-heeled ones to every leather-booted one of the male—and they were draped in so many jewels they had trouble lifting their arms or turning quickly. As for the men, they strode down the streets in tight slacks featuring huge jeweled cups covering their genitals. Men and women alike held their chins so high and their chests so puffed out they never even saw Jackie trolling around beneath them. Or, more likely, they simply had no interest.

Then, amid the bustle and hubbub, Jackie heard someone weeping. Drawn to the sadness like moisture to the earth, she angled her way out of the crowd, waited until the street emptied of people, and made her way to the nearby house that seemed its source. She had to climb a spiky shrub to see inside the first-story window. But it was worth it, for there, sobbing underneath a waterfall of silky black hair, was a young woman not much bigger than Jackie. She was slumped over on a bed much too large for her and was brimming with a sorrow so deep if flowers had been in the room they surely would have wilted in empathy. Jackie could not turn away. Even when a fat giantess burst into the room.

The giantess was squeezed into a shiny pink dress and teetered on ridiculously high-heeled shoes. Her expression was twisted with rage. "I am so ashamed of you, Ivy! Twenty-two years old and still not married!"

A balding giant with large muscles and a huge gut was hot on her heels. "It's because she's a runt! What man would want her?"

"I had the Ragner boy all lined up!" A boil the size of a ripe plum bobbed on the giantess's upper lip as she spewed the ugly words. "He was ready to take her. But what did she go and do? She told him she didn't want to marry him. Told him she would make a terrible wife! Honestly! The girl doesn't know what's good for her!"

The giant slammed out of the room, yelling, "I'm going to the Joining Ceremony! And you'd best come with me, Wife! Or people will talk."

"What about her?" the wife wailed.

"Let her stew in her tears. Maybe she'll cry herself into some sense."

The giantess sighed a sigh so long and so suffering the pictures on the bedroom wall rattled. "I'll tell people you're sick. That should keep them from coming after you. But you miss too many Joining Ceremonies and they're going to wonder."

The young woman, Ivy, lifted her head, revealing a beauty not even anger or the puffy redness of crying could mask. "I hate Joining Ceremonies! Half the couples getting joined are miserable!"

"Miserable beats alone!" the giantess said before storming out of the room.

Jackie longed to comfort the young woman, Ivy. Ivy! The name alone caused a curious feeling to rise up in her, a feeling of possibility, a feeling that maybe she *could* be happy—if only she could find a way to make contact. A gentle knock on the window? No. It would scare her; perhaps make her call out to her awful parents. Besides, there was such pleasure in simply gazing at her: her strong cheekbones, her long lashes, her lovely, full lips…

"What are you doing peering into Jorge Ingers's house?" a hulking giant snarled from the street.

Terrified, Jackie leapt down from her perch and sprinted her way down the street and through the crisscrossing avenues of the suburb, never daring to look over her shoulder to see if anyone was following. She continued on through the rolling green hills, her adrenaline pumping, heart thumping, and when she finally reached the hole in the road, she dove into the tunnel and all but slid her way down to the weedy patch in front of her house. Only then did she let herself rest, slumped on the ground, winded and exhilarated. What an adventure she'd had! What a peek into another world!

That night she was unable to sleep. She couldn't stop thinking about Ivy, about how sad she was. She became so obsessed with ways she herself might alleviate Ivy's unhappiness that she forgot all about her own discontent. She kept getting out of bed to look out the window at the beanstalk. Radiant with moonlight, the heart-shaped leaves glowed from within while the stalk lay hidden within the shadows. She cursed the lazy sun for taking its sweet time rising, cursed herself for being such a coward she'd scurried home at the first sign of trouble.

She picked up her palm communicator and messaged Marta. *What kind of bean was that?*

She was surprised when Marta messaged her right back. It *was* the dead of night. *You needed perspective.*

Irritated by Marta's elusiveness, Jackie messaged back a line of angry question marks.

Good luck with the bean was all Marta replied.

Jackie tossed her communicator onto the daybed and continued her pacing and sitting and pacing and cursing until dawn finally had the decency to break. Then she strode outside to the weedy patch, prepared to climb up the beanstalk, only to discover it had sprouted beans! Big beautiful green pods clung to the stalk like giant dewdrops. The beans made the stalk much easier to climb. She could use the pods to hoist herself up. When she reached the road this time, she took it at a quick clip, her mind whirring with scenarios of what she would say, or do, when she saw Ivy again.

The shepherd startled her out of her scheming. "Hey, Shortie! Where are you off to in such a hurry?"

"To seek out a friend!" she yelled back.

He waved a hand in the air. "Good luck!"

She continued jogging through the hills until she reached the suburb of oversized houses where she shifted to a brisk walk so as not to gain the attention of the giant passersby. When, at last, she came to that same street corner and that same shrub, she had to wait for a giantess pushing an enormous stroller with a pig-faced baby to make her way down the street before climbing up to the window.

Once there, she held her breath and peered into the room. Ivy was there! Sitting on the floor drawing in what looked to be a giant's notepad. She was even more beautiful than Jackie remembered, her black hair now tucked behind the cutest of ears. But once again Jackie was at a loss for how to get her attention. She'd spent the entire night coming up with plans for what she would do when she saw Ivy again, and now she couldn't think of a single one. If she could just get up the nerve to knock, she could—

But again the giantess of the house waylaid her by bursting through the door. "Put down that silly book of yours, girl!" Her face was covered in some kind of goopy beauty cream. "The widower Thompson has agreed to take a look at you. He's coming by tonight! Prepare yourself!"

"But he's twice my age! And was cruel to his last wife!"

"He needs a woman. His house is a shambles and he's been forced to eat nothing but tins of fish and peas."

"Would it kill him to pick up a broom? Boil an egg?"

"I don't know where you get these crazy ideas! Certainly not from me or your father. It would shame him to do such a thing. That's women's work and you know it! Just be ready!" The hag gave Ivy one last menacing look, then charged out of the room and slammed the door behind her.

Ivy flung her book on the floor, her eyes blazing with anger.

Jackie took a deep breath. Then another. When there was no courage to be found, she tapped lightly on the window anyway.

Startled, Ivy whirled around, but when her eyes met Jackie's her alarm appeared to melt into curiosity. Or Jackie hoped that was what her expression meant.

She motioned for Ivy to open the window.

Ivy shot a look to the bedroom door, then quietly walked over to lift the window. It was so large it took all of her body strength to accomplish. When at last she'd managed, all she said was, "This is different." But those three words wiped Jackie's mind clear of every single thing she'd planned to say; like sleeping butterflies roused by a ray of sunlight, her thoughts all fluttered away.

"Well?" the young woman said.

To Jackie's utter astonishment, she heard herself say something she had *not* planned to say: "I think I love you."

To Jackie's further astonishment, Ivy smiled a puckish smile. "In that case, come in. It's not often I have a woman knock on my window professing her love." She glanced toward her bedroom door once more before adding, "But be quiet. My parents are on a rampage."

Jackie scrambled through the window and did her best to jump lightly down into the bedroom. She was completely unprepared for how insignificant the enormous furniture would make her feel. How did Ivy manage? She noticed a stepstool by the light switch. Another by the dresser. But these concerns were minor compared to what she'd just confessed! Was she in love? Was that the fizzy feeling in her belly?

"I'm Jackie," she said, and stretched out her hand, a ridiculously formal move under the circumstances.

Ivy curtsied playfully and took her hand. "Ivy."

Then the two of them just stood there staring into one another's eyes, two ridiculous grins pasted on their faces, two hopeful hearts beating an unmistakable duet.

"Wow," Ivy said, at last. "It's amazing to be able to look into someone's eyes."

Jackie thought: *Amazing to want to look into someone's eyes.*

"So what are you doing here?" Ivy went on. "And more importantly, who are you?"

The amazing story of Marta and the bean came out in fits and starts, winding this way and that, like the beanstalk itself. Ivy appeared impressed if not entirely convinced by what she heard. "A giant beanstalk, huh? A place where everyone is my size, and a woman is not required by law to be joined to a man?"

"Women can be joined to women where I live," Jackie said, then felt herself flush.

Ivy raised an intrigued eyebrow. "Reeeeally…"

"Yup."

Unsure what to do next, Jackie picked up the sketchbook Ivy had tossed on the floor and handed it to her.

"Thanks," Ivy said. "My parents would kill me if they ever bothered to look at this. All art in Pureland must be sanctioned by the Committee for Moral Uprightness." An undercurrent of rage rumbled under her words, which Jackie found thoroughly compelling. Equally compelling was Jackie's ability to shift from the rage to the casual flipping of notebook pages for Jackie to see. She was so fluid with her emotions, flicking from one to another so effortlessly!

The notebook was filled with portraits, each one beautifully capturing a moment of private sadness.

"These are immoral?" Jackie asked.

"Unhappiness is considered immoral."

"But a person can't help if they're happy or not."

"That's debatable, but it certainly shouldn't be illegal."

"But your mom, your dad, they both seem sooo—"

"I know. It's this weird paradox…or denial…or double standard. I haven't quite figured it out. But it plagues Pureland. Everyone is unhappy, but they pretend not to be."

Jackie stared down at the ankle-high yellow carpet pile. "I used to think I'd never be happy."

"What changed?"

Jackie almost had the courage to tell her, but returned to the portraits instead. "Theses are wonderful." She worried that Ivy would notice her sudden shift of focus.

Ivy just laughed. "Of course you *would* say that. You came to me on a magic beanstalk professing your undying love."

"I just—" But the rest of Jackie's thought was kidnapped by a new one: She hadn't said undying, had she?

Ivy placed a hand on Jackie's chest. "Please don't apologize. Don't ruin this." Her hazel eyes were flecked with gold, her skin a sumptuous olive, her nose a small nut waiting to be… Unable to stop herself, Jackie leaned in to—

The sound of the front door crashing open thundered through the house.

Ivy stiffened. "My father. Back from his morning workout. He'll want breakfast."

"Can't he get it himself?"

"Just go."

"But…"

"Please. Go!"

"Ivy!" Her father's bellow shuddered through the house. "Where's my triple latte?"

Ivy bolted for the door, then spun around, took the few steps back, and cradled Jackie's face in her hands. "Thank you," she said, softly. "You've made today a much nicer day." Then she planted a whisper of a kiss on Jackie's lips. By the time Jackie regained composure, Ivy was slipping out the door, leaving Jackie to go out the way she came in.

She slunk around Ivy's neighborhood all morning, occasionally returning to the shrub outside Ivy's bedroom window, but alas, the room remained empty. She decided to do a little exploring and took one of the many moving sidewalks into the city. There she saw things that both thrilled and frightened her: beautiful mirrored skyscrapers next to alleys of trash and impoverished people, gorgeous store windows full of lavish merchandise but featuring live models whose lips and breasts were hideously augmented. But by far, the most puzzling thing was a torture device in the city's center that secured the offender's head, hands, and feet in a thick wooden block. Apparently it was used for punishing anyone deemed unhappy. A nearby broadside defined unhappiness as everything from failing to laugh at the mayor's jokes to sharing intimacy with one's same sex. Truly, the more Jackie saw of these giant people, the more she understood Iris's drawings. These people *were* unhappy—but they made great efforts to appear as if they weren't.

She returned to the suburb dispirited and just in time to witness the giant children returning home from school, giant backpacks slung over their giant shoulders, giant lollipops clutched in their giant fists. Their giant mothers herded them along like gaggles of unruly hippos, passing each other on the street gushing forced niceties—"Great day, huh?" "Doesn't get much better than this!"—their faces contorted into painful-looking smiles. The children taunted each other with cruel insults, but none of them ever dared cry.

Jackie was about to climb up the shrub when a melon-faced boy, as wide as he was tall, said, "Hey, you! I could squash you like a bug! Hey, Ronnie! Eno! Look what I found!" She tried to dissuade the bullies from their plan, but then one of them called over their dog, a mean, snarling thing; and Jackie, her depression now paramount, soon found herself trudging back to her own world at the bottom of the beanstalk. Only now her depression had a twinge of something new: anger. Not at the world, or Pureland, her usual practice, but at herself. How could she have given up on Ivy so easily? Was she really such a coward? Too wimpy to step up for someone she…loved?

Outside the pods were swelling with beans, some of them even bursting open and dropping their precious seeds to the ground.

Anyone could tell there wasn't much time before the magical plant began to die back, before she'd be cut off from Ivy forever.

She messaged the crone, Marta. *I have seen a place that lies beyond Utonia. It frightens me.*

You again? Marta messaged back.

Please tell me why you gave me that bean.

You needed perspective.

I can see that now. But I think I have also fallen in love.

Marta did not message back right away, which only added to Jackie's sense of urgency. When Marta did finally write back all she said was: *One does not "think" one has fallen in love. Either one has or one hasn't.*

Jackie knew that Marta was right. She also knew, as strongly as anyone can know anything, that she *had* fallen in love. She messaged this to Marta, adding the question: *How should I proceed?*

To which Marta messaged: *You're on your own with that one, dearie. Now I'm going back to my nap.*

Jackie stared out her window. The late-afternoon sun was turning the shadows long; the stalk showed signs of withering. It was now or never. So once again she forced her now-aching muscles up the beanstalk, which was beginning to shrivel and flake; and once again, she jogged down the road.

The shepherd shouted, "You? Again? Where are you off to now?"

"To rescue my love!" she yelled back, brazenly.

He smiled a snaggletoothed grin. "Good luck!"

"Thanks!" she yelled, and kept on.

When she returned to Ivy's house she was out of breath and her calves were burning, but she barely took note of these things, and slipped behind a tree while a couple of giant children on giant bicycles sailed past. Careful no one was watching, she mounted the shrub and peeked into the window only to find Ivy's room still empty. Her heart sank. Then she noticed the window was ajar. Determined to risk whatever it took to rescue Ivy, she wedged it open further and climbed in. Voices were coming from the interior of the house, one of them Ivy's. "I should warn you, I will make a very bad wife."

"Ivy!" her mother replied. "Manners!"

A man, the widower, Jackie supposed, chuckled and said, "I see I will have to teach you to be a good one."

"Show him the joining gown I made you," her mother said. "And the shoes."

A strange ka-thunk ka-thunk came toward the room. Jackie dove into the closet. The door opened and a weary, stilt-wearing Ivy stepped inside. Or that was what Jackie assumed, for Ivy was now close to ten feet tall and wearing one of the ankle-binding dresses of the Purelanders. The vision broke her heart.

She waited for Ivy to shut the door, then slipped from her hiding place.

Ivy recoiled, holding herself steady on the door frame. "What are you doing here?" she whispered. She ran her fingers self-consciously through her hair.

"I've come to rescue you."

Ivy laughed a numb laugh. "There's no rescuing me, my friend. My father has just signed the papers to hand me off to the Widower Thompson, a cruel man with bad breath and flaking skin."

"Then come with me! Down the beanstalk!"

Ivy sank down on the bed. "You're kidding, right?"

"No! I know it sounds crazy, but—"

"Ivy!" her mother called. "Are you almost ready?"

"Yes, Mother!"

Jackie hoisted herself unto the bed and knelt beside Ivy. "Didn't our kiss mean anything to you?"

Ivy's eyes pooled with tears. She blinked them back. "You have no idea…"

"So come with me."

"Ivy!" her mother yelled again. "Widower Thompson is growing impatient! And so am I!"

"Please," Jackie said. "I can't promise I'll always make you happy—but I know I can do better than this." She waited, aware that she was asking a lot. But she couldn't—wouldn't—doom Ivy to a life of unhappiness. Not if she could help it. She took a breath and played her last card: "I'm not going back without you."

Ivy met Jackie's gaze with such intensity if felt to Jackie as if her innards were being ripped from her belly. "You would forsake this wonderful world you speak of just to save me?"

Jackie nodded.

Ivy looked around her room once, then began lifting the heavy gold dress to wrestle off the hideous metal stilts. "Okay. Take me to this magic beanstalk of yours, this magic world."

Heart crashing in her chest, Jackie helped Ivy release the clasps, helped her wrestle off the gold dress and put on a short tunic. "Is there anything you want to bring? You won't be able to return."

Ivy thought for a moment, then said, "Nothing. Let's just get out of here."

"Ivy!" the giantess yelled.

Once on the road they ran side by side, matching one another stride for stride. It was getting dark and the streets were mostly empty of people. They hugged the shadows, Jackie praying that the beanstalk would be strong enough to hold them, worried what would happen if it weren't. At the outskirts of the city, an ear-shattering siren began to blare.

"They've found us out," Ivy said, breathlessly. "If they catch us we'll be stoned."

Jackie grabbed her hand and picked up the pace. She was having trouble telling how much farther they had to go—if they were even on the right road.

"Hey!" she heard a voice yell out from the shadows. "Where do you think you're going?"

Jackie breathed a sigh of relief. It was the shepherd. "Someplace better than this!"

"Lucky you!" he shouted.

A huge flying machine sputtered up behind them. *"Turn back! Now!"* an amplified voice commanded. In the distance dogs began to bark.

Jackie spotted the hole in the road and came to a halt. The tip of the beanstalk was drooping a good six feet away from the road.

"We're going to have to jump," she said.

Ivy leaned over and peered down the hole. Her eyes grew wide. "There really is a beanstalk."

"Yes. And if we don't jump now, our chance will be gone."

Ivy's eyes locked on Jackie's. "I don't know a thing about you..." was all she said. But it was enough. The two of them leapt, hand in hand, onto the top leaf of the beanstalk. It was brittle and dry, and Jackie worried it would disintegrate. But it held, the stalk bending gracefully downward and showering them in a downpour of confetti-like leaf flakes until it finally placed them gently into the weedy patch in front of Jackie's studio where they stood, gasping for breath, in the moonlight.

After a few rigid moments, Ivy released her vise grip on Jackie's hand and did a slow three-sixty. "Holy cats! You weren't kidding. Everything *is* my size!"

"I told you."

"I know, but—Look at that house! That tree! That...that"—she took Jackie's face in her hands—"that you!"

Ivy's touch lit Jackie up like a comet, the very air around her changing from dark and brooding to pure effervescence. Or, as the Utonians would later put it, "turned her from bulb to flower." The kiss that followed was long and lingering and bursting with promises of happily ever after.

Two elderly gentlemen on their evening constitutional stopped to take in the spectacle of the giant beanstalk dropping the two young women to the earth. Standing in the shadows, hand in hand, watching them kiss, the one said to the other: "That Marta, she sure knows how to cast a spell." His companion then kissed him on the cheek, and together they continued strolling down the magical, moonlit street of Utonia.

Allison Wonderland is one L of a girl. Her lesbian literature appears in the Cleis collections *Best Lesbian Romance 2013* and *2014*, as well as *Girl Fever*, *Girls Who Score*, and *Wild Girls, Wild Nights*. Besides being a Sapphic storyteller, Allison is a reader of stories Sapphics tell and enjoys everything from pulp fiction to historical fiction. Find out what else she's into and up to at aisforallison.blogspot.com.

This story is based on "Cinderella."

SWF SEEKS FGM
ALLISON WONDERLAND

*Single White Female Seeks Fairy Godmother
for shoe shopping companion and sappily-ever-after.
Must be able to work family-unfriendly magic with wand.*

Checks have mates. Glass slippers have mates. Even that repulsively scintillating stepdaughter of mine has a mate. Me, I've got bupkes.

As you know, I'm a widow. No, not a black widow—magenta is my color, I'll thank you to remember.

At heart, I'm a simple, vitriolic vixen in search of an animated sorceress who has the power to make my dreams come shrew.

That is to say, true.

I believe what we have here, my dear, is a self-fulfilling prophecy. Once upon a way to pass the time, I married Cinderella's father. We were not even on a first-name basis. I called him My Little Meal Ticket and he called me The Wicked Stepmother, the definite article of which I most definitely found flattering.

In spite of my bad reputation, I made him think my moniker was a misnomer. Damn, I'm good. So when he proposed marriage, I accepted. After all, if I put my mind to it, I could chateau the line.

Everything was Luciferric, until my husband croaked like the Frog Prince of a man that he was. Gone were the days of living it up. On the upside, I could once again live up to my nickname.

And did I ever. I looked at that looker Cinderella and thought: *I'll terminate her, too*. Oh, please don't misunderstand me—while my name is Lady Ptomaine, I am by no means a murderess. A villainess, sure, but I can assure you that every one of my husbands departed on good terms.

When Cinderella left—this palace, not this earth—we also parted amicably. I had been so uncouth to the youth, to understate the obvious, yet on her way out of her misery, she opted to hug me instead of slug me. If kindness could kill…Let's just perish the thought, shall we? With all the sincerity I could summon, I wished Cinderella a fond farewell, all the while hoping she would not fare well at all.

But she did, because of course she would. She's the underdog, the heroine. You've all been manipulated into adoring her and abhorring me. It's the age-old tale of good versus evil. When that revoltingly talented songbird brain opens her mouth, it's good verses for her and the evil eye for me.

Why am I so evil? Being mean is a picnic, a cakewalk, as easy as pumpkin pie. When you see, go evil: narrow your eyes like a feline. Mine offers an excellent example. When you hear, go evil: eavesdrop on the conversations of those who are similarly sinister. When you talk, speak pro evil. Use four-letter words such as "hate" and "hurt" and adopt a curt tone when executing commands. You see how straightforward that is?

Speaking of which…going forward, I am no longer straight. Herein lies the reason for my lies, my manipulations, my machinations. I took to playing cat and mouse with people's feelings as a means of subjugating my own.

I suspect I've always preferred the fair sex to the fair and middling sex—ladies and gentlemen, respectively—but in this kingdom, subjects are expected to exhibit a proclivity for heteronormativity.

Those who do not find themselves attracted to the opposite sex find themselves trapped in the tragic kingdom, scorned and mourned by young and old alike. It's a small-minded world, after all.

There are two ways of looking at this. I could, as one song advises, blame it on the reign. Or I could take the advice of a more refreshing refrain and believe that gray skies are gonna queer up.

I've put on plenty of things in my day: airs, the blame on others, myself on a pedestal. But a happy face? I wasn't sure that visage was even viable.

Still, I decided to fold up the social ladder and give it a whirl. And do you know what? I triumphed over adversity. Now all I've got to do is triumph over what some might call perversity.

Which brings us to the ad I placed in the personals column of our kingdom's underground newspaper. Where I come from, Fairy Godmothers are legendary, lauded for their altruism and affection and tenderness toward others. A Fairy Godmother, I reasoned, could give me a complete makeover. Internally, of course. Externally, I'm quite fetching, yes? She's mysterious, I'm imperious. She's everything nice, I'm everything vice. We'd make a consummate couple.

That being said, we can't consummate our coupledom until we become a couple. Thus far, I've received a single response to my ad. She telephoned last week, and at first I cringed at the sound of her voice, its treacle tone headache music to my ears. Nevertheless, I provided my address and we agreed to meet today at—

Oh! Queer she is now!

I hustle my bustle to the door and issue greetings and salivations.

That is to say, salutations.

I believe what we have here, my dear, is love at first sight. It is necessary that I describe this magical creature standing before me: in lieu of that joke of a cloak that constitutes the Fairy Godmother uniform, she is outfitted in a black gown that showcases her pleasantly plentiful proportions. Her hair, habitually hidden, is not only visible but luminous and voluminous. I put on a sappy face and glue my gaze to the blue hue of hers.

"You must be Wicked," she says.

"Is that an order," I reply, "or an observation?"

She shakes her head. The expression on her face can only be described as a cross between empathy and enmity.

I offer my arm. She takes it, her grip predictably delicate.

"So you're the devil woman," she remarks, as we embark on our short journey to the sitting room.

"Yes," I swoon, "which is why I am in desperate need of a guardian angel."

Godmother rolls her eyes, a response that seems quite out of character for such a winsome woman.

"Why don't you come over here and sit a spell?"

Her laugh is polite and probably patronizing, but she accepts the invitation, taking a seat on the sofa.

"May I offer you a beverage?"

"No, thank you. I have only a thirst for knowledge." So saying, she leans forward, inspecting the selection of hag rags spread out on the coffee table. She skips over *SinStyle* and *Women's Stealth* and picks up the latest issue of *Good Mousekeeping*.

"That's Lucifer," I gush, pointing to the handsome, hissy-faced feline on the cover. "He was voted Pussy of the Year by his peers."

"I'd love to meet him," she says, but I can tell she would sooner meet her Maker.

"I'm afraid I can't let him out of the bag. But you know what they say: when the cat's away..." It is then that I notice the magic wand tucked between her breasts. "I envy your bosom friend."

She smirks. "I believe the tail end of that expression is 'the mice will play.'"

For the first time in my life, I hear no evil, only good. "Will they?"

She shrugs. "Will they? Won't they? All perfectly preposterous inquiries that mandate either/or."

"In that case," I snicker, and hope she won't bicker, "are you a man or a mouse?"

"Neither/nor," she answers in all seriousness. "Lady Ptomaine, Bea Strait."

I feel my blood run colder. Is she going to cast aspersions on my perversions? Take that magic wand and poke my eyes out for making eyes at her? "Listen here, you little Fairy Godmotherfu—"

"Don't curse in my presence!" Godmother gasps, her mouth agape like a mask of tragedy.

I rush to my defense. "How else should I react when you're making insults?"

"I was making introductions," she clarifies, still shuddering in shock. "Bea isn't a verb. It's a noun. A proper noun, to be precise. My parents named me after the beauteous Bea Arthur."

"Oh," I whimper. There's something disturbingly delightful about being disciplined. "God'll get me for that, won't He?"

Bea chuckles. "He'll send you straight to Shady Pines, you shady Lady, you."

I blush. Being red feels a lot better than seeing red.

Bea reclines against the sofa, properly propping her feet up on the coffee table. I gasp, my mouth agape like the ruby-colored peep-toe shoes Bea wears.

"They're from the Friends of Dorothy Zbornak line," she shares.

"Speaking of which, I would like to apologize for the way I treated a certain friend of yours. It was nothing personal. Cinderella and I, we just got off on the wrong foot, that's all. She really was a shoo-in for the throne. Meanwhile, my girls couldn't even get the shoe on, which should come as no surprise to me because—"

"Put a sock in it, would you? I liked you better when you were unapologetically unapologetic."

Words fail me. I don't know whether to have a good feeling about this or a bad feeling, although truth be told, I wouldn't know a good feeling if it...I don't know, felt me up.

"Am I your type or your stereotype?" Bea asks, surmising my surprise. "If you were expecting me to be the guardian angel to your devil woman, I'm afraid your great expectations are going to grate on my nerves. Oh, that reminds me: Cinderella is expecting."

I blink, experiencing a hint of happy-for-her. It's a foreign though not altogether unpleasant emotion. "A baby?"

"No, the unexpected. Yes, a baby. I'm going to be the baby's godmother—lowercase for the time being, in case somebody else wants the job. I can't hog all the humans, you know. Oh, *that* reminds me—I just love the power of suggestion—before you and I get involved in...an involvement, I've been hearing rumors that you're dating Beauty *and* the Beast."

"I can explain."

"And you will."

I could get used to this, this business of taking orders. As it turns out, it's quite a turn-on. What's more, it's compatible with my motto: It's better to receive than to give. "Well, you see—"

"Mother!"

"What?" we respond in unison, then chuckle in tandem.

"I have company," I call, in the mother of all motherly tones. "Can it wait?"

"I suppose," one of the girls grumbles. They aren't twins, my daughters, but their unfortunate features render them difficult to look at and, therefore, almost impossible to distinguish. Regardless, I hope they'll accept the Sapphic side of me. They had no choice but to accept the bad side of me, so if need be, I'll simply make the choice for them this time, too.

Right now, however, I am choosing to focus all my attention on the very good company sitting beside me. "This rumor, it's unsubstantiated. That Sea Witch started it after I spurned her advances. What could I do? We weren't right for each other. Besides, with as many arms as she's got, she'd never be satisfied with just one octopussy in her garden."

Bea's lips curl like Lucifer's tail. "So you believe in monogamy?"

"Of course. I may be immoral, but by no means am I amoral."

"Well, it's good to know that you're still evil. I've got a thing for bad girls," Bea confesses, and pats my leg just below the thigh. "The Bea's knees," she teases, and squeezes.

For the first time in my life, I have a good feeling, and it feels so good. "What do you say we make like our clothes and take off?"

"Cool your jets, Lady," Bea advises, but her tone sounds enchantingly enticing.

"You mean we have to keep things G-rated?" I pout, hot under the lavender collar of my dress. "That G—isn't it short for G-spot?"

"Not...officially," Bea murmurs, coming closer.

"Just think," I reply, when she's close enough to feel my wicked cool heat, "if and when we do...that, you too will be known as an evildoer. But in a good way."

J. Leigh Bailey (jleighbailey.net) is an office drone by day and the author of young adult LGBTQ romance by night. A book-a-day reading habit sometimes gets in the way of…well, everything…but some habits aren't worth breaking. She writes about boys traversing the crazy world of love, relationships, and acceptance.

This story is based on *Alice in Wonderland*.

A Hero in Hot Pink Boots
J. Leigh Bailey

My brother always says my stubbornness will get me into trouble one day. Turns out today's the day. Or night, rather.

To be honest, though, stubbornness didn't cause my current predicament. Nope. My first foray into the lives of the popular people isn't turning out at all like I imagined it. The momentary pleasure of being invited and the knee-jerk acceptance of an invitation I had no business accepting might end up costing more than I can afford.

Not that I can afford much of anything. I have a whopping fourteen dollars to my name, all singles, all folded up in the mostly empty wallet in the pocket of my nicest jeans.

I glare at Paul, and when he smirks, I look at Todd. They both look fantastic, of course, the height of modern high school fashion, wearing the trendiest, fanciest clothes money can buy.

My nicest jeans and coolest T-shirt don't compare. Not by far.

A warehouse looms behind them, heavy bass pounding and neon lights flashing. A muscled mass of human stands by the door, beefy arms crossed over a beefier chest.

"Twenty bucks?" I cringe. "I didn't know I'd need that much." My shoulders droop.

Paul looks at me like I said something particularly pathetic. "This is *the* party this weekend. It's an underground rave, special invite only."

"We thought you could use the experience," Todd adds. "It's like our good deed for the year. Broadening the horizons of the less fortunate."

My face burns. In shame. In humiliation. But mostly in anger. *Less fortunate?* "I don't have twenty dollars." I barely get the words out through my clenched teeth. I would give just about anything—including the fourteen singles in my wallet—to not have had to say that. Besides, didn't raves go out of style with the Spice Girls?

Paul and Todd share a look that squicks my stomach. A silent conversation passes between them and my blood chills by the second. This won't be good. Todd licks his lips and nods. They turn back to me. "I can pay your way," Paul says with a reptilian smile. "But you don't get something for nothing these days, right?"

"Right." Todd nods.

"I'll pay for you, but you'll have to do something for me." His hand trails down his bony chest and I know exactly where it's going to stop. I stare, really hoping I'm wrong. But I'm not. He cups his junk and tilts his pelvis suggestively.

Oh. My. God. *Gross.* Bile creeps up my throat. I throw up a staying hand. "You know what? No. Just…no." I back away, and after a dozen steps, I whirl around and keep walking. Todd's and Paul's cold laughter trails behind me.

Ten minutes later and I'm completely lost. I squint at the nearest street sign. Somehow I've ended up in a mostly deserted part of Chicago. Alone. At night. Not the Magnificent Mile, either. Grit and grime edge the streets and I'm about as far from the Gold Coast as I can get without stumbling into the ghetto.

I should have stayed. How bad could a party like that be? Sure, drugs and alcohol aren't really my thing, but I could cope for one night, right? Better that than be accosted by some homicidal maniac while wandering the city in the middle of the night. I blame it on high school.

High school is okay. Being poor at a high school in a wealthy suburb is less okay. Every day I'm surrounded by people who think nothing of shelling out hundreds of dollars for a pair of shoes and who drive BMWs or Mercedes. Then there's me. Stuck with public transportation or the "generosity" of my big brother.

No lights glow up ahead or to my left, so I turn right. There are lights, but no other signs of life. To make matters worse—not that they need it—I don't even have my phone to call my brother for the ride. Because, like an idiot, I'd been so jazzed about the invite, I'd forgotten it on my dresser where I'd left it to charge. I need to find someone—preferably someone not homicidal—with a phone so I can make the call. So not looking forward to that. My brother will hold the favor and the inevitable I-told-you-so over my head for years to come.

What possessed me to agree to go to that party? It's not like Todd and Paul are friends. We're barely on a first-name basis.

Okay, I know why I agreed, but it's humiliating. I was so flattered to be asked that I said yes without thinking it through. That'll teach me.

So here I am, lost. In a sketchy part of Chicago at nearly midnight. Yep, worse and worse.

My foot catches on an uneven break in the pavement and I sprawl forward. Concrete scrapes against my palms and I barely miss hitting my chin. "Damn it, Kevin." Yes, indeed. Worse and worse. I push myself up, wincing at the sharp ache in my knee.

"Look what the cat dragged in," a melodic voice purrs.

I turn to face the speaker, crouching defensively.

One glance and alarm turns to awe.

A guy—maybe a year or two older than me—stands on the top of the stairs to a brick town house. He is the most beautiful creature I have ever seen—tall with long arms and legs, and a loose-jointed stance that reminds me of a cat. His dark skin shimmers in the orange glow of the front light. His full lips are slicked up with some kind of lip gloss and his eyes are lined and dusted with gold eye shadow, making them look positively huge. A skintight black shirt that might be made of spandex clings to his narrow shoulders and chest. His pants—apparently made of the same stretchy material—sport gold and black tiger stripes on a white background. Somehow the stripes at his hips point straight to his crotch. My tongue sticks to the roof of my mouth, but my gaze doesn't linger there. No, I am completely caught up in the guy's boots.

Hot pink, patent leather, knee-high boots stacked on four-inch sparkling gold platforms.

He really should look ridiculous, but I'm not amused. I'm awestruck. He is…magnificent.

He poses at the top of the steps, one hand on his hip, body tilted to show it off to the best advantage in the dim light.

"Uh, hi," I croak out, my aching knee forgotten.

As if that's his cue, the other guy comes down the steps. No, he doesn't *come down* the steps. He sashays down with all the swagger and swaying hips of a contestant on *America's Next Top Model*. In those boots he towers over me by several inches.

"Aren't you adorable?" he drawls.

I try to clear away the obstruction in my throat. It's not as easy as it should be. "Uh, thanks?"

"What's your name, sweetheart? I'm Cedric." He holds out a long, slim hand and I take it without thinking. The skin is soft and the contact sends tingling sparks through my veins. I try not to react—really, I do—but when Cedric glides his thumb down the back of hand, my toes curl. Seriously, like some teeny-bopper-chick-flick heroine being swept up by local heartthrob. Ridiculous.

"Kevin," I say in a rush of breath, remembering his question at the last second. There is something very wrong with this picture. I look up and down the street. I don't know if I'm searching for an escape route or a camera crew. Surely Cedric can't be for real.

"I hate it when the sidewalk jumps up to trip me like that." After one last, lingering caress of thumb, Cedric releases my hand. I make a fist, trying to hold on to the sensation, and realize the scraped palms no longer burn. Lust as an anesthetic?

Heart stuttering in my chest, I gaze into Cedric's beautiful face. The cocoa-colored skin looks so soft… I bite my tongue, hoping the sharp pain will be enough to clear my head. It is, but not by much. I've lost my mind, that's all there is to it. I shouldn't stand here like an idiot, gawking at some exotic guy, a stranger in more ways than one, in the middle of a dark street in an unfamiliar part of the city.

"I've got to go," I manage to say around a tongue that doesn't quite seem to work right. Not because of the bite, but because Cedric is just that awe-inspiring. "But it was nice meeting you." I keep staring, willing my feet to move. One step is all it will take, I know it. Just one step.

Cedric grins, but it's not any mundane twist of lips. No, he has the mysterious smirk of Mona Lisa and the smug, all-encompassing smile of the Cheshire Cat, all wrapped together. "Excellent," he says, linking his elbow with mine. "Tonight was turning out to be such a bore. I *have* to get out of here. Where are we going?" Wide, impossibly bright brown eyes meet mine.

"Excuse me?"

"Where are we going?" Cedric repeats, as if that's what I mean.

"No, I mean, I'm going to find a phone and call for a ride." A thought occurs to me. "I don't suppose you have a phone I can use?"

Cedric steps far enough away to spread his arms and juts his hip. "Honey, does it look like I have a phone hidden somewhere?"

No. The answer is definitely no. The skintight clothes and the form-fitting boots leave little—nothing—to the imagination. The only way he can be carrying a phone is if there is a secret compartment in the platforms of his boots. I sigh. "Of course not. Well, if you point me to the nearest twenty-four-hour pharmacy or a grocery store or someplace that has a phone, I'd appreciate it."

"I'll do you one better," Cedric says. "There's a place a few blocks over that should still be open. I'll take you."

"Oh, but I'm sure you have something better to do." He must be dressed up to go out, right? No one dresses that way all the time. "You can just tell me which way to go."

"Are you *trying* to get rid of me? Why would you want to hurt my feelings like that?"

I start to apologize, to reassure him that I want him with me. Except the guy freaks me out, and not in an altogether bad way. I've never been attracted to feminine or androgynous guys before; usually I crush on the jocks with their powerful muscles and loads of self-confidence. Cedric is confident enough for twenty jocks, but instead of bulging muscles, he's sleek and sinuous, like an exotic cat. A leopard maybe, or a jaguar. A jaguar in hot pink boots.

I concede. "If you've got nothing better to do, I suppose you can show me the way."

"Yay!" With a hop that shouldn't be possible in those boots, Cedric bounds forward and links elbows with me again.

A block and a half or so later, I catch sight of another person for the first time. A slouching hulk of a guy leans against a wall on the other side of the street, smoking a cigarette and watching the block. When his eyes land on Cedric, the guy spits out the cigarette and crushes it under the heel of his boot. "Hey, boy," he calls out. "You need to decide whether you're a man or a girl. 'Cause that pretty little princess thing you've got going on, it's whacked."

I stiffen as unfamiliar protectiveness surges through me. No one should talk to, or about, Cedric that way. And why do I care? I barely met the guy five minutes ago.

Cedric isn't disturbed, though. "Shut your trap, Jamal. You need to watch who you're talking to."

"And who's that?" Jamal asks, taking a step into the street. "Some pussy-boy wearing Barbie doll clothes?"

Cedric waves that aside. "Oh, you don't need to worry about me. My friend here"—he runs a hand along my arm suggestively and I have to grind my teeth together to keep from shivering—"knows how to take care of business."

I blink. What the hell is Cedric talking about?

"Oh yeah? And who's your friend?" Jamal folds arms that are about the same size as my legs across his bull-like chest.

Cedric seems genuinely surprised—and worried—that Jamal doesn't recognize me. "Don't tell me you've never heard of Marcus Carabas? Massacre Marc? The Master?"

I look over my shoulder, but no one else is around. Who is Cedric talking about? Jamal eyes me warily.

"Isn't he the one—" Jamal begins.

"Exactly. Now scurry along." Cedric wiggles his fingers in dismissal. "If you're lucky, Marcus won't be offended by your disrespect."

"Hey, dude, no disrespect meant. We're cool, right?" Jamal takes a few steps away from the street, leaning toward the shadows at the base of the building. He stares six inches over my head, fear emitting from his wide eyes and slack jaw.

Cedric pinches my ass and I jump. What the hell? He glares meaningfully at me and then at Jamal. "Oh! I mean, yeah, we're cool." I try to infuse my words with some of the swagger that Jamal had at the beginning of the conversation.

Jamal backs up until he can duck into the building, slamming the door behind him.

"What was that all about?" Now that Jamal is gone, I rub at my bruised butt, massaging away the sting.

"It's nothing." Cedric waves his fingers again.

"Seriously." I fold my arms over my chest. "Who is Marcus Carabas and why would you want that Jamal guy to think I'm him?"

"*You* are Marcus Carabas."

Not for the first time during our brief acquaintance, I wonder if Cedric isn't a little bit out of his mind.

"Or at least he thinks you are, and that's what's important."

"Yeah, but what about me?" I point to my chest. "Are you trying to get my ass kicked?"

"I have better things to do with your body. I'm not about to let anything happen to it, or you." Cedric smirks. When Todd smirks, it creeps me out. When Cedric smirks, my blood boils.

I try to swallow my tongue. At least that's what it feels like. My whole body flushes with embarrassment and eagerness. As soon as I'm sure my tongue is not, in fact, stuck in my esophagus, I say in a humiliatingly weak voice, "That's reassuring."

"Now tell me," Cedric says, strolling down the now-empty street, pulling me along while I struggle to keep up without stumbling, "what has you wandering through the streets alone on a Friday night?"

I don't know why or even how, but the next thing I know, the whole story comes pouring out. About the rave. About Paul's offer. About my limited cash. The whole time Cedric watches me with luminous eyes, nodding occasionally.

As we walk, the dark city changes. The shadows slinking along the sidewalk and around building no longer look eerie and threatening. Instead, they look mysterious, almost magical. The occasional streetlight we pass spotlights Cedric in all of his flamboyant, tiger-striped, pink-booted glory. It's like I am trapped in a fairy tale, one where boring teenagers become infamous badasses and magical, colorful creatures walk the streets.

My stomach sinks a bit when we turn a corner and I see the glowing sign for the twenty-four-hour pharmacy. I cringe at the yellow light from the front window that heralds the harsh return to reality.

"I guess we're here." I rock on the balls of my feet, tucking my thumbs into the waistband of my jeans. I glance at Cedric from the corner of my eyes.

"Who are you going to call?"

"My brother, I guess." Once again, my legs don't want to move. Maybe I don't need to worry about Cedric's sanity. My own mental stability is obviously in question. I finally manage to take a step and immediately jump back when a panicked face appears in the store's doorway.

"I don't want any trouble!" the clerk, a skinny middle-aged man in a blue vest shouts even as he twists the dead bolt, locking us out.

"*What?* I just need to use your phone." I push at the door, which doesn't budge.

"Leave now!" The clerk backpedals, holding out a warning hand. "I'll call the cops!"

Cedric steps up behind me, wrapping his arms around my waist. "He must have heard about Marcus."

I try to ignore the shivers his breath in my ear causes. "Marcus? But Marcus doesn't even exist!"

I catch a whiff of something sweet, like vanilla or sugar cookies, and inhale deeply, relaxing against Cedric's lithe body. Without conscious thought, I turn in Cedric's arms to try and get a better sample of the scent.

"Marcus is whoever you want to be."

I close my eyes, basking in the moment. It doesn't feel awkward at all to be standing in front of a store while Cedric's arms hold me. "You're not altogether sane, are you?"

"Honey, I'm as sane as you are."

Somehow that's not very reassuring. Right at this moment, I don't care, though.

I order my arms to release Cedric, and as much as I don't want to, I move out of his embrace. "I still need to find a phone."

"There's an all-night restaurant a couple of blocks up, one of those pancake places. They should have a phone you can use."

I keep my pace slow as we walk away from the pharmacy. I reach over and take Cedric's hand in mine before I even know I intend to. I've never done anything that ballsy in my life. Always I wait for someone else to make the first move. Not sexually or romantically—I'm a complete novice in all things romance—but in anything. I was so psyched when Todd invited me along. It didn't matter that Todd and Paul weren't friends of mine, or even friendly, or that parties in the city aren't my style. The fact that someone—anyone—had actually approached me made me giddy as hell. Maybe it's some kind of self-esteem thing. It's a risk, isn't it, taking the first step. It doesn't matter if it's an offer to be lab partners in chemistry or a date, rejection sucks. But here, with Cedric, the cautioning voice that keeps me from initiating any kind of interaction with others is staying silent. No, not silent. Gone.

The voice is gone.

And Cedric isn't rejecting me.

The thought makes me a little dizzy. Sure, Cedric is a little odd, but he's gorgeous and confident and doesn't look at me as though wondering who I am or why I'm here. Heck, I'd bet there are people I've gone to school with for years who probably have no idea what my name is. I'm that easily overlooked.

Maybe that's my fault. Maybe if I take more chances, initiate more contact, that can change. How far am I willing to go to test this newfound understanding and confidence?

"Cedric?"

He squeezes my hand. "Hmm?"

Screwing up my courage, I blurt out, "Willyoukissmeplease?" I bite back the groan at my own idiocy at the last second. I want to dissolve into a puddle and sink into the cracks of the sidewalk. Let people walk all over me. It's exactly what I deserve after that flop of a request.

When Cedric stops, I let myself be pulled to a halt, too. I fix my gaze on the tips of his boots, focusing on the glint of moonlight on the golden sparkles of the platforms. The heat from Cedric's hands on my face burns away the blush I know is staining my cheeks. "Say it again." The soft/rough texture of Cedric's voice washes down my spine, scrubbing away embarrassment.

I lick my lips and try again. "Will you kiss me? Please?"

The smile that blooms across Cedric's face shines brighter and broader than the moon above. "Yes," he says simply.

It's a soft kiss, a sweet kiss, everything a first kiss should be. And, good God, it rocks my universe. Tingles, starting from where our mouths touch, spread down my back and explode in my brain. Fourth of July sparklers dance under my skin, making me stand straighter, taller, prouder. Maybe it's because of the way Cedric purrs as he changes the angle of the kiss, deepening it. Yeah, that's probably it.

Cedric breaks away, leaving behind the lingering flavor of vanilla-scented lip gloss. There's an old saying about cats in the cream and another about cats who eat the canary. So much satisfaction pours off Cedric he resembles the cat who double-dipped the canary into the cream before eating it at snack time.

"Give me a fricking break."

A bucketful of muddy water in the face wouldn't have knocked me out of the moment as fast as those harsh, disgusted words.

"*That's* Carabas? Is this some kind of joke?"

Like an amateur presentation of *West Side Story*, a small group of thugs—complete with leather jackets and motorcycle boots—pose under a streetlight in perfect V-formation. The guy speaking stands at the apex, of course.

I count seven of them, and they all stalk forward, menace in every step.

"You know these guys?"

Cedric nods. "Unfortunately. Troublemakers. Not real dangerous, but *very* irritating."

I'm not sure I can trust Cedric's assessment. After all, if I am the threatening, mean-as-a-snake Marcus Carabas, then these guys he calls merely irritating are either as dangerous as kittens or as deadly as a South American drug cartel. Whichever end of the spectrum they fall on, irritating probably doesn't cover it.

The leader of the *irritating* gang stops in front of me, bringing with him the scent of leather and tobacco.

"Smoking's bad for you, you know." It takes me a second to realize what I said. What am I thinking? Nothing. Clearly I'm not thinking at all, to spout out that kind of idiocy.

"What's that supposed to mean?" The leader of the pack looms closer, glaring down a long nose that gives him a ferret-like look. "Is that some kind of threat?"

"Carabas doesn't make threats," Cedric says before I can get my brain to fully engage. "He makes promises."

"Um...Cedric?" I take a small step back as the thug presses even closer. "Try not to aggravate the wildlife, please," I mutter under my breath.

"Who are you calling wildlife?" The thug lunges forward, beefy hands reaching for me.

I lean away too quickly, my back arching *Matrix*-style to avoid the thug's grab. Unlike Keanu, my body isn't used to such contortions. My left leg kicks out in an effort to counter-balance my upper body weight and lands with significant force between the thug's legs. He bellows, hunching forward and cupping his balls. Cedric slips an arm behind my shoulders to keep me from falling backward.

"Ouch." Cedric's voice lacks all sympathy. He sneers at the thug as he helps settle me on my feet.

Thug #2 objects to Cedric's obvious amusement. He charges forward in nearly an exact replica of the first guy. He swings his fist at my head and Cedric nudges the back of my knees. I collapse into a squat even as Thug #2's punch flies over my head. The force of his swing pulls him around into an awkward pirouette and he spins into the first thug. Both of them fall to the ground in a tangle of arms and legs.

Cedric reaches down and pulls me up by the collar of my coolest T-shirt. I'm beginning to feel like Cedric's Kevin-shaped puppet. Of course, if his manhandling keeps me from getting my ass kicked, you can call me Pinocchio.

Thug #3 and Thug #4 dart forward and try to help the first two up. Somehow, all four end up on the ground, a writhing mass of denim and leather. I can't stop the bubbling laughter that creeps up my chest and through my throat. It's a slapstick comedy of errors. Whenever one tries to gain any kind of traction on the asphalt, their boots or hands or whatever slip and the whole lot of them fall back into place. Moonlight glints off some kind of shiny substance. Iridescent swirls of color show at certain angles. They landed in some kind of oil. What are the odds?

I don't even try to stifle my guffaws. Not only do they look ridiculous, they are unable to do anything more than glare at me. The other three thugs, the ones still standing, look on helplessly. They exchange glances. Questions are clear in their expressions. What should they do? Help their buddies? Attack? Retreat? Clearly, they don't want to come near me. The same fear I saw in Jamal's and the clerk's eyes shines in theirs.

I shake my head and link elbows with Cedric. "Let's get out of here."

"The restaurant?" Cedric asks.

I think about it for a second, about the call I'll have to make to my brother. And about the surprising things I've learned about myself tonight. "You know what? No. I'll just go back to the rave and haul Paul and Todd out of the building. I don't need to put up with their crap."

Cedric purrs. Lord, I love that sound. "Confident men are so sexy." He leans in close, wrapping both hands around my arm and resting his head on my shoulder. He has to stoop to do it, what with the difference in our heights and the added inches from his boots. It feels natural, though. Right.

We take our time. Now that I'm not in a hurry to get home, we can afford to dawdle. I want to extend my time with Cedric. I suspect I won't get to see him again. After all, he is clearly a creature of the urban jungle, and me, I'm banished to suburbia.

But if I've learned nothing else over the course of the last two hours, I did discover my backbone.

"Cedric?"

"Hmm?" It's a sigh of contentment more than a question. He rubs his head against my shoulder, like a cat scent-marking his favorite human.

"Will I see you again? I mean, after I go home?"

Cedric lifts his head and plants his pink-and-gold-covered feet. He turns to face me, flashing that Mona Lisa/Cheshire Cat smile. "Do you want to?"

"Well...yeah."

"Then you will."

"I wish we had a piece of paper or something. That way we could exchange phone numbers at least." I pull out my wallet and peer at the meager offerings. My ID and fourteen ones. Not even a receipt. I consider sacrificing one of the dollar bills—what's a buck in exchange for future interactions with Cedric?—but I don't even have a pen.

"Oh, well, here." Cedric reaches down to unzip the pink patent leather of one boot shaft and pulls out a slim phone. "Just put your info in my phone."

He has a phone? How did he— "Wait a minute! You told me you didn't have a phone!"

Cedric taps a finger to my nose and grins. "Au contraire. I asked if it *looked like* I had a phone on me."

"Then I could have called my brother at any point?"

"Yeah, but wasn't this more fun?" He tilts his head and looks at me through heavy-lidded golden eyes. "I know I enjoyed getting to know *you*."

I don't know whether to be upset or flattered. Who am I kidding? I'm totally flattered, and unlike the shallow flattery I felt at Paul and Todd's invitation, this time I know Cedric did this to spend time with me, not out of some kind of bet or humiliating prank. The whole Marcus Carabas thing is a little weird, but maybe it's for the best. Cedric might be a little crazy, but maybe I need a little crazy in my life. Especially when crazy makes me feel confident and worthy.

"You are," I say, standing on my tiptoes and kissing Cedric's cheek, "the most fascinating creature." I grab his phone and quickly enter my contact information. "Let's walk around some more. I think I want to spend more time getting to know my own personal hero."

It's nearly dawn by the time I return home. I have learned three things over the last several hours, though. First, I can spend weeks in Cedric's company and will never fully understand him. Second, Paul and Todd are the worst, weakest kind of bullies. I channeled a bit of Carabas and they practically fell over themselves to drive me home, all the while promising to leave me, and anyone else they might have wanted to mess with, alone. And third: I have standards. I have self-respect. And now I can add self-confidence to the mix.

It may have taken a catlike hottie in tiger-striped spandex and pink and gold platform boots to bring him out, but I really do have a little bit of Marcus Carabas in me. I'm not going to hide him behind baseless insecurities anymore. And if I tried—I stroke a hickey on my collarbone and grin—Cedric will just haul him out again. Which is exactly how it's supposed to be.

Andi Marquette (andimarquette.com) is an award-winning author of mysteries, speculative fiction, and romance. Her latest works include the novels *Day of the Dead* and *The Edge of Rebellion* and the novella *From the Boots Up*.

This story is based on "Little Red Riding Hood."

Red
Andi Marquette

Flesh and fur were slow to burn, and Rebeca knew the odor too well. From her vantage point on the steps of the church she could see the pyre in the town square and hear the pop and hiss of wood and wolf. She descended the steps two at a time and pushed through the crowd until the stench of death and heat stung her face.

"How many?" she asked a boy who stood to her right. She dreaded his answer.

"Two, miss."

She stared hard at the forms in the flames, but the blackened remains told her nothing of their past. She smelled no enchantment in the air, and she knew these were mere wolves, targeted because they might be something else, something much stronger, something tied to earth, blood, and magic. She'd once hunted them, too, roamed the forests in her scarlet cape, arrows tipped with silver, seeking to stop the beasts from spreading the bite and ravaging the landscape with fear.

She was an excellent shot and had brought several of the beasts in without killing a single true wolf. But, she thought as greasy black smoke rose from the pyre, she'd let old stories blind her, as they did so many. She realized it when she met Isadora.

"They'll be going out again," the boy said. "Another hunting party."

Rebeca looked down at him.

"Will you go with them?" he asked. He motioned at her cloak, recognizing it and taking her for the huntress she used to be.

"Not today. Sick friend."

"Tomorrow?"

"Perhaps," she lied.

"Lost the taste for it?" said a man who had appeared next to her. A large man whose dull brown hair hung to his shoulders and whose cheeks always appeared as if he'd been out in the wind too long. He stared down his long nose at her and grinned.

"Perhaps I'm just busy."

"Aye. With a sick friend." He gave "friend" a sarcastic emphasis, then looked at the bonfire. "Shot one of those myself. One bolt." He looked back at her, as if expecting her to challenge him.

She did. "I hope your friends were there to put the poor beast out of its misery after you'd missed all the vital organs with your one shot."

The boy cleared his throat, like he was trying to cover a laugh, and the man glared at him, then back at her.

"Stay out of the forests, miss. Do what women should, and find a man."

"And are you making yourself available, Robert?"

He scowled and spat on the stones underfoot. "Watch yourself." He turned and strode away.

She stared after him, wondering whether his last statement was a warning or a threat. The boy scampered after another group of boys and Rebeca gathered her cloak around her and slipped out of the crowd. The smell followed her, and she tasted bile in her throat as she hurried down a series of alleys until she arrived at a particular door. She hesitated to knock, afraid that this time, there would be no response from within.

She stood long enough outside the door that a woman across the way lingered in her own doorway, watching. So Rebeca knocked, dreading what she might hear. Or worse, what she wouldn't.

The door opened a crack and an eye, blue like a gemstone, appeared. Rebeca exhaled in relief. A whispered greeting sounded within and the door opened enough to let her in.

"Isadora," Rebeca said as she pulled the woman to her. She

kicked the door shut with her foot. "They're burning two more wolves in the square."

"Pity." Isadora clung to her.

"You can't stay here."

"Shh." She stroked Rebeca's cheek with her fingertips.

"I mean it. It's too dangerous."

"And too dangerous to be in the forests while they hunt." Isadora smiled, but her expression was haunted and pained. "I am too weak, love. I wouldn't last a night."

Rebeca reluctantly released her and glanced around the cramped, darkened room. It smelled of fatigue and weakness, a heavy, cloying odor. Underneath it she caught an acrid scent of scorched metal, not Isadora's usual. Dark enchantment. A bottle stood on the nearby table. She picked it up and held it near a weak slash of light that snuck in past the shutter. "How much have you had?" She jerked her gaze back to her, worry rippling through her chest.

Isadora looked away.

"Tell me."

"Enough."

She held the bottle up again. Over halfway gone. "It's too much." She set it down. "It'll kill you." She tried to keep the fear out of her voice, but from Isadora's expression she had failed. "Does it no longer work at the smaller dosage?"

"No." Isadora wrapped her arms around herself, and Rebeca saw, in the dim light, how frail she was, how the elixir had done what the old woman had said, but how it had indeed exacted a price.

"You must stop taking it." She returned to Isadora's side and gathered her into her arms. How thin she seemed.

"If I do, I'll die anyway. You know that."

"Then we'll leave. We'll go somewhere safe, where you won't have to hide from the moon. Or take poisons to ward it off."

Isadora laughed, but it lacked humor. "The hunts are not merely confined to this village. Or to these forests. Where, dear one, will we go?"

"There is a place—" She stopped at Isadora's expression.

"No."

"You'd be safe. We both would. Morgayne would ensure that."

"There's always a price for magic."

"You're paying a price now." Rebeca gripped her arms and stared into her eyes, fierce. "Every moon, you have to take larger amounts of that—that poison." She jerked her head toward the table. "I don't want to lose you to that."

Isadora lowered her head.

"Please. It's the one part of the forest the huntsmen won't go."

She sighed in resignation. "Of course they won't. She's a witch."

Rebeca stroked her face. "She's also my grandmother. And she owes me."

Isadora stepped again into Rebeca's embrace, and Rebeca knew that she'd won this argument. "We can leave before dawn. Can you be ready?"

"Yes." She pressed her lips against Rebeca's, a fleeting, teasing warmth. "You'd best go. Not all mind their business."

Rebeca kissed her forehead. "Keep the door latched." She slipped out and saw that the neighbor woman watched.

"She taken sick?"

"A touch of fever," Rebeca said.

The woman grunted, suspicion underneath the sound.

"Good evening to you." Rebeca nodded once and made her way out of the alley, out of the chill and darkness that collected between the buildings this time of day.

"Still about?"

She bristled at Robert's voice.

"So why is it you've not been on a hunt in at least a year?" he asked, catching up to her.

"Busy."

"There're rumors about you."

"There always are." She sped up and left him behind.

"And about your sick friend."

She slowed.

"Best hope they're not true," he said, a gloat in his voice.

She clenched her teeth and passed the square, where the flames had collapsed into embers around two blackened skeletons. Rebeca averted her eyes and quickened her pace.

❖

A day's journey felt more like a week's, and Rebeca saw each hour's pain in Isadora's eyes, in the grimace that seemed frozen on her mouth. She'd saved more than enough in the hunts for the horse Isadora rode, one the stablemaster had laughed off as not worth half what Rebeca offered. She didn't know much about horses beyond basic care, but she'd spent some time around the stables, and she saw in this one patience and endurance, and maybe even a bit of gratitude.

"Should we stop?" Rebeca asked after another long stretch of silence between them, broken by the horse's solid, slow hoofbeats on the hard-packed earth of the road and the chattering of birds in surrounding trees.

"No."

"You should eat. Have a bit of water."

Isadora managed a tight smile. "I'd prefer to keep going. Nightfall is not long off."

Rebeca stopped the horse. "Let me at least give you something to eat while you ride, then."

Isadora didn't reply, so Rebeca took her pack off, mindful of the crossbow she'd fastened across its front, and rummaged through it. She handed a hunk of dark bread up to Isadora along with a chunk of dry cheese. Next she passed a waterskin up.

"Put that around your shoulder, so it doesn't fall. You need to drink more, to flush out the poison."

Isadora laughed, but it sounded forced. "The poison is all that keeps me from hurting you."

"I don't believe that. Not anymore." Rebeca took the reins and gently tugged the horse forward.

"I wish I felt the same."

Rebeca didn't answer, instead clucked her tongue softly. The horse snorted in response and she automatically reached over and touched the horse's jaw, offering comfort to them both.

By the time evening announced itself in the angled rays through the forest canopy, the miles no longer seemed to pass beneath Rebeca's boots, but rather weighed them down. She checked on Isadora again—almost obsessive at this point—and studied her features for any change. Isadora dozed, fortunately, still upright on the horse's back, but slumped forward a bit, her dark cloak wrapped around her.

Rebeca scanned the surrounding forest and sniffed. Moss and damp, decaying leaves. Wild onions. And the thick, pungent scents of plants her grandmother might use in her medicinals.

She sniffed again. There. Barely discernible. Like what a wind chime might smell like, light and crisp, clean metal. Magic. The breeze shifted and the smell with it, stronger. They were close. She patted the horse's neck and urged her on with an encouraging click of her tongue. She needn't have worried. The horse hadn't wavered on this journey.

And finally, the sounds of birds and breeze stopped. She slowed, and to her right, the thick growth parted just enough to reveal a narrow path, wide enough to accommodate both her and the horse, if she walked in front. She again checked on Isadora, who still slept, and led the horse off the wider road.

Here, the deep shadows pooled beneath huge ancient trees, limbs gnarled with age, decorated with thick layers of moss. Rebeca knew they weren't alone. The prickle of a hundred eyes raised the hair on the back of her neck. She looked up, into the latticework of branches. Ravens watched them from their perches, silent and unmoving. And then one leapt from its branch and took flight, skimming gracefully ahead through the tangle of trees until its dark form was swallowed by darker shadows.

A sentry. Rebeca gripped the reins a little tighter, catching a hint of magic on the breeze left in its wake. She recognized the signature, faint as it was, and relaxed. Not quite dark, not quite light. Her grandmother had always walked the border between worlds. She checked on Isadora, still asleep, moving with the horse's slow, steady rhythm, hooves making muted thumps on the path, layered as it was with fallen leaves. That was good, Rebeca thought. Easy on both horse and rider.

She pressed on, thinking about the last time she'd come this way. Not so long ago. A year, maybe. She'd still been hunting then. And good thing, because even witches could be ambushed, as she'd discovered when she emerged into the clearing that sheltered her grandmother's home that day a year ago.

"Red?" Isadora's voice, soft and rusty with sleep.

She smiled at the pet name. "Here, love."

"Where are we?"

"Nearly there. Have some water." She looked back over her shoulder, pleased to see that the pain lines around Isadora's mouth had relaxed.

"I want to walk."

Rebeca stopped and the horse stopped, too, as if she had become attuned to her human guide. "Are you sure? It's not that far."

"I'd like to move a bit. And I'm sure the horse could use a rest." She smiled, and Rebeca saw more of the old Isadora in it, more of her familiar warmth and humor. She looped the reins around her left arm and stood on the horse's left side so she could offer support to Isadora as she slid to the ground.

"Oh, my. I've been sitting too long," she said with a grimace.

Rebeca motioned at the waterskin Isadora had slung over her shoulder. "Drink."

She complied with another smile, then unlooped the skin's string and handed it to Rebeca. "You as well."

Rebeca did, and waited as Isadora rummaged through a saddlebag and removed a small wooden bowl. She handed that to her, as well, and Rebeca filled it with water and held it for the horse, who drank until it was gone. She patted the horse's neck while Isadora returned the bowl to its pack, then waited for Isadora to join her. The two of them could just fit side by side on the path.

Isadora took Rebeca's hand as they walked, something she rarely did in the open. Rebeca looked at her and wondered if her color really was better or if the shadows masked her pallor. She sniffed and could only detect the barest trace of dark magic emanating from her. Instead, Isadora smelled more like herself, more like a mountain stream and cloves.

"When was the last time you took the potion?" Rebeca asked.

"Yesterday at midday."

"How are you feeling?"

"Better, but still weak. Tired."

"Am I walking too fast?"

"No." She squeezed Rebeca's hand.

They walked in silence until the path ended at a clearing occupied by a single house constructed of logs from the surrounding forest. Flowers grew in window boxes and the front door looked as if it had been recently varnished. Rebeca sniffed and caught the odor of magic and wild roses. Her grandmother was home, and probably knew she was coming.

Isadora sagged against her and Rebeca held her up with one arm while she clutched the horse's reins in her other hand. The horse snorted in a way that sounded relieved, as if she knew they'd arrived at the end of their long walk. Rebeca looked up at the surrounding trees. The lone raven sentry stared back at her. She took a deep breath and started across the clearing, moving slowly because she was supporting Isadora.

They had almost reached the door when it opened and a woman who might have been Rebeca's sister appeared. She wore heavy trousers, a loose rough shirt, and scuffed boots. Clothing like her own. Rebeca stopped and waited.

"To what do I owe the pleasure?"

"Gran. You're looking well." She always did. Magic ensured a timelessness. Her grandmother would never age.

"I doubt you came to discuss my appearance."

"You're right. This is Isadora." Rebeca motioned with her head, since both her hands were occupied.

Morgayne moved closer, took Isadora's chin gently in her hand, and examined her face. Isadora barely protested.

She stepped back and looked at Rebeca, disapproving. "When was the last time she shifted?"

"Three moons ago."

"Why has she gone so long?"

"The hunts have increased. It's not safe for her near the village."

Morgayne pursed her lips. "That ridiculous bastard magistrate again, letting his thick head get filled with lies." She didn't phrase it as a question. "Get her inside. And then I'll need to see what she's been taking."

"Thank you." Rebeca released the horse's reins and supported Isadora with both arms.

"Don't thank me yet." Morgayne arched an eyebrow imperiously but a smile twitched at the corner of her mouth. She took the reins and motioned at Isadora. "Put her in the room behind the kitchen. Then come and unload your steed."

Rebeca helped Isadora inside, where it was warm and smelled of fresh bread and some kind of stew. Her mouth watered. She hadn't eaten all day.

"Rest here," she said as she eased Isadora onto the bed in the room behind the stove.

"Red—"

"Shh." She took her pack off and helped Isadora into a nightshirt before she settled her beneath the blankets. "Rest. I'll be right back." She went outside to retrieve the saddlebags.

"Have something to eat," Morgayne said, and she took the horse behind the house and suddenly the house was much bigger, with another floor and a stable behind. Rebeca waited for the witchery to settle, then went inside.

❖

Rebeca watched Morgayne examine the contents of the bottle from which Isadora had been drinking. She poured a drop of it into a small metal bowl and coaxed its elements apart with the motions of her fingers. "Griselda's work." She looked up at Rebeca for confirmation, and Rebeca nodded. "Poisonous, over time," Morgayne added. "Typical of dark magic."

Rebeca didn't respond.

"How long since she was bitten?"

"Three years. I've known her a year. She's been able to shift until the last few months, when the magistrate expanded the hunts."

"Can she shift without the moon?"

Rebeca stared at her. "What do you mean?"

"A shift can be controlled, and without the use of potions." She waved her hand to stop another question. "You and I will talk, later. Was there another rogue in the vicinity that brought the hunts on?"

"One that I know of. I brought it down, but it didn't stop the panic."

Morgayne corked the bottle and set it aside. "It never does." She stared at the bottle for a moment. "One rogue ruins the whole lot." She looked over at Rebeca. "I'm grateful that you were here that day."

Rebeca remembered Morgayne's open front door hanging crazily on a hinge the year before, and the smell of blood. She'd had an arrow loaded and ready as she bolted across the clearing toward the house. The beast heard her and threw itself outside, snapping and growling, muzzle speckled red. She'd shot it without compunction, and when the silver-tipped arrow buried itself in the beast's chest, the rogue screamed and collapsed, smoke trailing from the wound. Black and acrid, like the pyres in the town square. She hadn't known the man the beast had been. She didn't recognize him, lying naked and bloody outside her grandmother's house. He was the last beast she'd killed.

"She needs to shift."

Rebeca looked at her.

"It will help with healing, and expel Griselda's mixture."

"I'm not sure she can."

Morgayne frowned.

"She's too weak. It might kill her if she doesn't have the strength to complete it." A cold fear dug into her heart.

"I'll make her something. Watch her. If she starts, we'll need to get her outside."

"I brought you more herbs. In the saddlebags. And the other things you like."

"Such a dutiful granddaughter," Morgayne said, not unkindly. "Perhaps you'll be visiting more often."

Rebeca said nothing and retreated to the room behind the kitchen, where she sat on a chair next to the bed, waiting. Morgayne brought a cup to her some time later and Rebeca coaxed Isadora to drink it. She handed the cup back to Morgayne and remained in the chair.

She didn't remember falling asleep, but something jerked her awake and she stared, disoriented, around the darkened room. She heard Isadora mumble something in her sleep, and beyond that, a tapping from the other room. She sat still, listening, and heard Morgayne open the shutter for a rustle of wings. She smelled a burst of magic.

From the bed, Isadora stirred.

"Red," she whispered.

Rebeca left her seat and leaned over her. Isadora gripped her arms.

"Get out," she said. "I don't want to hurt you."

"You won't." Rebeca slid her arm around Isadora's shoulders and sat her up. She had just managed to stand Isadora by the bed when Morgayne appeared in the doorway, a raven perched on her forearm, light from the other room spilling around her.

"Someone approaches."

"Who?"

"Three men on horses. Armed. With dogs."

"Hunters?"

"Most likely." She looked at Isadora and her brow furrowed. "We have to get her outside. Now."

"How close are the hunters?" Rebeca used her free hand to grab a blanket off the bed.

"A mile. As the raven flies. That gives us a bit more time. They'll be using the path. How long does it take her to shift?"

"A few minutes, when she's healthy."

"Red, please," Isadora said through clenched teeth.

"Out back." Morgayne moved aside as Rebeca passed her, supporting Isadora with one arm and holding the blanket with the other. Morgayne followed them through the house and opened the back door, grunting a little at its weight.

Rebeca hauled Isadora outside into the night, past the stable, into the forest. Isadora's breath came in short, sharp gasps that left puffs in the chill air, and Rebeca felt the muscles in Isadora's arm twitch. She lowered her to the ground, spread the blanket out over a patch of reasonably clear ground, and pulled Isadora onto it. Her sides heaved with painful exhalations, and in the waxing light of moonrise, Rebeca saw her muscles ripple and stretch, heard the muffled cracking of Isadora's bones. She tore the nightshirt off Isadora's body, leaving her naked and exposed to the moon.

"I…can't…" Isadora said, voice low and guttural.

"You can."

"Leave."

"No." Rebeca placed her hand on Isadora's back, willed her to find the strength to complete the shift. She stared as her fingers glowed red, as if they burned from the inside, and the smell of wet stone and earth surrounded them.

And then there was fur, thick and warm beneath her hand, but only for a moment as the beast that had been Isadora rose on her four legs, wolflike, but bigger than any wolf, moonlight glancing off the ebony of her coat. Isadora turned toward Rebeca, lips raised in a snarl, a low growl in her chest.

Rebeca remained on her knees and kept her eyes on the blanket, waiting for the two parts of Isadora to merge in the wake of transition.

Isadora growled again, then stopped and moved closer, sniffing. Rebeca exhaled with relief as Isadora nuzzled her face and licked her cheek.

"Go, my love," Rebeca said. "Hunt."

Isadora whined softly.

"Morgayne will take care of me. Go."

Isadora nuzzled her once more, then slipped into the forest, leaving only the smell of musk and cloves behind.

Rebeca gathered the torn nightshirt and blanket and returned to the house. She shoved them into the woodbin near the back door, noting that the stable was gone and the house was but a cottage again. She entered and pushed the door closed and barred it. When she turned, a much older Morgayne waited for her. The raven was gone.

"How long have you been using your magic?" She appeared pleased.

"First time for—whatever that was."

"Perhaps you should stay a while, rather than simply visit once a year." She turned away and Rebeca heard a man's voice outside, shouting a greeting. Morgayne turned back and took Rebeca's face in her hands. Heat shot through Rebeca's skull followed by a million pinpricks that faded as quickly as they had come. Morgayne released her, left for a few moments, and returned with a hand mirror. She held it up.

"Come, William. Someone hails us."

Rebeca stared. A young man stared back. Her features, made masculine. Her hand flew automatically to her chest.

"You're intact. But our visitors see what you do in the mirror. Come."

Rebeca followed her to the front door. She heard male voices beyond. Morgayne pulled the door open.

"Here, what's the fuss?" she asked. "Who goes there, bothering an old woman in her home?" she said in the reedy, tremulous voice of age.

"Apologies," said a man Rebeca knew. She swallowed a growl of her own when she saw Robert outside with two others she recognized from hunts past, all wearing thick, dark cloaks and carrying crossbows. Their horses stamped behind them, and one man to Robert's right held two leashes with straining hounds. The other man held a torch, as did Robert.

"Have you perhaps seen or heard any large wolves in the area?" Robert asked.

Morgayne moved aside so Rebeca could join her in the doorway.

"Haven't seen a wolf in months," Rebeca said, and her voice was the tenor of a man's. "Or the likes of you, for that matter. What village is home?"

"You're a feisty one," Robert said with a laugh.

"And you're a hunting party out after dark, trespassing. Are there bounties on these wolves?"

His eyes narrowed in the torch's light, and the man who held the dogs looked first at Rebeca, then at Robert.

"No need to concern yourself with that," Robert said, danger in his tone.

"Seems it is my concern, should you kill one on my grandmother's land." She felt Morgayne's hand on her arm, gripping hard.

"Now, lad, no need to get saucy," said the man to Robert's left.

"My grandson is protective." Morgayne tsked. "We had some trouble with another hunting party a few weeks back. Not from a village we know."

Robert shrugged. "No need to worry on our account. We'll make camp elsewhere." He turned away just as a long howl floated over the trees.

Morgayne's hand dug harder into Rebeca's arm.

"No wolves, eh?" Robert laughed. "The bounty's ours, lad. Unless you beat us to it." He jogged to his horse and mounted in one swift motion as his comrade released the dogs. They ran, baying, into the forest, and the men on horseback followed.

"That sounded like Isadora," Rebeca said, voice as tight as her chest.

"They must be stopped."

"I know." Rebeca retrieved her crossbow and cloak. "I'm going after them. If Isadora smells me, she'll smell them, too, and know to stay away." She didn't wait for Morgayne to respond and instead slipped into the forest, following the sounds of the horses and dogs.

And then there were beasts. Three? Four? They moved parallel with her, slicing through the moon-dappled darkness like knives, the only evidence of their presence the tang of magic.

The torches bounced like will-o-the-wisps ahead, and one man shouted in triumph. Rebeca was running now, moving nearly as silently as the beasts, and a howl sounded, haunting and eerie, just ahead.

Isadora.

The beasts ran past her, and the hoots of triumph became screams of fear. She heard the wet crunch of bone and the gurgle of blood before she came to the scene, two men already dead, Robert backed against a tree, shooting bolts as fast as he could load. The dogs ran yipping past her, away from the carnage, and she saw a flash of ebony in the light of a dying torch.

Isadora.

Robert raised his bow, took aim. Rebeca launched herself off the body of a fallen horse, threw herself between him and Isadora. The bolt caught her in the side, but the pain didn't start until she slammed to the ground and then that was all she knew. That and the dying scream of the man who had shot her and the anguished howl of a beast.

❖

Rebeca opened her eyes and stared at the moon. She tasted blood, and knew what that meant. Isadora whimpered beside her. "Are you hurt?" Rebeca asked. It hurt to talk.

Isadora whined and licked her face.

"She's not. But you are." Morgayne kneeled beside her, and a ball of pale blue light floated above her palm. "There isn't time enough to get you back home," she said. "The wound is too severe." She used the ball of light to further examine her. "Any movement will make this worse."

"I'm sorry," Rebeca said to Isadora. "But you're safe now."

Isadora whined again and nuzzled her face.

"She drew them away from the house," Morgayne said. "It gave me time to bring in some reinforcements."

Rebeca smelled the beasts, but she didn't try to see them. "Look after her, Gran." She coughed and tasted more blood. Pain filled her belly.

Morgayne laughed softly. "No, my dear, that will still be your task."

And then Rebeca heard the crack of bones and smelled musk

and wild roses. "Gran," she said in the light of the moon, stunned. "Your teeth."

"The better to bite you, my dear," came Morgayne's voice, low and guttural. And her fangs closed on Rebecca's neck, gentle, until they broke the skin and Rebeca felt a searing heat and then a sensation as if she were floating, watching her pain recede and the bolt emerge from her body, as if it was pushed from inside. She relaxed, exhausted.

"Rest," Morgayne said in her normal voice. "We'll talk in a bit, after you're healed."

Rebeca's eyes closed again and Isadora licked her face, and as she drifted to sleep, she knew the price she had paid for Morgayne's help.

It was worth it.

Rob Rosen (therobrosen.com), award-winning author of the novels *Sparkle: The Queerest Book You'll Ever Love*, *Divas Las Vegas*, *Hot Lava*, *Southern Fried*, *Queerwolf*, and *Vamp*, and editor of the anthologies *Lust in Time* and *Men of the Manor*, has had short stories featured in more than 180 anthologies.

This story is based on "Jack and the Beanstalk."

THE BEANSTALK REVISITED
ROB ROSEN

Jake awoke with a start at the sound of pounding on his bedroom door. "Time to get up!" his father shouted, repeatedly, until Jake flung his long legs out of bed and lumbered over to the door.

"It's Saturday, Dad. I don't have to get up early today," Jake grumbled, rubbing the sleep from his eyes as he slowly opened the door.

"Yes, but I do, and today is your mother's birthday."

"*Step*-mother," Jake corrected, as he always did.

"Semantics," his dad replied. "In any case, I'm sure you've conveniently forgotten to get her anything, so here's fifty dollars. Go buy her something nice."

His dad handed him the bills and was off in a flash. Jake could think of a million other things he'd rather do than go shopping for a present for his stepmother, especially on a weekend, but he knew he had little say in the matter.

When his real mother was still alive, birthdays were more fun than Christmas. Now very little excited Jake, especially anything that had to do with the woman his father married. Still, he did have fifty dollars, and that could buy a whole lot of things besides just a gift for his evil old stepmonster.

So Jake showered, dressed, and drove his beat-up Honda down the street to the local pawnshop. Mr. Harrington kept a rare collection of comic books that Jake couldn't normally afford. But normally he didn't have a wad of cash burning a hole through his jeans. And though Jake never did care for Mr. Harrington, he certainly liked his comic books well enough. He eyed them hungrily as soon as he entered the store.

"No reading in here, young man. You want it, you buy it," Mr. Harrington quickly admonished.

"No sweat," Jake replied, and flashed him the money. Mr. Harrington eyed him suspiciously, but stepped a few feet back to let Jake explore the collection. Mr. Harrington liked cash more than he hated teenagers; it was merely a question of priorities.

Fifteen minutes later, Jake was at the counter with several hard-to-find issues. Each cost ten dollars. That was five comics: a boon for any broke nineteen-year-old. But just before Jake paid for them, he remembered his stepmonster. She'd never believe the comics were for her, and, more importantly, neither would his father. So, with much thought, he dwindled the stack down to four and asked Mr. Harrington what he could buy with ten dollars for his stepmother's birthday.

Mr. Harrington reverently looked around the place and replied, "Son, you're lucky to get those comics for that price. You know, ten dollars doesn't go very far these days." Jake looked around the store as well, but all he saw was a bunch of junk. *Who'd want this stuff*, he thought, *let alone pay ten dollars for any of it?* But just before he started to return another comic to the rack, Mr. Harrington pulled out an item from beneath the counter.

It was dusty. It was banged up. It was on the small side. And it had a funny-looking angel-like thing along the side. More important, however, was that it was marked for exactly ten dollars.

"Bingo." Jake exhaled with relief. "What is it?"

"What is it?" Mr. Harrington said in mock surprise. "This, young man, is a harp. And a very unique harp at that."

"Then why's it marked for only ten dollars?" Jake asked, already leery.

"Because it can only be sold to a very special young man, someone like yourself, I believe, someone who can truly make it *sing*."

"Sing? You mean play, right?"

"No, for just the right person, this harp will sing," was the reply. "Do you know the story of Jack and the beanstalk?"

"The fairy tale? Sure, I know it. My mom used to tell it to me when she was, um…still alive." Jake looked down at his sneakers. He hated talking about his mother like she wasn't there anymore.

Mr. Harrington nodded. "Yes, the fairy tale. Though, like many fairy tales, this one is rooted in truth. Because this, my boy, is the actual golden harp that Jack stole from the giant. And it *will* sing, but like I said, only for a special young man like yourself. Or, well, a giant, but they're significantly harder to come by these days."

"Oh come on now," Jake said. "You're pulling my leg. It's just an old brass harp. Fairy tales are fairy tales, nothing more."

"No sirree. Lots of those stories are based in some way or another on real people and events. Take, for instance, Dracula. You know Dracula, right? Well, he's based on a real live person: Vladimir the Impaler. Ever heard of him?"

"Sure, I suppose so," Jake said, thinking that Mr. Harrington was even crazier than he first thought. "Still, Dracula isn't a giant beanstalk or a singing harp."

"Okay, how about Cinderella, then? And her evil stepmother?"

Ah, now Jake did indeed see something concrete in that example. He knew *they* existed. "Fine," he allowed. "I'll give you fifty for these comics *and* that banged-up harp."

"You got a deal, my boy. But I'd be careful with that harp if I was you. No telling what'll happen if it ever starts singing again."

"Yeah, yeah. Whatever. Just wrap it up so I can get home before my dad does."

A few minutes later, Jake was back in his car and heading home. "Crazy old man," he said with a laugh as he raced down the street. Still, far in the back of his mind he couldn't help but think about the story of Jack. *You never do hear what happens to that harp of his*, he thought. *The goose that laid the golden eggs is surely dead by now, but what about the golden harp? This one here looks old enough, doesn't it?* "Oh man, Jake, now you're as crazy as that old coot," he said to himself as he pulled up to his house a short while later.

Still, to be on the safe side, he polished it up so that it practically glowed, made it appear like it really could be made of gold. It did look, in fact, that it was worth the fifty bucks that had been given to him. His father would never be the wiser about that one. And when they'd finished with the cake that night and it was time to hand over the presents, Jake was sure his stepmonster would love it. Not that he cared, but he did like to make his dad happy.

Their reactions to his gift, as it turned out, were mixed. Jake didn't think that either really knew what to make of it. And he relayed Mr. Harrington's story word for word, just to be on the safe side.

"But your mother doesn't know how to play the harp," his dad said.

"Well, it is pretty," his stepmother interjected. "Thank you, Jake. It's a very thoughtful gift."

"And it made Jack rich, so there's no telling what it will do for us."

"Yes, well, okay, time for bed," his father said, placing the harp on the mantelpiece. "I think the only things rich around here are the cake we just ate and that story Mr. Harrington told you."

Jake laughed even though he was hurt by his father's remarks. His stepmonster, at least, seemed to like the thing, and it was her birthday, after all. And yet, there was still something nagging at him.

So once the house was silent, he tiptoed back into the living room and brought the harp back with him to his bedroom. "Mr. Harrington said that someone like me could make it sing," he said to himself as he sat with it on the floor. "But how do I make it sing?" That was when he remembered the story his mother had told him so many years earlier. The giant had commanded the harp to sing. "Maybe that's all it takes. Okay then, Harp, sing. Sing, Harp, sing."

Jake waited. And waited. And waited some more, all the while commanding the harp to sing. But nothing happened. Not a peep. "Maybe she's been asleep too long. Maybe it'll take a while for her to wake up. And maybe the whole thing is just a fairy tale after all." Jake moped back to his bed and sadly drifted off to sleep. He slept a deep sleep, filled with dreams of giants and golden eggs. He slept a sleep so deep, in fact, that he didn't hear, sometime in the middle of the night, the tiniest little voice coming from the floor.

"Master?" the voice squeaked out. "Master, are you there?"

Nothing. No one was there, the harp realized. So she sang, knowing that her master always came to that. But she had been asleep for so many countless years that all she could muster was the smallest of pitch-perfect peeps. And still nothing. No one came for her, neither her master nor anyone else. So she shut her eyes and simply waited.

And that was how Jake found her in the morning, just as he had left her, with her eyes closed and her voice silent. But something was different, all right. For there, outside his window, in full, lush greenery, was a massive beanstalk. Jake rushed to his window, opened it, and then stuck his head out, eyes wide as saucers, jaw hanging limp. He looked the enormous thing up and down. It stretched as far as his eyes could see, all the way up and into the clouds, in fact.

"Holy cow!" he shouted. "Look, Harp. The beanstalk! You must've sung while I was sleeping, Harp. Sing again. Sing, Harp, sing!"

And lo and behold, the harp once again opened her eyes, and this time she let out a painful shriek. She screamed as loud as her little frame allowed her, "Master! Master, help!" Well, that simply would not do. Jake didn't pay ten dollars for a shrieking harp. So he ran from the window, scooped her up, and climbed outside so as not to wake his parents, who surely wouldn't understand a screeching harp *and* a giant beanstalk.

When he was outside, he closed the window behind him and looked sharply at the harp, which he could still hear screaming even behind his muffling hand. "Okay, listen here, Harp. You have to shut up before you wake up the whole darn neighborhood." But she kept right on screaming behind Jake's hand. "Okay, okay. How about I take you back to your master? Then will you shut up?"

The harp stopped screaming and looked up at Jake and blinked. "I'll take that as a yes," he said. He removed his hand from her tiny golden mouth. "Okay, I guess we're going up the beanstalk, then."

He knew his parents would never allow that, so he didn't tell them his plan first. Besides, he reasoned, the giant was already dead, or so the story went, so how could there be any danger? And maybe there'd be more golden egg–laying geese up there. Then he could buy as many comics as his heart desired.

So he climbed. And climbed. And climbed. Until at last he was at the tippy-top of the beanstalk and high, high, high above the clouds. Miraculously, when he finally hopped off, he was standing on solid ground. "Thank goodness for that," he said, and then made his way toward the castle that sat a mere few hundred yards away. He figured he could leave the harp on the doorstep and go searching for any animals, geese or otherwise, that laid golden eggs.

But before he could leave the harp by the door, she once again shouted out, "Master! Help, Master, help!" And from behind the door Jake could hear the sound of feet fast approaching.

The door creaked open. On the other side wasn't a giant, but another young man just like Jake. "Fee fi fo fum, I smell the blood of an Englishman. Be he alive, or be he dead, I'll grind his bones to make my bread!" the stranger roared.

Jake scratched his head. *You and what army?* he thought. "Um, yeah, I'm just here to return your harp is all."

The stranger stared down. "Harp? Is that you, Harp? Sing to me, Harp!" he commanded. And the harp sang, sang and sang in fact, a song so beautiful as to bring a tear to both the young men's eyes. "Why did you steal her?" said the other man, when the song was at last finished.

"You've got the wrong person. That was Jack; I'm Jake. And I'm returning the harp, not stealing it."

"Jake, Jack. Sounds the same to me," he said and started to raise his fists in the air.

Jake couldn't help but laugh. "Not going to grind my bones with those, you know."

The stranger nodded and sighed, his arms and fists falling to his sides. "Guess that only worked for the master." The sigh repeated. "He's been gone so long now. Him and the goose." Again he stared down at the harp. "But at least I'll have her company again. Thank you for that." He held his hand out. "Pete."

Jake took Pete's hand in his, a spark of electricity suddenly rising up his spine, a swarm of butterflies let loose inside his belly. "A pleasure to meet you, Pete."

Pete nodded, their hands still clasped together. "Same here, Jake."

"You made the harp sing," Jake suddenly realized. "I was told you had to be special to make her do that." The gap was suddenly closed between them, hands still as one. "What's so special about you, Pete?"

There eyes were now inches apart. "Same thing that makes you special, I believe, Jake." And the gap was suddenly completely closed; the two men's lips joined, tongues thrashing as the harp again began to sing for them.

In seconds, they were both naked, not to mention hard and thick as the beanstalk itself, both dripping considerable amounts of sap. Finally neither one felt all that alone, the harp seemingly bringing them together,

As they stood entwined outside the massive door, it was almost impossible to tell where one ended and the other began. Both men sucked and stroked and kissed and licked and prodded and poked with abandon, exploring the other's body as if was made especially for them.

And perhaps it was. Perhaps the harp was made for them as well. For when she finished her song, they finished their acts of love, their bodies drenched with sweat, sticky with that aforementioned sap, lips locked, vise-tight, eyes afraid to blink lest the other disappear.

A short while later, as they again sat there on the front stoop, dressed once more, catching their breath, they both heard a shout coming from the beanstalk. Jake looked up and spotted his stepmother frantically running their way.

"Don't hurt my son!" she was shouting.

Jake sat there stupefied. In the years that they'd been together, he'd never heard her refer to him as her son. And he'd never expect her to risk her life for his, that was for sure. Especially considering the way he normally treated her, which was with indifference at best.

"Um, don't worry, I'm fine," said Jake. "But where's Dad?"

His stepmother was still clutching her chest and was still breathing hard. "Last I saw, he was fast asleep. I thought I heard something, so I got up. Then I spotted the beanstalk, saw that you were missing, and came climbing up here to find you." Just then, Jake saw his father climbing up and off the beanstalk, and then he too was running over to the group of them. He grabbed his son and his wife and hugged and kissed them on the top of their heads. He didn't even notice Pete.

"Um, Dad, you're embarrassing us in front of my, uh, my new friend here," Jake said. And then he grinned, a smile so bright as to light up the sky itself. "See, Dad, I told you the harp was magic. And you should hear her sing. Just like an angel."

"Sing, Harp," Pete commanded.

And the harp did sing. And she did indeed sound like an angel, just as Jake had promised. And all four of them stood and watched and cried as she sang her beautiful song, until there were no tears left and it was time to go. But not before Jake asked Pete to come back with them, so he'd never have to be lonely ever again, so neither one of them would have to be.

Oh, Pete loved hearing that, for he was truly tired of being alone. "But wait," he said to the happy family just before they all started their descent down the beanstalk. "I have a gift for you all."

Pete ran around to the back of the castle and came around the other side in no time flat. In his hands he held a fat, honking goose.

"Wow, look at her!" Jake shouted. "I wonder how many comic books I can buy with a golden egg?"

"Oh," said Pete, "sorry, but there was only one goose that could do that. This one lays plain old goose eggs. But they do make the richest cakes in the land."

Jake frowned, but his parents laughed just the same and patted their son on the shoulder.

"Okay, real funny," Jake said. "Let's get home, then, and start baking. I'm starved. Dad, you go first, then me, then Pete, and then Mom."

"You mean stepmom, right?"

"Semantics," Jake said, with a sheepish grin.

And the four of them climbed down the beanstalk and they all lived happily ever after. Especially once they started baking cakes professionally. See, that goose really did lay some rich eggs. Now Jake and the Beanstalk bakeries can be found far and wide.

And that ain't no fairy tale.

Veronica Wilde (veronicawilde.com) is an erotic romance author whose work has been published by Cleis Press, Bella Books, Liquid Silver Books, and Samhain Publishing.

This story is based on "The Snow Queen."

HEARTLESS
VERONICA WILDE

The Snow Queen puts on her makeup at midnight in front of an old-fashioned vanity. Supernaturally beautiful, she needs the makeup to look human—to pass as a human woman done up as a gorgeous freak. As if past her dominatrix club owner persona, she still goes to bed at night worrying about her credit card bills and romantic troubles. Just a normal girl at heart.

But the Snow Queen, who has no heart, knows she will never be normal. Her flawless skin is a pale baby blue all over her long and curvy body, except where her nipples are a deeper blue, her pussy a flushed bluish violet. Her hair is a platinum waterfall and her lips are a deep rose red, the better to show off her movie-star smile. But her eyes are what disturb her club guests the most: the dark navy of a winter midnight, fathomless except for the gleam of a star.

Because she is beautiful, bespelling others is effortless for the Snow Queen. Love in the traditional sense might always stay a foreign language to her, but slavery is a substitute she doesn't mind at all. She lives to seduce the butch young dykes who most please her taste, enjoying the slap of their hard muscles on her stomach as they fuck, the infatuation swimming in their eyes. It's as good as love, she thinks. She drinks in their smitten adoration like nectar until her icy touch drains it out of them.

She herself has never experienced such emotions. Just once she would like to feel what they feel; just once she would like to become as intoxicated with one of her pets as they become with her. Yet the reverse always seems to happen instead. Instead of her absorbing their joy, they gradually become contaminated by her coldness. If they spend enough nights with her, they become little more than sullen zombies. Then it's time to find someone new.

The Queen smooths on her lipstick and leans back. In the vanity mirror, lined with pink lightbulbs, she is as beautiful as a star. She puts one hand on her chest where her heartbeat should be. As always, there's only silence.

She rises. It's Saturday night and time to go downstairs and oversee her nightclub.

❖

Outside, the city breathes and drips humidity. The heat has been rising for days, a blistering glare that empties the sidewalks in the afternoons and keeps everyone miserably awake each night. Electricity flickers across the city, hinting at an imminent blackout.

"I know it's around here somewhere," Gerda says. She's reading a map on her phone. "Maybe down this way."

"Just admit you lost the address." Kai usually never snaps at her girlfriend, but the heat has made her irritable, and she doesn't want to go to this party anyhow. It's too hot to be wandering around the city trying to find Gerda's old roommate's new apartment.

"Don't yell at me."

"I'm not yelling, Gerda. I just think it's time to call it a night." What Kai really wants is an ice-cold beer and cool cotton sheets to sleep naked in.

"We're going to this party!" Even in her anger, Gerda looks beautiful, her cheeks flushed with heat.

"You're going," Kai says, pushing back her rumpled blond hair. "I'm going home."

She stalks off without waiting for Gerda's reaction. The humidity has worn out her patience. Taking a different downtown street in search of a cab, she's mildly wary when a stranger stops her.

"Hot out tonight," he says.

"No shit, Captain Obvious," she mutters and goes around him.

"Hey!"

His tone is so urgent that she turns. "What?"

But whatever he wanted to say is lost. Instead he blows something like mirrored splinters into her eyes. She recoils and instinctively rubs her eyes—yet there's no pain. She blinks.

He smiles and points up the street, to the blue lights of a nightclub looming over the sidewalk. Its luminous coolness beckons like a promise. "Come with me," he says. And in a daze, Kai follows.

The bouncer gives the man a strange smile and waives the cover charge. Kai hesitates but goes in. Just one beer, just to get out of the heat for a few minutes.

The club is the arctic sanctuary of her dreams. The walls look like ice, and hundreds of fiber-optic stars in the ceiling suggest a nocturnal heaven. The bar glows blue. She shivers in her damp muscle shirt, looking at the dozens of shadows twisting on the dance floor. When the bouncer taps her shoulder and makes a *follow me* gesture, Kai tenses, but the bouncer only says something about meeting the owner and leads her to a staircase in the back.

They descend into a separate basement club lit by the flickering of electric torches. With a jolt, she sees that almost everyone is naked. A collared man is bent over a spanking stool, while other women and men are shackled to the walls or strapped to examination tables. The snap of a riding crop makes her jump.

Kai swallows. She's never been into the BDSM scene, but she can recognize a dungeon when she sees one. "Sick," she mutters and backs up. But when she turns to leave, she's facing the most beautiful woman she's ever seen.

In the dungeon light, the Snow Queen glows like a goddess. Tall and voluptuous, with a platinum flow of hair, her skin appears a soft blue. Enraptured, Kai stares into her dark blue eyes. Meeting her gaze is like falling into an ocean with no bottom.

The Snow Queen smiles.

Kai stumbles on her words. "Uh, sorry. Hi. I'm Kai."

Without answering, the Snow Queen takes Kai's hips in her

hands. Her fingers are cool even through Kai's jeans, but she's too struck by her lips to notice. They are a full, deep rose and all she can think about is feeling them on her pussy.

The Snow Queen kisses her. Her mouth is hot and tender in the dark dungeon. "Now you're mine," she says, but Kai thinks she must have misheard her over the music. Her head is swimming. She struggles to gather her wits. *Be a challenge; that's the way to impress a woman this beautiful.*

"I'm on my way out, actually," Kai announces brazenly. "My girlfriend is waiting for me at home."

Distant fire flares in the Queen's eyes but her voice stays cool. "I understand. This scene is a bit much for a vanilla girl like you, anyway."

Kai bristles. "I'm not vanilla! I've—I've done all this stuff before." She gestures grandly around the room.

She regrets the lie as soon as she says it.

The Snow Queen arches her brows. Slowly she pulls Kai's muscle shirt up to her neck, twisting it into the collar to leave her nipples and hard abs exposed. Kai jerks a little with the instinctive desire to cover herself. Everyone has stopped to watch them.

"So you're one of us," says the Snow Queen. "How nice." Circling Kai, she touches her nipples, the base of her spine, until Kai's muscles jump beneath her fingertip.

A predatory smile spreads across the Queen's face. She's always had a taste for boyish girls, butches with insolent attitudes and cocky grins, but this specimen puts her former pets to shame. Everything about this one, from her chiseled sun-browned torso to her bluish green eyes, is mouthwatering. Tonight she has her dream butch in her hands.

She strokes Kai's jugular, the beat of her pulse. Her skin is hot and the Queen wants to bite and suck her everywhere. Withdrawing her cool-bravado essence will be like drinking honeyed nectar. But the Snow Queen controls herself.

"So you've done 'all this stuff' before..." she baits.

"Yeah, of course." But the boast in Kai's voice flickers out into fear.

In one smooth move, the Queen undoes Kai's jeans and pulls them with her underwear down to her knees. Now the thick silicone cock she's packing is on full display to everyone in the dungeon.

Kai's face turns pink.

"Your ass is as pristine as a baby's," the Snow Queen says, turning her around in a circle. Kai stumbles in the half-lowered jeans. "You've never been spanked in your life."

"I…" Her voice dies in her throat.

"It isn't nice to lie, Kai."

The Queen sits on a stuffed velvet chair and pulls Kai over her knee. That taut body is rigid as a board, but as the Queen delivers the first blow on the right cheek, then the second on the left, Kai begins to struggle. But the Snow Queen's nightly predations have made her strong, and she continues to spank Kai's firm white cheeks until her handprints mar the skin. A blood-red heat is filling Kai's face but she doesn't stop.

A crowd has gathered to watch. Kai twists in mortification, which amuses the Queen. Scratching her nails over the inflamed skin, she can only to think of how sexy Kai will look gagged.

The spanking goes on and Kai's protests turn to groans. That silicone cock is lodged between the Queen's thighs and the heat of Kai's skin is intoxicating her senses. The Snow Queen wants to dominate and devour every inch of Kai's squirming hard body, then ride her cock into exhaustion.

Grabbing a fistful of the silky blond hair on her lap, the Snow Queen lifts Kai's head. Her greenish blue eyes look enamored already, and as the Queen kisses her for the second time, she can feel Kai's essence filling her like liquid stars.

She slaps Kai's bottom again. "Walk."

Kai is dazed but willing as the Queen marches her off to a private dungeon. Finally they're alone together. Stripping Kai of all of her clothes, the Queen shackles her to a St. Andrews Cross. She's had many naked butches displayed like this, but none as handsome as Kai. She pinches her thighs, runs her fingernails across her stomach.

"Please…"

The Snow Queen lightly slaps Kai's mouth. "Silence." Then, holding her shackled arms for balance, she slowly impales herself on Kai's cock.

This is the moment she cherishes: that first incredible sensation of throbbing heat pushing into her pussy. It lights her up like fire, an electric charge going straight to her clit. She moves slowly on Kai at first, sliding her arms and legs around her as she gradually adjusts to the toy's thickness. Beneath her, Kai jerks against her shackles. Her struggle only makes the Queen wetter.

She slaps Kai's face with her breasts. "Don't talk. Just show me what you can do with this big, pretty cock of yours."

Kai's dick feels huge inside her. It connects the fiery buzz in her clit to the stiffness of her nipples, until her entire body hums with excitement. A soft groan escapes her as she begins to ride Kai faster, smoother, their rhythms meeting in perfect sync. Kai's hips bang against the cross, driving into her over and over until she wants to scream. They're fucking hard and fast with all their power now, and she strokes her clit until her pussy feels almost incandescent. Then they're coming hot and wet, together, as a rush of power fills her like a thousand fireflies.

She buries her face in Kai's chest, drinking in the fresh smell of her skin, like sun-baked sand. Slowly she forces herself to slide off and undo the shackles. Kai sprawls on the floor, her blond hair a mess of sex and sweat.

Perfect, she thinks. *This one is just perfect.* From her narrow hips to her boyish frame to the beautiful sex-flush across her cheekbones, Kai is having an effect on the Snow Queen that she's never experienced. This one's energy tastes so sweet, so succulent. The Queen looks at her again, half-puzzled.

Kai gazes up at her with smitten eyes. "You're the woman of my dreams."

All of her pets fall in love with her, but Kai's words cause an odd flutter inside her chest. She'd describe her heart as a butterfly trying to get free, if she possessed a heart.

She masks it with a cool smile. "Don't move."

Kai obeys as the Snow Queen finds her camera. She always

makes it a point to photograph her pets early on so she can remember them later, after they're ruined and lifeless. Her photographs are her trophies, a way of preserving forever what she knows will always be temporary.

Kai's body is committed to photographic posterity, from her toned thighs to her bitten mouth. Then the Snow Queen links their fingers together and leads Kai upstairs to her home on the top floor. "This is where you'll live now."

Kai seems so different from the others. Maybe she won't be drained as quickly as the others; maybe she won't turn cynical and lifeless. Maybe, the Snow Queen thinks, she can keep this one a long, long time.

❖

The Snow Queen arranges the day's new daffodils and roses. She has flowers stocked daily: tiger lilies, irises, delphiniums, and of course, roses of every color. She loves their beauty and freshness because unlike her pets, her cold touch does not drain them. Every day she has new ones delivered so she never has to watch them fade.

She glances at Kai, who's staring into her vanity mirror. It's a self-absorption that makes her uneasy. Kai's begun showing signs of the same atrophy all her other pets went through; lethargy, indifference. Lately she's incapable of real conversation, except to tell the Queen how beautiful she is. Only sex interests Kai.

Who isn't quite the swaggering, handsome young butch she used to be. Her tan has faded and her silky hair has gone dull. Oddly the Snow Queen feels more attached to her than ever. Her other pets revolted her when they turned ugly. But she adores Kai so much that she knows she will care for her no matter what.

She leaves the flowers to slide her hands down that sculpted chest, toying with her nipples. Kai sighs and leans back into her. "I'm so wet for you…"

The Queen begins to rub her pussy through her jeans. "What were you thinking just now?"

A slight frown creases Kai's face. "That I don't look like me anymore. And it's been..." Kai trails off as she tries to calculate how many days she's been living there, or has it been it weeks? "Never mind." A sweet smile breaks across her face, making the Queen melt a little. "You're the perfect woman, you know that? You have everything."

"Except a heart." The Snow Queen meets Kai's eyes in the mirror.

Kai turns around and jokingly lays her hand on the Queen's chest, pretending to listen for a heartbeat. When she doesn't find one, her hand jerks away—but she laughs anyhow.

"As if. You're the most incredible woman I've ever met. You're..."

"Beautiful," the Queen says. "Yes, I know."

Kai stands and buries her face in the Queen's neck, biting her throat the way she likes. She's taught Kai well over their weeks together. As the Snow Queen sinks into her vanity chair, Kai kneels obediently. Her mouth ascends her thighs, sucking here, nibbling there, until her tongue is working the Queen's pussy with masterful skill. Still, the Queen wishes Kai would show some spontaneity. That she would come up with her own ideas of how to fuck her and worship her and make her come. She can't stop thinking about the night they met and the defiance in Kai's eyes, the struggle of lust and willfulness that made her so irresistible.

She closes her eyes, pretending Kai is still the same. Pretending that gorgeous butch with the cocky smile is kneeling before her right now, her tongue and her heart given freely. But that can never happen now. The only way to bring that dashing person back to life is to return Kai to the real world forever.

A pang twists inside her.

"You whore!"

Both she and Kai look at the door, where a girl with long black hair is starting to weep. This must be Gerda, the ex-girlfriend. The Snow Queen glances at Kai, who's still on her knees with a dazed expression. She can handle this easily. One push of a security button and Gerda will be removed from the club.

"I've been looking for you in this neighborhood for weeks," Gerda sobs. "Who is this bitch?"

"Um..." Kai struggles for words until Gerda pulls her away.

"Look at me!" she cries and as her tears fall into Kai's eyes, flushing out the shards of mirror, The Snow Queen can see the two possible fates before her. Keep Kai and watch her fade, or let Gerda save her.

She does nothing to intervene.

Confusion wrinkles Kai's brow. "Gerda...I was...I was..."

The Snow Queen feels a new and crushing pain that she suspects is grief.

"Why are you acting like you're drugged? I'm getting you out of here. And as for you, you freakish blue bitch..." Gerda grabs a lush red rose and stabs its longest thorn between the Snow Queen's breasts.

The rose clings to her blue skin. All of them watch as it begins to melt in streaks. Water glistens on the dark red petals; flesh and flower fuse together in a bloody, cloppy whirlpool of viscera. Then the rose is sucked into the Snow Queen's chest.

Brilliant colors light up her navy eyes like an aurora borealis.

Gerda finds Kai's pants. "Let's go. Now." She grabs her hand and pulls Kai out the door.

Alone, the Snow Queen falls to her knees on the marble floor. Her face works in contortions of an anguish she's never known. The walls are beginning to melt in trickles, much like the tears streaming down her face, though she doesn't know if she is weeping from sorrow or joy. Her mouth, when she opens it to cry, is full of rose petals. Her pale blue body shakes with the convulsions of transformation as deep in her chest begins the telltale, rhythmic thumping of her new heart.

Juliann Rich is the author of three affirming novels for young adults: *Caught in the Crossfire*, *Searching for Grace*, and *Taking the Stand*, coming out with Bold Strokes Books in 2015. She lives in southern Minnesota with her husband and two chronically disobedient dachshunds.

This story is based on "Little Briar Rose."

The Ivy and the Rose
Juliann Rich

Ivy backed out of Lord Ainsworth's bedchamber, a chipped porcelain pot clutched in her small hands. She turned to find her master standing in the hallway beside a stranger dressed in a shimmering charcoal robe, a bulging money purse hanging from the belt that circled his fiercely thin waist. Ivy stood and waited for her master to speak as the scent of his urine, hours cold, seeped from the chamber pot in her hands and filled the hallway.

"She might be the one you seek." Lord Ainsworth bobbed his fat head. "She stumbled onto my grounds, spewing some nonsense about standing inside the castle with the cursed Princess Ambrosia one second and outside my gate the next. Claimed she'd been transported here by magic. The nonsense! But never you fear, I showed her what happens to chambermaids who hold with thoughts of magic. She's tame now." Lord Ainsworth frowned at the strands of long red curls that always escaped Ivy's bonnet no matter what she did. "Well, tamer."

"M'lords." Ivy curtsied. In a flash she imagined it, the pot tipping and spilling its stench onto the master's shoes in front of the stranger he was so keen to impress. She hid her smile under the wide ruffle of her bonnet.

She stole a quick glance at the stranger.

"Inside the castle one minute." The stranger tapped his bony fingers together and murmured, "And here the next. How clever... and yet how ignorant. To think they could hide the key from me!"

Neither who they were—clever or ignorant—nor what key they had hidden did the stranger say as he swept down the threadbare rug. The master chased after him. Or, more's the truth, after his money.

But Ivy didn't have time to wonder about such things. A whole morning of chores made more complicated by an unexpected guest lay before her. Best not to dawdle with questions that didn't concern her.

Ivy stepped out the kitchen door and flung the contents of the chamber pot. Three doves—one a babe still covered in fluff, one plump and glistening gray, and one with pure white feathers—watched her from a branch in a nearby tree. "Danger," the white dove seemed to coo. And then, "Beware."

"Oh, hush with ye!" Ivy left the doves, preening their plumes, and stepped inside the kitchen.

"Who's the rich bastard what's got the master drooling?" she asked Milli, Lord Ainsworth's cook.

"It don't matter who the master's entertaining!" Milli's large brown eyes, usually calm and kind, widened with worry. "What matters is that I'm to produce a grand meal for two from this bitty chicken!"

Ivy plunged her hands into the wash bucket and scrubbed until the filth was gone. "Now don't you fret. You take a deep breath and calm yourself."

Milli closed her eyes and inhaled deeply. Her fingers, clutching the counter, unfurled.

"That's better." Ivy smiled. "How can I help?"

Milli opened her eyes and gestured toward a platter filled with piping-hot scones and a steaming pot of tea. "You could bring that tray into the dining room. With any luck they'll gorge themselves on sweets and won't even be hungry."

Milli's hands still trembled, poor thing. Ivy picked up the tray and spoke, her voice steeped with the magic of goodwill and friendship. "You'll cook a meal fit for King Alexander and Queen Alexia, you will!"

Though how her friend would accomplish the feat, Ivy had no clue. Lord Ainsworth's kitchen was empty as his heart. A few overripe vegetables on the counter, a small sack of barley in the larder, and one stringy marsh hen on the counter. It would take a magician to turn such poor offerings into a meal fit for a king. "You'll think of sumfink, Milli. I know you will."

Milli's eyes glazed like she was near asleep. Then they narrowed. She glanced toward a week-old loaf of bread atop the garbage bin next to the kitchen counter. "Dare I? Oh, I don't know. If the master ever found out...perhaps he mightn't, though, if I cut off the bits of white and cubed it. Yes, and with a pinch of sage and a splash of broth made from its liver..." she muttered to herself, reaching for the moldy loaf of bread.

Milli's voice stopped Ivy at the door. "Promise you'll keep your thoughts to yourself for once," Milli said, her hands busily shredding the bread to wee bits. "I've the worst feeling, I have!"

"I promise," Ivy said, leaving Milli in the kitchen muttering about apples and chopped nuts.

The master's guest sat at the far end of the dining room table. Such an odd-looking one was the stranger, with black hair that hung to his waist, cheekbones so sharp Milli could have carved a ham on them, and fingers as thin and gnarled as a bird's talons.

"I simply cannot let the girl go for less than one pound two shillings," her master said. "You must understand. I have years invested in the girl. Why, I've given her a proper training, I have." Lord Ainsworth reached out and swatted Ivy's rear just as she was about to put the platter down.

She lurched forward and the tray skidded across the table.

"Obviously." The stranger traced the fresh scratch in the wood with the tip of a fingernail, the point of it sharp as a dagger. "There is, of course, the matter of the debt you owe the crown."

Lord Ainsworth's head jerked toward the stranger. "Debt? What debt? I've paid my taxes, every last shilling."

Ivy poured two cups of tea and handed one to her master, who snatched it from her hands. Whether Lord Ainsworth's scowl was due to the scratched table or the talk of debt made no difference. There would be hell to pay no matter the cause. She handed the other cup to her master's guest, who accepted it and stared until she flushed red and stammered, "Will there be anything else, m'lords?"

"Stay, by all means. I have questions for you." The stranger lifted the cup to his lips and sipped.

She curtsied and backed a step away from the table.

The black-haired man turned his attention to her master. "But first, Lord Ainsworth, let us settle the matter of your debt. It is true you owe the crown nothing for this house and your land. But for privilege of having your fires laid, your chamber pots emptied, and your meals served to you by one who remains in the employ of our king, sleeping or not? No, I am afraid, sir, your debt has run quite high on that account."

The master looked at her then, stone-cold fury in his eyes. "Is it true, girl? Are you in the king's service?"

"Yes, m'lord." She jutted out her chin. "As I told you when I came to your door."

"And when was that?" The stranger leaned forward.

"I believe it were two years ago exactly on the morrow, m'lord." How could Ivy not know the passing of time to the second since she'd seen her girl? It carved itself on her soul.

"Two years ago exactly! You *are* the one!" The stranger's voice pitched high as a woman's. His eyes flashed. "Quick, tell me! How did you escape the curse?"

She opened her mouth to answer him, but it was Milli's voice she heard in her mind. *Promise you'll keep your thoughts to yourself.* Ivy stared at her scuffed shoes and shook her head.

The master pounded his fist on the table, rattling the cups, the saucers, her bones. "Two years I've tried to teach you silence and now you learn the lesson? Oh, for the love of King Alexander, may he wake soon, speak the truth, girl!"

So she spoke, though not the truth. "I were already running away, you see. From Mrs. Babcock, the head housekeeper what caught me peering behind the curtains and under the bed for the princess when I should have been laying her fire, but Mrs. Babcock dinnit understand. She dinnit know that were our game. I tried to tell her, but she got so red in the face and gave me such a fright when she swung her hand back that I ran from the servants' quarters and never looked back."

THE IVY AND THE ROSE

It crawled up her throat then, everything she'd swallowed down for two years.

Rushing through her morning duties.

Stealing away to the forgotten room.

Flinging open the door.

Expecting to see her girl lighting up the darkest corner with her smile.

Finding her lying on the floor next to a spindle, a drop of blood glistening on her fingertip.

Her Rose, her girl.

She gulped it in.

The rush of a breeze on her face when she'd flung open the window in the tower room and cried into the sky, *Try to touch her, I dare you! Lay one finger on my Rose, and I'll tear you to bits!*

She gulped and swallowed, gulped and swallowed, but they surfaced nonetheless, the memories flavored bitter by grief.

The windowsill biting into her legs. The closer to fling her curses to the sky. *I'll pierce you till your blood runs cold!*

And then—not—as the wind rushed past her.

Fingers dug into Ivy's arms and shook her till her teeth rattled in her head. "Collect yourself, girl! I have need of you!" The stranger's voice, high and sharp, sliced through her memories.

She opened her eyes and stared into the face that floated just beyond the stranger's shoulder.

"Can you ever forgive me?" She looked into eyes she alone could see. "It were *my* fault! It were *my* idea for us to meet there seeing as how the room were all but forgotten. I dinnit know there were a spindle there. How could I have known? Oh why, Rose, why did you leave me?" The sob ripped through her, leaving her unable to hide from the truth any longer. For she was the one who had left her girl inside the castle. It was a terrible, awful truth, and it crushed Ivy utterly.

"In what part of the castle does Princess Ambrosia lie?"

Ivy stared into the distance, the stranger's words naught but a mumbling of sound with no meaning.

"Where? Tell me, where is she?" the stranger screeched.

• 115 •

But she couldn't answer him. Grief, or maybe guilt, had turned her mute. The stranger shook her, and when that failed, he raised his hand and took aim. "Return to your senses! We must leave tonight if we are to awaken Princess Ambrosia in the morning!"

He didn't need to strike her.

"Wot's that you said?" She blinked and looked into his eyes. "Awaken the princess? But how?"

He reached into his pocket and withdrew a small glass vial. "I've discovered the cure for eternal sleep, my dear."

She stared at the liquid inside the vial. Glowing golden light. Could it be?

"But I need you, in possession of your senses, in front of the castle wall on the morrow. Now quickly, go prepare for the journey."

She forced herself to look into his cold black eyes. "Why do you need me, m'lord? Weren't nuffink I could do to save her when I were there."

His lips curled back into a grotesque smile that sent chills down Ivy's spine. "You, my dear, are going to part the wall of thorns for me, of course."

Ivy had seen the wall once when the master sent Milli and her to town for supplies. She had even seen the men who tried to reach Briar Castle, their decaying bodies ensnared in branches stained dark from their blood, and she had smiled. Because they would never reach her. Never touch her.

Her Rose, her girl.

"Impossible!" Ivy turned to leave the room.

The stranger dug his fingers into her shoulder and swiveled her to face him. "It has been foretold by the wise women! *And on the dawn of the second year one will stand before the wall who the curse will recognize and the wall will part.*"

Her head spun. It couldn't be. "But..."

"Fool! Don't you see? You were inside the castle when the curse fell. You are the one! We must leave this very night!"

So they did, right after Lord Ainsworth and the stranger devoured Milli's feast of stuffed hen. Right after they declared it a meal fit for the king. Right after Lord Ainsworth offered his chambermaid as payment for any outstanding debt.

The willow-thin stranger tossed Ivy onto the back of his horse and they rode away.

She righted herself and held on for dear life, her arms circling his waist as he kicked his steed past mercy or reason. Somewhere, miles behind them in the space between her master's house and the castle, the chambermaid's cap flew off and Ivy's long red hair streamed behind her.

It did not even dawn on her to look back.

❖

They rode throughout the day and the long night that followed.

They rode until the space between Ivy's legs chafed from rubbing against the back of the stranger's saddle.

They rode through farms and villages, until dirt roads turned to cobblestone and the clacking of the horse's hooves quickened the beating of her heart.

They rode together, but Ivy schemed alone.

She cooed questions into the stranger's ear, the way Milli soothed a chicken meant for the ax and afterward, when he tossed his answers into the wind where they floated back to her, she plucked as many details as possible.

"My name is Lord Kerberos," he told her. "It was I who restored order to the kingdom in the days after the curse when only chaos reigned. Those silly people in the village with their petty disputes? They would have sent the kingdom into civil war, so I, a simple apothecary with a modest shop, took it on myself to listen to their grievances and pass fair judgment. Not six months later they begged me to officially stand in the king's stead and look after all his matters." Lord Kerberos patted the fat purse that swung inches from Ivy's outstretched fingers. "I like to think I have been worthy."

She liked to think of a day when she would be a lady at court, worthy of her girl. But even Ivy, a simple servant girl, knew that thinking a thing didn't make it so.

"It's just a temporary post. Mine until the princess wakes, and with her, King Alexander," Lord Kerberos said.

In the distance Ivy saw the castle's spire rising high above the rest of the city. Her stomach clenched to think of her girl lying inside the tower, a thick layer of dust gathering on her lashes, her lips, her long golden braid into which Ivy had woven each strand of their forbidden love. The horse leapt with joy at seeing his home. Lord Kerberos's money pouch, freed from his belt by fingers practiced at lacing bodices, slipped through her hand and plunged toward the ground. Ivy snatched it midair and held it tight, as tight as she held her dream to run away with her girl to a place where they could simply be two girls in love. Surely, such a place existed somewhere.

A crowd had gathered in anticipation of Lord Kerberos's arrival. The people peered at Ivy, their curious glances and voices pelting her like stones.

"Is she the one? That girl what rides behind Lord Kerberos?" A man with white flour in his hair spoke, a baker from the look of him.

"Are you dazed, man? She's naught but a chambermaid!" Another man, his apron splattered with blood, glared at Ivy. She cringed to think of him with a butcher knife.

"Why else would Lord Kerberos bring her to the wall?" The baker waved a hand toward the hedge of thorns.

"I don't know, but it's going to take more than a chambermaid to part—"

The butcher fell silent, as did the rest of the crowd, when long ribbons of gray and white streaked above the castle.

"Quick! They are coming." Lord Kerberos thumped to the ground and pointed at the sky. "Open the wall!"

Ivy waited until the world wobbled into one fixed place and then she too slid from the horse's back and stood in front of the villagers, Lord Kerberos, and the castle. "Who's coming?"

"The wise women. Quickly! There is no time!"

Ivy glared at the swirling mist that drew near and remembered the story, now legend, about the cursing of Princess Ambrosia. There had been four fairies, in that time, who watched over the kingdom. But King Alexander, disgruntled with one of the fairies, had invited only three to the princess's christening. The three fairies, as the story went, had arrived in a shimmering mist of dove gray and pure white. The first fairy, naught but a young girl, bestowed the gift of beauty on the baby princess, for she prized beauty above all else. The second, a robust woman, bestowed the gift of strength on the princess, for she had experienced the hardship of life and prized strength above all else. The third, a frail elderly woman with pure white hair, was just about to bestow her gift on the princess when the fourth fairy arrived in a swirling cloud, black as her heart. The evil fairy faced the king who had slighted her and spat her vengeance.

"On the day when Princess Ambrosia's heart quickens from true love she will prick her finger on a spindle and die," the fourth fairy said, turning into smoke the color of charcoal and flying out an open window.

"Not death, but sleep." The third fairy, her power diminished by age, could only soften the curse.

Ivy glared at the shimmering mist that drew near. "Them's your wise women? Them ladies what gave gifts to my princess when she was born? Ain't nuffink but a bunch of busybody fairies what cursed my gir—the princess."

Lord Kerberos nodded. "Yes. Exactly! *They* are the ones who trapped the princess in eternal slumber! Now hurry before they try to stop you!" He took a step toward the wall. The hedge of thorns shuddered and shrank tighter than ever. Fog descended until Ivy could no longer see anything, and when she breathed the air was moist and thick.

"Lord Kerberos? Where are you?"

When at last she heard a voice, it did not belong to Lord Kerberos.

"She has returned!" A girl spoke and clapped her hands, her voice pitching higher with each word.

"The one from within!" Another woman spoke, her voice steady and strong.

"And on the dawn of the second year!" An old woman's voice shook.

Their voices tumbled, one atop the other, until Ivy's head grew light and she considered floating away on the fog. But then she remembered.

Her girl. Her plan.

"You won't stop me with a few thorns, you hear?" She slipped her hand into her apron pocket and clutched both purse and purpose.

They murmured, the chorus of women.

"She hasn't changed!" the girl exclaimed.

"Not one bit! Look how brightly she still burns!" the woman in her prime agreed.

The old woman chuckled. "Do you not see what she keeps in her pocket? Oh, she has changed. She has grown strong enough to bear secrets!"

Ivy reached the end of her patience with fog and fairies.

"Stop poking around where you never was invited!" She waved her arms, parting the mist.

The fog drifted away. She had expected to see them, the wise women, but all she saw were the backs of villagers running from the voices and Lord Kerberos poking at the wall of thorns with his dagger.

"Where'd they go?" She walked toward him. "I weren't done telling 'em what I think of 'em. Blasted fairies!" This last part she shouted into the sky, in case they were perched in a nearby cloud, listening.

"Look, it's opening!" Lord Kerberos pointed his dagger toward the section of the hedge near her. Some branches pulled to the right. Others to the left. But pull they all did, creating the smallest of gaps. She took a step toward the wall. The gap widened. And another. It widened farther.

"Out of my way!" Lord Kerberos charged, his dagger waving as he rushed the wall. The thorns clamped onto the dagger just as it penetrated the gap, narrowly missing his hand.

Lord Kerberos took a step back and stared at the hilt of his dagger held captive by the thorns. "I'd say ladies first, except…"

"I'm no lady." Ivy spat on the ground between her feet.

She almost did it. Almost darted through the hedge, quick like a fox, leaving him behind with nothing but his made-up title of lord. But then she remembered he held the cure to awaken her girl. She stepped toward the wall. The branches relaxed and the dagger fell into her outstretched hands.

"Follow me." She ducked through the parting branches without so much as a glance backward. "And stay close or I'll leave you to the thorns."

❖

Ivy's fingers caressed the letter *A* on the shining gold crest that marked the heavy oak door of the castle. *A* for Alexander. *A* for Alexia. *A* for Ambrosia.

"She weren't never your Ambrosia. She were always my Rose," Ivy whispered, wrapping her fingers around the handle and heaving with all her might.

The door shuddered and swung open.

"Oh, well done, girl! Now lead me to the princess!" Lord Kerberos's breath was hot against the back of her neck.

Ivy turned and shrank from her first glance at Lord Kerberos since they'd entered the hedge of thorns. Red streaked his face and arms and dripped from the tips of his long fingers. Strange, the thorns had let her pass without so much as a scratch. His eyes begged no mercy, and she had none to offer.

"Same rules as before. I lead. You follow," she told him, stepping inside the castle.

She was prepared for dust.

Flecks of dust. Layers of dust. An entire tomb filled with darkness and dust.

But there was no dust. Instead, there was light.

Light that flared to life from the candlesticks on the entry table the minute her foot crossed the threshold, as if the castle itself were a living thing, awake all these years, and rejoicing at her return. Lords and ladies, fresh from the hunt, had fallen to the ground in the entrance hall, their bodies and cloaks lying in crumpled heaps. Ivy donned a thick robe and slung a second around her arm.

"I thought better of you, girl, than plundering the spoils." Lord Kerberos eyed Ivy suspiciously.

"The princess is likely to be chilled, ain't she? What with lying in a room with the window flung open these past two years." The truth of her words hurt Ivy, but that wasn't the reason she took the cloaks. They would have need of them before the night was over.

Light burst from the stacked logs inside the hearth the moment she stepped inside the kitchen where the second houseboy slept, a broken twig still clutched in his hands.

Lord Kerberos frowned when she disappeared into the larder and returned with a basket filled with aged cheeses and bottles of wine. "Now we're stopping for a picnic? Do you want to awaken Princess Ambrosia or not?"

"The princess is likely to be hungry, ain't she?" Ivy avoided Lord Kerberos's eyes.

More light flared from the lanterns in the great hall and glinted off the golden thrones where King Alexander and Queen Alexia slumbered. A thorn stabbed Ivy to the heart. Or just as good. She walked into the hall and knelt before her king and queen.

"Now what are you doing, girl? Stopping to pay your respects to *the king and queen*?" Lord Kerberos spat and Ivy's hand twitched to slap the words off his bony face.

"Aye, I am!" Her voice rang out through the hall.

Ivy knelt before King Alexander, leaning forward to press her lips to the royal ring on his limp hand. It was a hanging offense, she knew, to steal the king's seal. She withdrew and slipped the ring into her apron pocket next to the pouch of money. Both would offer some measure of protection for the princess. *That* was a thing worth dying for.

Three doves flew through an open window and perched on Queen Alexia's throne. "Oh, shoo, you bloody birds!" Ivy waved her hand at the doves, but they blinked at her and refused to move.

Ivy straightened the crown on Queen Alexia's brow. Leaning close, she whispered, "I won't let nuffink harm your girl, Your Majesty. I swear I'd die first. 'Cuz she's my girl, too."

The queen, still slumbering, smiled and shifted on her throne. The doves cooed and fluffed their feathers.

Footsteps echoed throughout the cavernous room. Ivy turned, but not in time to avoid the shocking impact of the bony hand across her face. She sprawled to the ground at the foot of her queen.

"I have had enough of these games! I demand you lead me to Princess Ambrosia this instant!" Lord Kerberos towered above her, his rail-thin body shaking with fury. He drew his foot back as if to kick her.

Ivy curled into herself and covered her body with her arms. This was not the first time she had been treated thus. But the blow never landed.

Lord Kerberos flailed like he'd taken leave of his senses. The doves flung themselves at him in a flurry of feathers. They pecked at his eyes, his mouth, his gashes from the thorns, and Lord Kerberos lashed with his fists. And then the smallest dove, hardly more than a chick, fell. It landed on the stone floor beside her with a sound so faint it near as broke Ivy's heart. The faintest chirp seemed to say, "Strike." And then another, "Now." The young dove shuddered and lay still. Ivy stroked the gray feathers of the dove's chest, soft as silk, and felt tears flood her eyes.

Lord Kerberos took aim at a pure white dove, old and wobbling in its flight. His hand struck out. "You thought you could stop me? By letting her sleep instead of die? Do you not understand? You made it *easy*!" The dove lurched away, taking the blow on its tail feathers. "You tried to stop me with your hedge of thorns, but I found your key and she let me into the castle. I will make the girl lead me to the princess if I have to break every bone in her body! Do you not understand? Once I kill Princess Ambrosia, everyone within these walls will die as well. Fools! You've handed me the *kingdom*!" Lord Kerberos spun in a circle, his long hair waving out in his madness. His laughter pealing into a woman's cackle. The edges of his gown began to dissolve into smoke the color of charcoal, and Ivy knew. Ivy saw.

It was not Lord Kerberos who stood in front of her, but the evil fourth fairy.

It was not a cure inside the vial, but poison.

The mist crawled up the cloak, freeing the fairy from the vulnerability of a mortal form.

Ivy charged, the dagger in her outstretched hand. The evil fairy turned and aimed a bony hand at her, muttering an evil incantation. One dove darted in and pierced the evil fairy's cheek. The other dove aimed for the hand. It flew away with the nub of a pinkie finger in its beak. Black blood spurted from the wounds as the evil fairy shrieked and did not see Ivy leap, plunging the dagger deep into a still-beating, still-human heart.

The evil fairy fell at the foot of the sleeping king and queen, an inky puddle seeping from the corpse.

Ivy exhaled, long and slow.

The corpse convulsed. A pitch-black raven burst from its chest and flew at her, its sharp talons drawn.

Ivy screamed and the two doves swooped in, flapping their wings to shield her face. The raven turned and sailed out the window, cawing, "Damn you. Damn you all!"

Ivy wrapped her arms around herself. When the quaking stilled, she stepped over the body and walked to the staircase that led to the tower room. She paused for only a second to look back at the fallen dove.

❖

Ivy spread the cloak across the princess's body, cold as death itself, and wept. No cure. No hope. No plan. Not anymore. She brushed her fingers over her girl's lips and bent close to whisper into her sleeping ear.

"It were always you, Rose, what warmed my heart. Ain't nuffink worth nuffink in this life if I can't share it with you."

Princess Ambrosia stirred and reached for Ivy in her sleep.

Ivy caressed the softness of the princess's skin, the satin of her lips, the silk of her hair. Each touch was a good-bye. She stood and walked to the window, still flung wide.

She gulped the air as it rushed her, crisp and sharp, savoring the last taste of life as she stared into the vast blue sky above and the hard earth below. Ivy spoke no words as she swung her legs through the window, the sill biting deep into her flesh. She was past the point of threats or pleas. She inhaled deeply, leaning forward. She was ready, and then she heard a voice, ancient as time itself.

"I thought you wanted to save your girl."

Ivy turned toward the voice and almost lost her balance. A strong hand grabbed her, belonging not to the old woman she assumed had spoken, but to a strong woman in her prime who stood beside her.

"I do, but she sleeps and I can't do nuffink to wake her." Ivy shook off the woman's hand and turned back to the window.

"In fact," the old woman's voice warbled, "you are the only one who can wake the princess. If you choose to do so, that is, after you learn the truth."

Ivy climbed out of the window and studied the old woman who stood before her. Wisps of pure white hair that flew about her face. Eyes, blue and clear as the sky, surrounded by craters of wisdom. She knew something. No, she knew everything.

"We have watched over you all these years, my dear," the old woman said. "The three of us. We have watched you and waited for you to know who you are. Some of us realize the truth early in life, like the young one who sacrificed everything for you."

The young one? An image of a dying dove flashed through Ivy's mind.

The middle-aged woman spoke. "Others, like me, come to the truth at the height of our lives. I found the choice difficult. I had children, you see."

The old woman continued, "And some, like me, are so old when we learn the truth that the choice is easy."

"What are you talking about? What truth?" A gust of wind blew in from the window, chilling Ivy to the bone.

The old woman took Ivy's hand. Her skin was smooth and paper thin. "To leave this life and join us. To become a wise one."

"Me? A fairy? Are you blinking crazed?" Ivy pulled her hand away. "I'm just a chambermaid!"

The old woman chuckled. "A chambermaid with the power to part a hedge of thorns?"

"That's right. 'Cuz I came from inside the castle. Or sumfink like that."

The old woman stared into the distance. "Try to touch her, I dare you! Lay one finger on my Rose, and I'll tear you to bits! I'll pierce you till your blood runs cold!" She quoted Ivy's words, spoken in this very spot two years before. "Dearest Ivy, you are the one who called the hedge of thorns into being. It was born of your love for the beautiful Rose and your desire to protect her. In all the world, there is no more potent magic. It was the first time you wielded your powers, but not the last. Think, child. Remember."

Ivy thought and remembered. Her fall from the window that had ended at Lord Ainsworth's gate. Milli's miraculous meal fit for a king. So many other mysteries she'd never been able to explain. Until now. Could it be?

The old woman nodded. "You may use that gift to awaken the princess. You may even have the life with her that you wish right here in the castle." She sighed, the tired sigh of one who has lived centuries. "But know this, if you choose to live as a mortal, your body will age and die, though your magic will live on in some form. Join us now and you will live forever, watching over all of humanity and lessening the suffering of this world."

Ivy glanced at her girl. "But if I join you?"

"She will sleep, forever protected by the hedge of your love."

It was barely a choice at all. Ivy strode across the room to the princess. "Awake, my girl." She kissed her gently.

Princess Ambrosia, thereafter known throughout the kingdom as Princess Rose, opened her eyes and smiled at the one whose love had quickened her heart. "Why, Ivy, it's mean of you to make me wait so long! You took such a time with your chores, I must have fallen asleep."

Ivy cradled her girl in her arms. "Forgive me?"

"Always," the princess whispered.

THE IVY AND THE ROSE

❖

Life changed for Ivy, who was named Princess Rose's royal consort. Nights with her girl were a delight, but the long days at court? That was another matter. The ladies were silly. The lords, boorish. But the kitchen became a place of respite when Ivy brought Milli to the castle and named her head cook. And as for Lord Ainsworth, Ivy's former master? He finally settled his debt to the crown...after two years of servitude spent emptying all the chamber pots in the castle.

Following the king and queen's deaths, Rose and Ivy ruled with wisdom and kindness and lived well into the sunset of their years, neither parting from the other for more than hours at a time. And on the terrible day when two graves were dug, the kingdom mourned and planted a bush of roses at one and a vine of ivy at the other. It is said that before the sun fell on that day of mourning the vines had entwined, one within the other.

You can see it, if you are brave and worthy and willing to leave this world of logic and reason. You can trudge through the forest until you reach the castle where a hedge of roses blooms, but beware. It is a place where a cook can become a magician, a lord an evil fairy, a princess a mere girl, and a chambermaid a queen's royal consort. Or even a wise woman.

Who knows what you will become?

But if you do risk the journey toward truth, tread softly. For you, like others before you, may catch a glimpse of the rare Briar Castle mourning dove, marked by blazing red feathers.

"My Rose, my girl," the dove coos as it perches on the princess's grave.

Still.

Sasha Payne (Morsus@virginmedia.com) is an English writer of gay erotic fiction and romance. She is a lifelong speculative fiction and fantasy fan and most enjoys working within the genres of speculative fiction, fantasy, or historical fiction.

This story is based on "Goldilocks and the Three Bears."

Goldie and the Three Bears
Sasha Payne

It was raining like the end of days. A constant downpour that turned distant sirens into the wail of lost souls and cloaked us all in heavy gray mist. I was glad of the mist that night, glad to be one more anonymous Joe wrapped in a rain-slicked trench coat. Private dick was always a job on the edge of respectable, beyond the edge some might figure. Sure, I sailed close to the wind, but I was no scum sucker, and that was one night I was paying for it. I needed somewhere to hide until the heat wore off and Titchy McGee decided to turn his wrath on someone else to cross his path.

From where I was standing, soaking wet and jumping at shadows, the Cabin looked like a mighty fine bolthole. It was closer to a dive than a nightclub—entry was through a back door off an alleyway—but that suited my mood. I'd never get into any high-class gin joint any way.

The beady-eyed gunsel behind the counter drank me in like I was a tall glass of cool water. But he was on duty and I was in a hurry to get into the thick of the action. I gave him a rain check and pushed into the club. The lights were low and a fog of smoke filled the air. Whatever kind of club you're thinking of, that was the Cabin. Chippy boys in shorts and tight shirts swished around, selling cigarettes and their souls. The bartenders were dames with short, slicked-back hair and men's suits. Up on the stage, a pair of canaries in low, tight dresses and killer heels were crooning to a dirty little jazz number. I knew the trombonist some, he was a switch-backer out of Brooklyn with a taste for cheap scotch and expensive card games. I'd met him in another club, another time, and I'd fingered his slider before he mouthed my piece.

I flicked a deuce at the nearest drink slinger and she sashayed across. She poured me a dirty martini and waved back my green.

"It's been paid for."

I followed her gaze to a booth by the band. My benefactor was a suit I'd seen around. Tall, broad, with long, dark hair and a beard I could have crawled into. I pegged him as a Russian, or maybe a Pole. A traveler from the ice looking to get warmed up. It would've been rude not to go over, so I did.

He grinned as he watched me walk across. I was glad to know my quality still held.

"Aren't you going to drink it?" he asked as I slid into his booth.

"Figured I'd come thank you in person."

I took a gulp; it burned like an angry lover.

"My name is Mischa," he said, getting good and close. He smelled of cigar smoke, leather, and fine brandy. There was a bottle on the table, newly plundered and already half-drunk. My host was a man of large appetites.

"You can call me Goldie," I said.

His fingers, thick and covered in heavy rings, tipped up my hat. "Because of your hair."

"Sure."

I finished my martini and another appeared at my elbow. He waved off the chippy boy with an ass slap that must've left a mark. The chippy jumped, rubbed his rump, and lammed off before Mischa could make it double.

"I don't get a brandy?" I asked.

"Brandy is expensive."

"And you pegged me as cheap goods?"

He smirked and drank me in. "I believe you are beautiful… goods."

Mischa rolled the word around his mouth, letting it linger. I could see he like the taste.

"I'm not in the market for a daddy bear to take me home to his cave."

Mischa finished his brandy like it was water. His hand dropped to my thigh and explored the landscape. If the damp material bothered him then he didn't show it. His hand was hot and insistent. I felt steam rising where he handled me.

"A shame," he said, figuring to sound like he meant it. "Have you played in the rooms here?"

"You booked one?"

Sure, I'd played here before. Everything from broom closets to ballrooms were just waiting for playmates. I was pretty sure there were secret snappers hidden away, but that was no skin off mine. I hadn't the green to be blackmailed.

Mischa grinned and I saw gleaming white teeth.

He stalked into the room ahead of me. He was that kind of pick-up. The room was a temporary possession, just like I was. I figured we'd both be having a fast, rough night. The room was a decent size and glam for what it was: thick carpet, soft lights, and a bed the size of a football field. Mischa took off the heavy fur he was wearing and hung it up, neat like. Underneath, his suit was pin sharp but couldn't stop him from looking like a circus strong man on his day off. I took off my hat and hung up my suit; I put my piece in my jacket pocket and hid my knife under my pillow. Sure it was dangerous. I already had a crew after me, and here I was climbing into bed with a gee sure to ride me hard and put me away wet. Thing was, Mischa's interest was all on the surface. Better some bear you know wants to maul you than some dish that stabs you in the heart.

I heard the door lock, but when I checked it the key was still there. Day some pick-up hides the key is the day I stop picking up.

Mischa was just finishing airing his fur: He had a great barrel chest, rolling stomach, and meaty thighs. Where his skin wasn't covered in dark, curly hair it was smothered in green and blue tattoos. He was eating me up with a spoon and I wasn't minded to kick him out of the room neither. I liked what I saw: the muscles, and the smile, and I liked the thick, long, half-hard cock.

He prowled across the room toward me. He had a look in his eye like a tiger circling a lost lamb and a predatory smile like he could already taste me. He pinned me up against the wall and kissed my neck with his warm, soft lips and softly bristling beard.

"I'm going to fuck you, Goldie," he growled into my ear.

"Figured you might."

He pawed my ass with one hand while the other tangled thick fingers in my hair.

"Do you liked to be fucked?" Mischa asked. "Do you liked to be fucked very hard while you squirm?"

I leaned back a little. No reason he should get it all his own way.

"Hard as you like sweetheart, but I'm not promising any squirming, nor weeping, begging, or screaming."

Mischa grinned and took my wrists between his thumb and forefinger. Not painful but firm.

"I like to make men squirm."

"I like to make Swiss cheese and bacon sandwiches, I don't see that happening here either," I said. "You're not tying me up either." Sure I was horny and maybe I was a little reckless, but I wasn't insane.

Mischa gave me a hard kiss and a soft lick along the side of my face. Tasting it like he tasted the idea of owning me.

"Tie you up!" he said, backing toward the bed and pulling me after him. "I do not need a rope or chains to control a man." He flipped me onto the bed and pinned me down. He had my arms above my head, wrists held, and his heavy thighs were making me real intimate with the mattress.

"You wanna test how controlled I am?" I asked.

I was nervous, sure, but I didn't show it. The mood was still light. Two guys having fun.

"I think we will both enjoy this," he said.

He lowered his head to bite and lick my neck. His heavy beard was a light tickle against my skin. His free hand squeezed and teased my nipples before trailing down to my gut. He used his fingertips as he scoured my body like he was searching for gold. I'm no dummy but it took me a couple of passes before I tumbled to his game: looking for a ticklish spot. He was real wedded to making me squirm. He gave up on my torso and walked his fingers up to my pits. I tried to play it cool some more but busted my flush with the first card. I tensed and he chuckled.

He drew his fingers slowly over my skin, looking for the sweet spots. It wasn't the most undignified position I'd been in but damned if it wasn't in the top ten. He had me pinned while that old mix of irritation and delight, pain and pleasure, at the tickling sensation was getting close to unbearable.

"Ha ha!" he cried. Thrilled.

Damn it.

"Doesn't mean a thing," I drawled.

My punishment for raining on his parade was that he kept it up. Round and round, light, teasing touches, until not reacting was its own agony.

Then he spun me over onto my front. For a second or two I felt spun out of whack. Then I felt those slicked, thick fingers tug out of me. Mischa was a maestro of doing what he wanted with other men's bodies. His left hand pawed my hair and pushed my face into the pillow. I could see nothing but the tiny whirling pattern on the cheap cotton. The scent of carbolic soap filled my lungs. My arms scrabbled for purchase but came up with nothing. Mischa's right hand slapped my ass, then grabbed and squeezed like he was measuring me for market.

Then he fucked me. The great length and weight of his cock slammed into my ass. He grunted. I felt him move his legs and then his right arm slid under my thighs. He lifted me up. Lifted me up and fucked me again, deeper. He had me dangling so he could get a better, deeper angle. His left hand kept my face pressed into the pillow. His weight was behind his thrusts as he played with the angle, played with my body as he looked for the best way to fuck me as deeply as he wanted. Each thrust was deeper than the last, harder than the last. I felt like I was splitting. His balls slapped against my ass and he murmured happily. He was finally deep enough to bury himself inside me. I was light-headed. He was finally ready to really start fucking me, just the way he wanted. It was hard and it was deep and it was fast. The impact slammed me against the pillow over and over. It felt like a road drill. I ached where I hung over his arm. My legs throbbed from his weight. My head was sore from the pressure of his finger. Most of all my cock was aching. He was fucking me hard and deep, like he owned me, like a possession, and my cock was hard. Hard for him. Hard for it.

He came with a groan, and his arm tightened around me while his fingers clenched in my hair. I heard myself creak like an old door, then he let go. I fell onto the sheets in a mess of aches and confusion. I sat up and regretted it; that hadn't happened in a while. Mischa had wandered into the shower. I heard him start singing as he turned on the water. Fucker had plowed me, literally dropped, and walked away. I knew there were weak-willed Joes who'd take that as a cue to try harder for reciprocation. Maybe crawl into the shower and flutter their eyes at him.

Me, I jacked over his shirt. Then I got my knife, dressed, and left. I didn't much care if he came after me sore over his shirt. Big never bothered me anyway.

I went back out to the bar and ordered two fingers of scotch. I knew I smelled of sex and I didn't care. Around here it was just another cologne. As I was sipping my whiskey I saw two mooks shoulder their way in. Titchy McGee's men—I'd seen them eyeballing me in his office, just before I jumped out the window. Since I didn't see any windows in easy reach, I headed for a booth before they saw me. I ducked into the first half-occupied one I saw. A small, nervous-looking guy with chipmunk cheeks, a small mustache, and a neat little beard.

"How's it cooking, Chief?" I asked.

"Um..."

"Buy you a drink?"

"Uh, sure," he said.

He was a doll, in a boyish way, and looked happy enough to have me pressed up against him.

I sent a chippy boy for a drink and introduced myself.

"Sean Weiss," he said. "You come here...uh..."

"First time picking up?" I asked. "You don't have to say anything smart. You don't have to say anything if you're not in the mood." I slipped the chippy a deuce to watch out for Titchy's mooks and sipped my drink while Sean sucked down his like it was going out of style.

"Something smart was never an option," he said. "If I don't talk, what do I do?"

"Talk's overrated." The chippy was gesturing at me wildly. Titchy's mooks were prowling nearby. I put my hand on Sean's knee and he blushed like a Catholic schoolgirl. I kissed him hard and he squealed. I kissed him soft and he moaned.

"Should we...um...the screen..." he murmured.

Figures I wouldn't have seen the privacy screen. I pulled it shut. We could still be heard but between the canaries, the band, and the general hubbub I didn't figure that a few moans would make much of a dent.

Sean was hard already, so I worked my hand down his pants and into his underwear. Felt like cotton boxers, comfortable and straightforward.

"I've never...um...how do we..."

"Quit yammering. Never helps."

I kissed him. He moaned like a ten-dollar whore. I got the feeling maybe this wasn't just his first time here. Sean grabbed his seat and thrust against my hand. He panted out his piece and filled my hand. As he fell back against his cushion I found his handkerchief and cleaned us both off.

"Oh, oh...um..." Sean smiled sleepily. "Do you, uh, should I?"

I unbuttoned my pants and freed my dick. I was half-hard. "Got no complaints, I hope."

He shook his head and put his hand on my thigh. I threw a cushion on the floor.

"On the floor?"

"You, sure. I'll stay here," I said. "You played the flute before?"

Sean's eyes were round as marbles. He knelt down and rubbed his paws on his thighs.

"My first time in a duet," he said.

There was something real pleasing about the way his eyes brightened and his cheeks flushed. When you're a guy in this town, you take what compliments are thrown your way.

Sean wet his lips and I put his hand around the base of my cock. I stiffened in his hand.

"Better?"

He nodded, wide-eyed, and then lowered his face. He closed his eyes and slowly licked along the underside of my cock. I put my hand on his shoulder and pulled him a little closer. His breath was warm against my skin as he swirled his tongue around me. Sure, he was a little sloppy and a little fast, but he was enthusiastic and excited. I tipped back my head as he murmured happily and took me into his mouth. He squeaked a little as pre-come squirted into his mouth.

The sound of the club receded as I relaxed back against my cushion. I closed my eyes and concentrated on the feel of his mouth and the little sounds he was making. My other hand found his shoulder and then slipped up into his hair. It was smooth and sleek and gave me no purchase. Sean's other hand stroked my thigh and then he walked his fingertips into my crotch.

I heard myself groan and I tensed. Sean was new to it, sure, but the boy was a natural. He stroked my balls with his fingertips as the tip of his tongue circled my slit. I felt my balls rise and heard Sean's little "oomp!" as he realized. The only things going through my mind were the texture of his tongue and the warmth of his mouth. I think my eyes opened. I figure maybe I pulled his hair. I'm sure I grunted something meaningless as I came in his mouth.

We had those quick, few seconds where you aren't quite sure if you should say "thanks" or "get out." Then I emptied my drink and headed for the screen.

"Thanks for the fun," I said, as I pulled it back.

"Maybe another time," he said.

I waved him off as I went. He was a sweet guy, sure enough, and the world does terrible things to sweet guys. Starting with introducing them to guys like me.

It was getting early, which is like getting late if you're the kind of cat who wakes at noon and sleeps at dawn. I didn't see Titchy's mooks, so I headed for the back door. My luck being what it was, I got halfway there before the cops raided the joint. Most days we'd all put up our hands like good little boys and girls. I had no reputation to ruin, and most that did had the money to make sure they didn't. That was most days. That particular night three mob goons were shaking down the owner and Stripes Gonzalo was sucking sausage—not an event he wanted discussing on the street. All four of them had heaters and they all used them. The cops fired back and then the whole caboodle went to hell in a handcart. I headed to the basement, me and a good dozen others. There was a hidden door down there, used back when the place was a speakeasy. The trombonist had told me one time the band used it to grab cigarette breaks without any customers grabbing them.

It was crowded in the basement as a couple of bar staff were still fighting with the door.

"Breathless suits you."

I turned; it was the trombonist, all dolled up in his penguin suit and holding his trombone. I tried to remember his name. It was something foreign. He was dark, strong, and handsome. I remembered his accent; he'd been born in America but his mother tongue still trenched his words now and then. "Javid," I said. "Been a while."

"I've been touring."

The door opened and we pushed through, shouldering our way out of the fetid basement into the dark, smoky air beyond.

"You got wheels?" I asked.

"I have feet," he said, and smiled. He had a smile like sunshine on glass. "Nobody would call you slow to put yourself forward. I'm in a flophouse around the corner. If you're nice, I'll let you come with me."

"I'm always nice."

He laughed as we walked along the sidewalk; he was carrying his trombone still. If any of the cops swarming around had given us a real look they'd have us bang to rights.

"I saw you hiding from those goons," he said. "The little skinny one with the hat and the bald one with the limp."

"A couple of Titchy McGee's boys," I said. "He's sore I wouldn't pony up some snapshots."

I followed Javid into the building. It was exactly the sort of place a traveling musician would flop.

Javid shook his head. "Blackmailing Titchy McGee, Goldie? There are easier ways to kill yourself."

"I don't play that game. Some broad calling herself Mitchell offered me two hundred to hide out and snap her old man playing pat-a-cake with a dancer. Turned out to be McGee."

"The dancer?" he asked.

"Funny guy."

Javid grinned and opened up his room. His clothes were hung up neat but that was it. There was a whole stack of records on the floor, the player was on the bed, and a truckload of skin magazines were on the couch. He put his trombone down in its case and pushed the magazines onto the floor. I nudged the record player with my foot. "Making sweet music?" I asked.

"You keep that up and I'll hand you over to Titchy myself." Javid lit a cigarette, sucked down smoke, and let it linger. He blew it out in one long, slow breath. "You want a drink?"

"Only when I'm conscious."

He had great gams. That was the third thing you noticed about him. The first thing was how beautiful he was, then how dark he was, and finally how long and shapely his legs were.

He poured us both a gin and offered me a cigarette.

"I only smoke after sex," I said.

"So stash it for an hour," he said. I did.

We neatened up the couch and sat down. There was darkness coming through the dirty windows and the whisper of traffic was loud when we were quiet.

"You must need a rest," he said.

"Say what?"

Javid smirked and sucked his cigarette. "When I was up onstage I could see you. When you're up on stage you can see what everyone's doing. You'd like it."

I kicked off my shoes and took off my jacket. The gin was burning away some of my tension and the warm thigh pressed against me was helping with the rest.

"What's your point, Javid?"

"I saw the little teddy bear blowing you," he said. "He's been sorely missing a playmate for a while. It was good of you to indulge him."

"Wasn't any great charity."

Javid slipped off his shoes. "I'm curious about the Russian you started your evening off with."

"Mischa."

"Is that his name?"

"So he said. He could've lied, I wasn't minded to check his drivers' license."

Javid's eyes sparkled as he wriggled out of his jacket. "But then how would you find him again?"

"I've no compelling reason to," I said.

Javid crushed his cigarette in the ashtray. "I heard he doesn't take lovers."

"No?"

"No, just slaves." Javid turned to face me and ate me up. "Were you his slave, Goldie?"

"I'm nobody's slave." I finished my gin and put down the glass. "He wanted it rough, no problem. But he didn't want to scratch my back after I scratched his. I don't much care for that."

Javid slid closer and unbuttoned my shirt. "Maybe he thinks slaves don't deserve it. Perhaps you were supposed to beg."

"I'm nobody's slave and I don't beg, not for a pretty face, a stiff drink, or a warm blanket on a cold day." Javid was real close now and I could smell his hair oil and his aftershave.

"When you say rough," he said delicately, putting his hand inside my shirt and stroking my gut, "how rough?"

I lay down and pulled him with me, so we were side by side. "How rough a story would get you out of your pants?" I asked.

"A please would do that."

"Please."

He took off his pants and threw them on the floor. Mine followed, then the rest of our clothes.

"What position?" Javid asked. His breath was moist against my face.

"This is good."

He grinned. "The Russian."

"Facedown. Ass in the air. Being fucked like a jackhammer."

Javid whistled. "Lucky boy." He put his hand on my hip as he leaned in to kiss me. His skin was burning. He had fine, dark curls of hair along his forearms and across his chest. As I pulled him closer his hair brushed against my skin. Our dicks nestled together, same size or near as damn it. "Did you ever kiss his sheets?" I asked.

"He made a play, I wasn't interested." Javid winked. "I think I hurt his feelings."

"You didn't like his manner?"

Javid shrugged all graceful, like a ballet dancer. "No. Too demanding. Too loud. Too grabby. Too much."

"No argument there."

"What about the little bear, how did you find him?"

"His name is Sean," I said. "Not demanding enough. Not loud enough. Not grabby enough."

Javid laughed. "What a shame."

We kissed, good and slow. He tasted of gin and breath mints. I wondered when he'd used those, and for who.

"Your pistol must be running hot," Javid said, stroking my cock.

"It's good for it." I was getting hard. I'd say it was quick but that'd be a lie. I'd been fixing for this more or less since I saw him onstage.

"I hope I can keep up," he said and caught my mouth with his. They fit well. We fit well, like two cogs interlocking. I heard quick breathing but didn't know if it was him or me. His hands were smaller than mine but his fingers were longer. They played along my arm as we thrust together, hard cocks sliding against each other. My hand was splayed against the small of his back. The jets of his backbone felt like a submerged rock path in a stream. I tried to think about the feel of his skin and the heat of his breath. Anything but how close he was. Javid grabbed my arm, his fingers digging into my skin. His body was juddering a little, like the ground right before a quake. I tried to think of baseball or math problems. But we were both close and neither of us was going to last. Javid moaned my name and pulled my trigger. I grunted out my little death as he was splashing his across my thighs.

We lay quiet for a bit, cooling and uncomfortable but not enough to move.

"I hope they don't charge me to clean the couch," Javid said.

"Who's going to clean us?" I asked.

Javid poked my gut with his finger. "Be cheaper to buy new than clean you."

"Cheaper, sure, but who wants to live cheap?"

Javid sat up and stretched. "Your Russian was too much and your little bear wasn't enough. What was I?"

"What do you figure?" I asked.

"Just right," he said with a grin.

Stacia Seaman has edited numerous award-winning titles, and with co-editor Radclyffe won a Lambda Literary Award for *Erotic Interludes 2: Stolen Moments*. She has essays in *Visible: A Femmethology* (Homofactus Press, 2009) and *Second Person Queer* (Arsenal Pulp Press, 2009).

This story is based on "The Little Match Girl."

Final Escape
Stacia Seaman

It was a bitterly cold night in Detroit. The wind had picked up and the snow started falling as soon as the sun went down. Laima had no plans for New Year's Eve—all she wanted to do was make some money to buy something to eat, then find a place to stay warm, stay dry. She wore almost everything she owned: T-shirt, sweatshirt, the old woolen navy pea coat she'd found at a thrift shop, faded jeans. Her tattered boots, taped with duct tape, were scant protection against the slick, icy pavement. She paused to tuck her tangled hair, once so thick and lustrous, into her tattered beanie.

The street was deserted, lined with the burnt-out shells of houses—testament to the thousands of residents who'd abandoned the city when its economy collapsed. This area was so different from the suburban neighborhood where Laima had grown up, with its green, tree-lined streets and large cookie-cutter homes, the brand-new American cars in the driveways. It wasn't safe to go into most of these houses; though they were dark, that didn't mean they were empty, and the people inside weren't usually friendly.

Snow was starting to accumulate, on the grass, on the pavement, and the cold had driven everyone indoors. Laima couldn't see another soul on the street. Alone, hungry, and miserable, she shivered as she continued walking. On a night like this, she wanted coffee with sugar. And maybe some soup or, if they had it tonight, chili. There was a diner a few streets down—it was open twenty-four hours, but perhaps not on New Year's Eve.

But if she didn't make some money first, she wouldn't eat anything. She had put together more kits yesterday, so she had plenty: Baggies, each with a new syringe, a bottle cap, a cotton ball, and an alcohol pad, that she sold for a dollar each to other addicts. If she sold five, she'd have dinner.

Laima bowed her head against the wind and started down a small side street. She took in the boarded-up windows of the houses; usually there were signs of life in at least a couple of them, but not tonight. It was cold, it was dark, and anyone who had a warm place to stay was unlikely to venture out. She knew better than to knock on any doors. On the street people knew her and bought kits from her; on a night like tonight, though, with no one around, they'd think nothing of taking her kits, her stash... She didn't allow the thought to continue.

With every step she took on the way to the diner, her hopes continued to dim. Not only did she not encounter any other homeless addicts who might buy some works, but she didn't see anyone who might be a diner patron, someone she'd be able to hit up for a dollar or two. Finally Laima reached the diner. It was silent, deserted, almost eerily dark without the garish neon that usually lit up the entire block. A handwritten sign in the door informed her that she'd arrived during the only twenty-four hours of the year the diner was closed, but they would reopen the next day at noon, "a Football Free Zone!"

With tears running down her cheeks, Laima crossed the street, then walked down a ways to where two buildings overlapped, forming a sheltered corner. One of the buildings jutted out just far enough to block the wind, and the sidewalk there was dry and free of snow. She sat, drawing her knees up to her chest, and tried to think of what to do next.

Laima fingered the balloons in her pocket. Nothing in her stomach, nowhere to warm up, no one to talk to. She pulled out one of the balloons, then carefully zipped her pocket closed. Turning her back to the street so nobody could see her, she prepared a dose. She shivered as she pulled her arm out of her coat, but quickly felt the rush of warmth once she'd finished giving herself the injection.

She closed her eyes and leaned her head back against the brick. Her feet were finally warm, as though she were sitting in front of the fireplace in her parents' living room, wearing thick woolen socks and sitting under the old plaid blanket they kept draped over the back of the sofa. Her cat, Zemi, lay curled on her lap, purring. Laima sank her fingers into Zemi's thick fur, rubbing her back, scratching behind her ears. That last day before the holiday break, in school, she'd sneaked a look at Emilia during biology class. Emilia had smiled at her, shyly, and it was all Laima could do to keep her hands folded on her desk and not reach across to link her fingers with Emilia's. She sighed happily and continued to pet Zemi. In the background she heard the preparations for the holiday meal. New Year's Eve in her family was a joyous occasion—tradition held that the year would continue the way it had started, so everyone wanted to be happy, singing and talking and enjoying each other's company.

How long had it been since she'd enjoyed her father's company?

How long since she'd been welcome at her family home?

How long since she'd seen Emilia?

The fire vanished; Zemi's purrs faded into the darkness. The warmth had worn off. The cold seeped into her toes through her cracked boots. Once again chilled, Laima curled up against the brick wall of the building behind her. She slipped her hand into her pocket and fingered the balloons. It was too soon, she knew, but she had felt so good. For that one moment, everything had been good again.

She prepared another dose, then injected it. As she leaned back against the building behind her, the brick wall in front of her began to waver—from solid to translucent, then it vanished completely. As she looked into the room beyond, she saw a family. Her family. There she was, a young girl with long, wavy dark hair that tumbled down her back as she ran from her father, screaming with laughter, clutching a new toy she'd received as a Christmas present. The dining room table was laden with food for their holiday meal; the smells made her mouth water, her stomach rumble.

And there, sitting in the comfortable chair closest to the fire, there was her mociute, her father's mother, the person who knew and understood her best in the world. Even as Laima watched, the view changed: her grandmother's wrinkles deepened, her shoulders bent under the weight of her years. And there was Laima, a year ago, at her feet, her grandmother's hand gently stroking Laima's hair as she told her stories of Laima's senelis, her father's father, who had died before Laima was born. She smiled and pulled Laima close as Laima told her about Emilia. Beautiful Emilia, with her golden hair and her caramel-colored eyes, her sweet sweet kisses and her poet's soul. Laima told her grandmother about their days together at the DIA, how Emilia loved the modern American artists while Laima herself preferred the Europeans. They would go to Europe one day, Laima said, her and Emilia, and see more art, more museums, visit the village where Laima's mociute and senelis had met and fallen in love. Love, Laima's grandmother sighed, love was such a gift to see shining in her Laima's eyes. Would Emilia be coming to share in the New Year's Eve celebration?

Through the invisible wall, Laima saw herself smile, the glow of happiness that Emilia would finally meet her grandmother. Saw herself pulling out her phone, sending a text message. Moments later she was greeting Emilia, inviting her into the house, hanging up her coat. Taking her by the hand, Laima led her to the chair by the fire and introduced her to her grandmother, watching them exchange holiday greetings. In this glimpse into the past, Laima saw herself full of contentment that the two people she loved most in the world were here, with her, on the most important night of the year. What joy the new year would bring! Then, after Emilia bundled up to return to her own home for her family's holiday meal, the two girls stole a kiss under the mistletoe.

Laima closed her eyes as she remembered; she could still hear her father's roar, feel his hands on her arms as he tore her away from Emilia. Hear Emilia's sobs as she turned and ran out the front door. Laima still felt the sting of her father's hand, the burning imprint of his palm on her cheek.

Hot tears on her cheeks brought her back to the present. Behind her the wall was cold and hard. This time she didn't hesitate. She shot up a third time, needing the warmth of the past to help her cope with the frigid loneliness of this New Year's Eve.

This time the warmth drifted down over her. Looking up, she saw a Christmas tree; the trunk was in the corner beside her, and she was sheltered in its branches. It was the most magnificent tree she'd ever seen. The boughs danced with sparkling lights and colorful ornaments. Some had photographs of Laima, her parents, her mociute...Last year Emilia had given Laima a special gift, an ornament with a picture of the two girls together, which she'd wrapped in tissue and told Laima to put away for the future, when they would celebrate together. She'd had to watch as her father, over the protests of his wife and his mother, had broken the ornament into bits and told Laima to leave his house and never return. She'd barely had time to stuff some clothes into her backpack before he'd slammed the door in her face—"You've disgraced us all"—and she'd stumbled out into the cold. Her grandmother had beckoned her to the back of the house, where she'd pressed a roll of bills into Laima's hand and hugged her close.

Laima blinked and saw Emilia's ornament on the tree before her, but as she reached for it, the tree began to rise, higher and higher, into the sky, until the twinkling lights looked exactly like stars. She gasped when one of them began to fall, blazing into the night with a trail of fire behind it.

"That means someone has died," she said aloud. When she was little, her grandmother had told her that shooting stars were the souls of the dead making their journey toward heaven. Laima's eyes filled with tears. Every two weeks for the last year she'd taken the bus to the cemetery where her grandmother visited her husband's grave on Wednesdays. During those short visits Laima had once again felt loved, felt cherished—but one summer day she'd waited for hours, alone, and on her next visit, her grandmother lay in the ground beside her husband.

Laima had only one dose left. It was hours yet until daylight... She opened the balloon. As she held her lighter under the spoon, she looked up and saw her grandmother standing beside her on the sidewalk, smiling, holding out a hand. "Mociute, take me with you," she said. "Don't go away this time. You always go away." She quickly found a vein and injected herself. The rush was immediate—Laima's corner became as warm as a spring day, and her grandmother, strong and young, helped her to her feet. They turned to see Emilia, who greeted them both with a kiss and an embrace, and the three began to soar into the sky, shining, leaving behind a golden trail of fire.

Hours later, when the sun finally rose, Laima sat tucked into her corner. Her cheeks were flushed and she wore a blissful smile, yet she was ice-cold. Beside her on the ground were a needle and a spoon. "Another junkie trying to escape her life," said passersby. None of them could imagine the joy and the love of the new world she had entered in the new year.

E.J. Gahagan likes writing, reading, eating, sleeping, art, music and dancing. Not necessarily in that order. He lives in the Pacific North-West, but not one of the fashionable parts. Any resemblance between E.J. and anyone you know is purely coincidental. No, really.

This story is based on "Snow White and the Seven Dwarfs."

Sneewittchen (Snow White)
E.J. Gahagan

Long ago, in the time of the Great Burning, there lived a king and queen in a faraway land.

The king, though of royal blood, was a man much given to slothful habits and minor debaucheries, leaving much of his royal authority in the hands of the ministers appointed by his father. The king frittered away his days hunting in the royal preserve and his evenings immersed in games of chance and banqueting on all manner of rich foods and rare wines.

All but forgotten in her own wing of the castle, the queen worked on a tapestry that laid out the history of her own family. She was a witch descended from a line of witches older than the kingdom itself. She created this tapestry in the greatest secrecy. The room she worked in was suffused with ancient magic, hidden atop the tallest tower in the castle and protected by strong spells.

One day, while the queen worked on her tapestry, a raven landed in the window next to her. "Greetings, daughter of Morrighan," said the queen, "what errand brings thee hither?"

"Greetings to thee, beloved of Morrighan. I bring you a message."

"From whom?" the queen said, setting down her needle.

The raven bowed. "Cerridwin, Your Majesty."

"Please, continue."

"Seven days before the next full moon you must fast—not a morsel can pass your lips—bathe daily, drink purging teas, cleanse thyself inside and out, for on the night of the full moon you must lie with your husband and conceive by him. Unto you a daughter shall be born, skin as white as new snow, lips as red as fresh blood, eyes as blue as lapis lazuli, hair as black as a raven's feathers."

"A daughter," the queen said quietly.

"She shall be the future of your line and the hope of your kingdom. All that you know, all that you are, shall pass to her. Guard her well, oh Queen, from the danger that surrounds us all."

"And I must lie with…my husband?" the queen asked.

The raven shrugged her wings as well as a raven was able, as if to say, "It wasn't my idea." Then she flew away. The queen dwelt long on what she had heard; finally, with a deep sigh, she resumed work on her tapestry.

All was done as the queen had been directed to do. The birth of her daughter, named Snow White, was celebrated throughout the kingdom and beyond, particularly by the king of a neighboring realm. His was a poor, and poorly led, kingdom. Avarice, want, and fear ruled there in equal measure, but he was the father of a newborn son monumentally misnamed "Charming," a son who could secure for him the dowry of his wealthy neighbor's daughter.

But tragedy followed happiness when the queen died of a fever while Snow White was still an infant. The king turned her education over to his late queen's ladies-in-waiting. These servants, fully aware the queen was a witch but not being witches themselves, dared not teach Snow White anything beyond what girls of high station should know.

Of the queen's secret room and the tapestry nothing was said, so great were the punishments of witches in that evil time. And so Snow White grew to adulthood ignorant of her heritage and her latent powers.

Upon her coming of age, the king began to make inquiries concerning a suitable husband. His ministers, pursuing the desires of their own shriveled souls, pushed him to choose his neighbor's son. The king did not see great prospect in that match and said so, but the wily ministers pressed him so relentlessly that he finally agreed.

With that, the date for the marriage was set. But of all of this, Snow White knew nothing. Learning of her father's plans from Gretchen, the last living handmaiden of her mother's household, she despaired for her future. Never did she plan to marry, for she had no desire to be any man's wife. Many were the days she would climb the outside staircase to the top of the tallest tower, unaware of her mother's secret room below, and look away to the Darkly Woods, feeling a yearning she did not understand, and while she tended to all the duties and obligations of her station, she would feel an emptiness that nothing within the compass of her life could fill.

With the news of the impending marriage, she flew to her father's side to beseech him to change his mind. "Father, this thing cannot happen. I will have to go far away. This is my home, all that I know, what will you do without me?" she cried.

"Snow White," he said, "I love thee above all others, but the die is cast. What has been promised can not be un-promised. You shall have a rich dowry to take to your new family. They shall all be pleased and treat you with the greatest respect."

"My...new family?" Snow White said, her hands trembling as she tried to grasp her father's arm. "Father, I beg you, please..."

"If I may explain, Your Majesty?" said the king's vizier from the doorway of the audience chamber.

"Yes, please do," the king said.

"Your Highness would do well to remember that this is a matter of state," the vizier said in silky, yet ominous tones as he slowly approached Snow White. "A uniting of kingdoms. Can the misgivings of one girl be allowed to interfere? Your soul belongs to God, this is why you pray to Him. Your loyalty belongs to your father, to whom you owe everything, and your body shall belong to your new husband, so that you will bear him, and the kingdom, many children. This is your duty and your fate. I am greatly surprised that this must be explained to you."

The king took Snow White by the wrist and led her to the chamber door. "Go, my child, and prepare. All shall be for the best. Prince Charming is somewhat unschooled in life's finer pursuits, but bringing a wayward husband to heel is part of a wife's work. It is God's will and the natural order of things. This shall be made plain to you after you are married."

Releasing her and smiling benignly, the king firmly shut the door against his daughter.

Snow White ran to her room and threw herself onto her bed. Her tears flowed in a stream. The horror of her future had fully descended upon her. Seized by the blackest despair, Snow White curled into a tight ball and wished herself a swift death to release her from her fate.

Gretchen, hearing Snow White's sobs, entered the room and sat at her side, stroking her beautiful black hair and humming a nursery tune she had loved as a child. Snow White quickly turned to her and seized her hand. "Gretchen, what is to become of me? Marriage, marriage to a man I've never met. How can Father do this? And Prince Charming? What manner of man is he?"

"I have never seen him," Gretchen said, her voice trembling. "but many stories are told of him in the marketplace. He is a formidable man, quick of temper, proud, haughty, vain—in all these things he is his father's son, a man I met long ago, although I wish to God I had not."

"How can Father do this to me?" Snow White said, clinging to Gretchen. "I have obeyed him in all things, loved him without question or complaint, and now he sells me into slavery and calls it a marriage. I shall die, Gretchen. I shall die before I submit to this."

The old woman, her arms around Snow White, rocked her from side to side to comfort her as she had done when Snow White was a child. She then stopped so suddenly that Snow White looked up at her, puzzled.

"This thing shall not come to pass," Gretchen said. "There is something I must show you." She took from her apron pocket a ring of old, rusty keys. Holding one up, she put a finger to her lips and bade Snow White follow.

Silently and unnoticed, they passed through the castle and came to the tower; up the stairs they went till they came to a small door. The iron key opened it and the old woman bade Snow White enter. There was nothing in the room but three windows: one facing east, one south, and the last west.

Before Snow White could ask a question, the old woman touched the windowless north wall and whispered words Snow White could not understand. The wall vanished and therein was another staircase. The old woman held out her hand. Snow White took it and was led to her mother's secret room.

Snow White marveled at what she saw. It was easily twice as big around as the tower itself. How was this so? Many large windows circled it, and most astoundingly, there was no ceiling—the whole room seemed to be open to the sky. Snow White knew this could not be so, for she had stood on the roof of the tower more times than she could count.

The old woman lit a lamp and pulled her to the tapestry. She explained its meaning, Snow White's bloodline, down through the centuries, the millennia, to the beginning before the Beginning. Although the old woman talked for hours, no time at all seemed to pass.

Snow White trembled as she heard about her place in a world she never dared even dream about. That within her lay a great power whose source was her very being, and the key to that power lay in the choices she freely made about herself. Looking away to the north, she beheld the Darkly Woods in a way she never had before. The yearning within her for answers about herself, about her true nature, about her desire for a completeness she could not find in her father's world would no longer be denied. She knew not why, but she had to go north.

Snow White asked Gretchen to fetch her some food from the kitchen while she returned to her room to put on traveling clothes. When the old woman returned she was told of the plan and sworn to secrecy.

Gretchen walked with her to the edge of the wood, then stayed in that spot, peering into the forest long after Snow White had slipped away into the darkness.

When the king discovered his daughter missing he raised a terrible fuss. He ordered his men to search to the four corners of his kingdom. The old handmaiden was closely questioned, but the king believed her story and let her go. When the searchers returned empty-handed he offered a reward of one thousand gold marks to whoever could lead him to his daughter.

Snow White traveled as fast as ever she could. For three days and three nights she traveled down roads, then paths, and finally, goat tracks. So deep into the wood was she that the noonday sun did not reach her. Her food was gone, but she did not despair; she knew not where she was going or what she would find, but she did not weep with fear. For, in truth, she had never felt so free in all of her life.

On the fourth day she came to a clearing, where a small spring bubbled up from the earth. The water was cold as ice and clear as crystal. She drank much and washed her hands and face. As she knelt by the pool she thought on all that Gretchen had told her. Her mother was a witch, from an ancient line of witches. Could it be that she was also a witch? She could not be sure. How did it feel to be a witch? She didn't even own a broom, or a cat! It was all so confusing. She lay down in the soft moss next to the spring and fell into a deep sleep.

As she slept, a beautiful Naiad rose from the pool and examined Snow White closely. Placing a cool hand on Snow White's forehead, she turned to the north and sang a song in a trilling soprano. Presently, a raven arrived and the two of them engaged in a most melodious conversation, then the raven returned to the North.

The Naiad smiled on Snow White and gathered watercress for her to find when she awoke. She called on the woodland folk to gather nuts and fruits and lay them next to the watercress. Then she sank back into the pool.

When Snow White awoke, her hunger was such that the humble offerings of the woodland hosts seemed a feast. As she ate, the raven returned.

"Greetings to thee, Daughter of the Morning Star," the raven said, bowing till her beak touched the rock she perched upon.

Snow White bowed slightly in return. "Greetings to thee, raven. How comes it that I understand your speech?"

"Knowledge of my language, and much more, is in your blood," said the raven, hopping onto Snow White's knee. "If you are rested, follow me, there is someone you must meet."

With that, the raven flew up to a low branch and carefully led Snow White through the trackless forest to a clearing in the very heart of the Darkly Woods. There before her was a humble cottage of most comforting aspect. Smoke drifted lazily from the chimney, and all around it was the most beautiful flower garden Snow White had ever beheld.

But the garden was but as an ash heap beside the beauty of the woman who sat near the front door, staring intently into a bronze basin filled with water. Her dress was a dark green velvet; her hair, the color of burnished copper, hung about her shoulders like a mantle; about her waist was a girdle of white silk embroidered most artfully with gold thread.

Snow White approached the edge of the garden and stopped. Her uncertainty rooted her to the spot. When the woman looked up from her basin, Snow White's heart was in her throat.

The woman rose and walked to Snow White, curtsying deeply before her. Snow White could scarcely breathe, let alone speak. She felt a heat begin to build deep within herself.

"I bid you welcome, Snow White. My home is yours for as long as it pleases you to stay," the woman said.

"You know my name?" Snow White asked.

"The raven told me you were in the forest. I feared that you might become lost, so I asked her to guide you here. Stay or leave as you choose, your freedom in this forest is absolute."

"And your name, my lady?" Snow White asked, curtsying until her knee touched the ground.

"I have more than one, but here, in this forest, you may call me Druantia," she said, smiling. It was a smile that filled Snow White with the most exquisite warmth.

"I thank you for bringing me here, Druantia. I was indeed lost and out of food," she said, bowing again.

"Do you wish to return from whence you came? I can make it so, you shall be perfectly safe."

Snow White reacted sharply. "No, good lady. I was, I am, trying to go as far away from my home as I can."

Druantia gestured to a hereunto unseen bench engraved with the most fantastical creatures. They moved of their own accord, capering and chasing one another across the back, arms, and legs of the bench. Snow White had never seen the like, and she gasped in astonishment.

"Are you a witch?" she asked, more out of awe than fear.

"I am, Snow White. And also something more. But I am no greater or lesser a witch…than yourself."

"I? A witch?"

"Yes, you, as was your mother. I knew her well. Were you ever told of your family line? It is unbroken for uncounted generations," Druantia said, gesturing again for Snow White to sit.

"Until just a few days ago, I knew nothing of my mother's family. My father never told me," Snow White said, seating herself beside Druantia, her whole body rigid with indecision over what to do next.

"Your father never knew. Your mother fully realized that she would have to hide her true nature in order to be queen of her realm," Druantia said, taking Snow White's hand.

Snow White blushed deeply, hardly hearing Druantia's words. She knew in her heart, and her soul, what her mind had not yet accepted—that all she had yearned for was, literally, at hand. Her life before entering the Darkly Woods was already fading to a disquieting memory. The empty feeling that had dogged her days was fading as well, to be replaced with a certitude of purpose and a deliriously delicious desire to get as close to Druantia as she would allow.

"Are you quite all right?" Druantia said, giving Snow White a concerned look.

"In full truth, Druantia, I've never been better. Please continue." Snow White's mind, and heart, raced in a manner that she was wholly unaccustomed to.

"You look flushed," Druantia observed.

"Really? Fancy that," Snow White said with a giggle she could barely control.

"Yes, well," Druantia said, giving Snow White a sly half-smile. "Your mother accepted that, as did all of us who loved her. With your mother's passing it was desired that someone join your household who could teach you what you needed to know, but her personal servants were set against it. They greatly feared the punishments that would befall them if such a teacher were found out."

"That is done now. I wish for nothing other than to learn all that I can about my mother, her family, about me. Will you teach me? I would consider it the greatest honor." Snow White had taken up both of Druantia's hands and clasped them over her wildly beating heart.

"Nothing, or, I suspect, very little would give me greater pleasure," Druantia said, her own face turning red as an autumn leaf.

And so began Snow White's journey to reclaim her birthright.

As the days of summer grew shorter, Snow White's knowledge and powers grew apace. And as the women worked together, their love and passion for one another soared to the heavens.

It happened one day, as they made love in the sacred pool, that a woodsman who had lost his way spied them. He soon realized that the woman with black hair was none other than Snow White. Who the redheaded beauty was mattered not to the woodsman, although he did stay to watch.

One thousand gold marks would be his when he told the king what he had seen. Silently, he slipped away and soon found the road to the king's castle.

As he approached the castle it occurred to the woodsman that he should take care with whom he spoke. If he told a sentry or other servant, they would run to the king with the news and claim the gold that was rightfully his. As he fretted over his dilemma, a well-dressed gentleman approached the castle on horseback. Surely this fellow would take him right to the king. He stood off to the side of the road and waved a filthy kerchief at the Worthy Sir.

"M'lord, I am but a humble woodsman, but I would beg your

leave to escort me to the king. I bear news that he is most anxious for."

"Think you fit to speak to the king? Begone, cur, before I drag you behind my horse for a circuit of this castle," said the nobleman.

"Please, my lord, great is the news I bear, news known to no other but me," said the woodsman, dropping to his knees.

"What could you possibly know that would interest His Majesty?"

"News he greatly desires. News of his daughter, Snow White."

"Snow White? What of her?" the nobleman demanded, dismounting and bearing down on the now-trembling woodsman.

"I have seen her, m'lord. I must tell this to the king alone because he has promised a reward of…"

"A thousand gold marks," the gentleman finished for him. "Yes, this is so. Come with me, we shall see if you speak the truth."

"I will speak only with the king!" the woodsman cried. "It is he who offers he reward."

"Know you not who I am?" said the ungentlemanly gentleman, planting the sole of his boot firmly in the woodsman's face. "I am His Royal Highness, Charming, the man who will be Snow White's husband. I as much as His Majesty wish to know of Snow White's whereabouts."

"F-forgive me, Your Highness, I did not recognize you. I would never have spoken such a way had I known," the woodsman said, struggling to sit up.

"In speaking to me, you are speaking to His Majesty. Speak the truth and the money is yours," Charming said, motioning one of his aides over.

The woodsman eyed Prince Charming warily, then let out a sigh of resignation. He related all that he had seen, to the clear consternation of Prince Charming.

"This spring, you know of it?" Charming asked his aide, after kicking the woodsman in the face again to silence him.

"Yes, Your Highness, it's a haunted spring, night creatures dwell in it. The people thereabouts know where it is if only to avoid it. The redheaded woman, I've heard of her, she is supposed to be a powerful witch, but few have seen her and none know where she hides."

"If we find one, the other cannot be far away," Charming said, kicking the slowly rising woodsman again, apparently out of habit.

"The spring is fifteen or so leagues due north, perhaps twenty once we're on the forest tracks," said the aide.

"I want twenty archers, our best," Charming ordered. "Provisions and gear for several nights in the forest. We'll start as soon as everything is ready, but I want to take this witch early in the morning, while she still sleeps. No doubt she has placed a most unnatural enchantment on Snow White. Every care must be taken to see she is returned to us unharmed."

The aide bowed and hurried away.

"So, peasant, you saw Snow White, my future wife, your future queen, engaged in revolting acts of carnal congress with a minion of Lucifer?" Prince Charming said, slowly circling the woodsman.

The woodsman stiffened visibly. "I...I saw...something, Your Highness. It may not have been what I...I think I saw."

"What you think you saw?" the prince thundered. "Do you expect a thousand marks for what you think you saw? How know you it was even Snow White in that demon's embrace? Speak, you reeking piece of dog shit."

"It was...I saw Snow White, Your Highness, of that I have no doubts at all. As to what she was doing, it is far beyond my poor, poor powers to say," the woodsman said, whimpering in a most abject manner.

"Henceforward, woodsman," the prince said, leaning down and whispering into his ear, "it shall be far beyond your poor, poor powers to say anything at all."

And with that, Prince Charming slit the woodsman's throat from ear to ear.

It was at dawn of the next day that Prince Charming and his men found Druantia's cottage. No smoke rose from the chimney; the door and windows were closed. The prince deployed his men in a rough circle all around the cottage and yard.

He sent three men in to kill Druantia and bring forth Snow

White. These men approached the cottage in silence, then, in a thrice, were through the door. Those outside waited for screams, but nothing issued forth from the cottage except silence.

Presently, the three emerged, sheathing their hunting knives. The rest gathered around. "Empty, Your Highness," one of them said.

"And the hearth is cold. No one has been here for two, maybe three days," said another.

"She knew we were coming and she's run off. No matter, they are on foot, we'll track the witch down and send her back to hell in pieces," Prince Charming said as he rode his horse over the garden, trampling down the flowers.

"You owe me an apology for what you've done to my garden," Druantia said.

The men turned as one to face Druantia. She and Snow White stood on the crest of a ridge that ran behind the cottage. Both women wore dresses of the most dazzling white satin; on their heads were diadems of silver with a single round moonstone at the center.

Prince Charming continued to ride his horse back and forth through the garden.

"Snow White," he called out. "All is well now. Come down here and be safe. We will deal with this fiend from the pit."

"I did not ask you to come here, and no power on earth could induce me to go anywhere with you," Snow White said, putting her arms around Druantia's waist.

The sound of bowstrings being drawn filled the air.

"No man fire until Snow White is with us," Prince Charming called out. The men relaxed, but kept their arrows notched.

"Snow White," he said, in as gentle a voice as he could muster, "this woman has placed a vile enchantment upon thee, but once she is dead, all will be well again. Know you I? I am Prince Charming, your future husband. Your father, the king, is sore worried about thee. Come to me, Snow White, come to me and my life be forfeit before any harm should befall thee."

Snow White remained silent and tightened her embrace of Druantia, who put her arm across Snow White's shoulder.

"You loathsome whore," Prince Charming said, presumably to Druantia. "My men shall make great sport of thee before your head hangs from my saddle horn." He drew his sword and strode forward.

The sky quickly darkened, and a great wind rushed through the forest. The branches of the great oaks swept back and forth, bowling over the archers. Panic stricken, they threw down their bows and ran, horses and men, away into the forest.

"Do you think you can frighten me as you did those fools?" Prince Charming said, fixing a withering glare on Druantia. "I've sent over four hundred of your kind back to hell. Snow White is mine, her kingdom is mine, and you will be nothing but meat for my dogs when I'm done with you."

"A kingdom you covet, a kingdom you shall have," Druantia said, raising her hand, her oak wand materializing in it as she did so. "Hail to thee, Charming the First, king of the frogs."

She pointed the wand at Prince Charming. A great flash of light filled the glade. Of Prince Charming, nothing remained but a small, warty, toadish-looking frog atop the heap of empty clothing.

Upon the death of her father, Snow White ascended the throne, where she was beloved by all for her sense of justice and the wisdom of her decisions. Witches were no longer put to death but banished to the Darkly Woods, along with their familiars, which, oddly enough and quite contrary to popular belief, turned out to be other women rather than cats or budgies.

The menfolk were greatly put out by this, especially since so many wives freely, indeed, eagerly admitted to practicing witchcraft, but the law was the law. These women were sent into the Darkly Woods and ordered to never return. Except on market days. Or if they forgot something or had someone really, really, really important to visit. But after that they had to go right back. And on nights of a full moon, a strange hellfire glow could be seen in the heart of the Darkly Woods, with the sound of many drums pounding out unnatural rhythms accompanied by the howls, growls, shouts, and laughter of many women apparently suffering either the torments of the damned or something else entirely. No man dared venture forth to investigate.

Snow White and her closest adviser, a woman known only as "Dru," were inseparable as they traveled the kingdom together, seeking after the well-being of her subjects. Tongues wagged, as idle tongues are wont to do (no snickering, please). But...

They Lived Happily Ever After.

Alex Stitt is a British-American bibliophile with a Master's in Counseling Psychology, penning novels for the bright eyed and the queer-at-heart. Inspired by years as an international ally trainer, Alex writes gender-variant, culturally diverse fiction with a flare of bohemian magic.

This story is based on "The Red Shoes."

The Red Shoes
Alex Stitt

Like many in the South, we had lost our fortune in the great dust bowl, maintaining only our propriety and a useless hunk of land. It was the summer of 1936, remembered as another blazing heat wave thick with cicadas, screaming in the trees. I was only sixteen, but I, in our ever-shrinking town, was wed-stock—which is to say a qualified bachelor.

"Don't go flapping your gums at me, James," Ma said, still bossing Lenore, our only maid, through the vicarious process my mother called cooking. "You're going to the cotillion! When *our* mayor and *our* preacher fashion an idea, best you listen. Not everyone was invited, you know, but by the grace of God we have not been forsaken! People remember the Conahues. Good breeding is all we've got left."

Blinking, I watched Lenore bake an apple crumble my mother would later claim as her very own recipe, though I hadn't seen flour on Ma's fingers since Pa died.

"All right, Ma, I'll go," I said, looking down at my worn soles. "But I'll be needin' new shoes."

With a heavy sigh, she shook her head.

"Your pa's got some old loafers up in the closet—"

"Which I'm wearin'," I said, drawing her disappointment to all our spent reserves.

The cotillion was devised by Mayor Everglass, whose daughter had just reached an eligible age. Wanting to find a noteworthy suitor, not merely for the sake of his own dwindling fortune, he and our pastor had arranged a platonic social. It was to be a sensible, jazz-free affair for all the young boys to meet all the young girls, and so stitch our community back together.

I was going to need new shoes.

Defeated, Mother waved me into the living room, looking suspiciously at Lenore, who knew all too well Ma kept our money under a loose floorboard beneath her rocking chair.

"Tomorrow," she said, touching my face with hope and condescension. "And do buy something dapper. No more... *shenanigans*. Please. My heart can't take it."

Gifted a whopping three dollars from Pa's old cigar box, I smiled, kissed Ma on the cheek, and headed up to my room.

My wardrobe was the ghost of my father. Every piece of clothing I had, from my Sunday best to my work overalls, had belonged to him at some point, and they were all torn and faded long before I ever grew to size. I'd barely known my pa. He'd died when I was six, and so I'd spent my life watching his ghost on a wire hanger, waiting for the fateful days I'd fit a shirt, or a jacket, or a hat.

Turning away, I crept to my own private floorboard, one I'd pried open myself, secret even from Lenore. Inside, I kept my shenanigans, my shame, and my only genuine joy.

Unwrapping a bundle of paper, I looked down on a square fold of crushed red velvet, its neckline an intricate pattern of lace. Lifting the dress, I stood before the mirror, holding it against my front. Its soft fabric was a dream, a flattering fit I had found eight months ago, on a trip searching for work in New Orleans. But I was too young to hire, and too impulsive—my imagination quickly stolen by the flapper mannequins in the storefront window. I'd never seen clothes like that, their wooden heads adorned with feathered hats, their faux bodies layered in Chinese silk and French crinoline.

It was there, off Bourbon Street, I'd found my dream. I had gone in, just hoping to touch one of the dresses, to tangibly know what drew me, but I couldn't stop. Knowing my proportions by heart—Ma having measured my life against my pa's inseam—I'd walked in and inquired, quite sheepishly, if they owned anything with a 32-inch waist and 38-inch chest. I was promptly escorted to a rack of fineries, where I'd found this ankle-length number.

It was scarlet, like passion enfolded by nightfall, designed for evening soirees and candlelight. Its front was flat, yet diffident, but the back V-lined lower than modesty could own. So I bought it, then and there, using what little money I had. Jobless, I returned home, to this very same room, where I twirled in front of my mirror.

When Ma saw me, I was beat across the head for shame. The dress had a tear in it now. Learning how to sew, and finding myself rather good, I'd stitched it back together using Lenore's needles. When asked, I told Mother I'd pawned it.

The door creaked.

I spun about, dropped my dress, and ran to the corridor.

A plate of apple-cobbler waited on the floor.

❖

The next day I walked to town, watching the automobiles kick up dust as they rattled by. With sixty unmanageable acres to the Conahue name set on the edge of town, we offered Snellville a great deal *if* Snellville ever decided to expand. For what it was, the land was a good investment, but there was simply no one left to invest in it, hence the mayor's cotillion. There was nothing like matrimony to boost the economy.

The town was abuzz with excitement. Boys and girls of upper-class stock were coming from all over the state, and I was starting to wonder what chance Ma saw in any of it.

My imagination played on me, presenting dreams I could never fulfill. I saw the cotillion in my mind, all paper lanterns and confetti. I envisioned the boys in their tuxedo flair, and the girls in their gowns and dresses, their many styles like a corsage variety. And I saw myself, in crushed red velvet. In my mind, I wore matching mousquetaire elbow gloves, with long hair to complement, and a chest to rival. I did not think of myself as a girl, for a girl I was not, and who had ever heard of such a thing? But in my desperate hope,

I thought of myself as a beauty, warranting the adoration of those tuxedo boys, blushing so obviously against their white ties.

A car backfired. I shook my head. What was I doing? A boy dreaming about boys? Catching my reflection in a storefront window, I looked at my face, trying to find some recognition of self, but there was nothing there I knew, save an inherited suit belonging to a man I barely remembered.

Focusing, I looked inside, and saw, to my amazement, a pair of dark red shoes with a thin buckled strap. They were gorgeous, with an elegant heel not so high as to be intimidating and a closed toe polished to a radiant sheen. They were of burgundy depth, complementary to evening soirees and candlelight.

Pulling three crumpled dollars out of my pocket, I looked down at my scuffed loafers, then back to the display. They were on sale. Everyone was preparing for the cotillion, pulling their more adventurous line out of the back. I had never thought to see such shoes in Snellville, and without delay I ran inside.

The lady behind the clerk, whom I recognized as another nameless face from my congregation, looked at me awkwardly. I asked her what size they were, and she told me. For a moment I blinked, lost in gender's odd translation. I asked her what size they were compared to a man's foot, at which point she thought me a loon. However, there was money in my hand, and she was not one to refuse a sale, or a morsel of gossip to gab about later. Calculating with her fingers, she guesstimated, and my heart nearly melted over her cash register.

With change left over, I bought a jar of black boot polish and left with a box under my arm. Halfway home, I scrubbed my old shoes clean in our primarily evaporated pond, dried them off in the sun, then painted my pa's brown loafers black.

"Perfect." Mother clapped as I came in through the back door, modeling my remodeled shoes. I could only assume she thought my old ones were in the box. "Now what girl could resist you? I took the liberty of laying out a suit on your bed. Go have a look."

Lenore looked at my feet, noted the exact same tongue with the exact same laces, then went back to rolling dough.

THE RED SHOES

Upstairs, I found a real tuxedo atop my mattress. Like most of my hand-me-downs it was a size too large. The fashion was outdated, and it smelled of mildew, but it was a genuine black-tie ensemble. Disinterested, I threw open my box, unpacking my new red heels. They gleamed, even in my dim bedroom.

"James," Mother called up the stairs, looking wistfully at her wedding ring. "How is it? Do you like it? It was your father's. He only wore it once."

"I love it," I said, running my hands over the shoes' smooth red leather. Remembering myself, I quickly hid them under the floorboard, nestled atop my dress.

"Do remember to call in with Mrs. Bacon today," Mother added, returning to the kitchen. "She's digging up her garden, and you need the work."

With my secrets stowed away, I threw on my overalls and ran downstairs. With my painted black loafers deemed too nice to work in, and without any other shoes, I ran barefoot out the front door. The downside to this was that Mrs. Bacon really was digging up her front garden, and it was hard to step on a shovel with bare feet.

Awarded iced tea, fresh peaches, and fifty cents in gratitude, I headed home as the sun sank into the tree line and the shadows grew long. To my amazement, the house was empty. Lenore wasn't baking, Mother wasn't directing, and my heart sank.

Running upstairs, I pried up the floorboard, and stared, utterly confused. There was my paper parcel, my dress safe and sound, but the shoes were gone. Uncertain of my destination, I rushed outside, spied my mother and Lenore heading for the woods, and followed.

❖

"And you're sure about this?" my mother asked.

"Mrs. Conahue," Lenore sighed, leading my mother deeper into the woods. "I've known your family a long time, and James always was a goose. That's why I brought 'em. Soon as I found 'em."

"I can't take it anymore." My mother trembled, holding my high heels to her bosom. Above her, the sky was a tangerine glow, making the willows all the more black. Moss grew in unkempt patches, and the ground grew soft. "It's as if someone's bewitched my boy."

"All the more reason to call on a witch," Lenore nodded, searching momentarily to find her way. "Old Bashee's a coot, all right, but if anyone can help, it's her."

"But Voodoo? Is this why you never go to church? I always wondered, Lenore, but I never knew!"

"Hush your prattlin', Mrs. Conahue. We're here."

Ahead of them was an old plantation house, and by the size of the trees consuming its front porch, it had to be one of the first erected in the whole state. Remnants of white paint peeled off the walls, and the banisters, and the balustrades, but the wood beneath had rot, and all that kept it up was a brickwork chimney, smoking in the dark.

"Are you comin' in or not?" A voice piped up behind them as an old woman elbowed her way past. "Dinner's gettin' cold. You like calabash? Everyone likes calabash."

Bent with time and hard work, Old Bashee hobbled along, her stride lopsided, her dark Creole skin marked with strange, lacerated scars. Perhaps a dog or a gator had once bitten her face, or perhaps Old Bashee wrestled with creatures far worse every day. Her hair was a thick bundle of dreadlocks, wrapped so large atop her head my mother half thought she was carrying a bundle of sticks.

Apologetically, Lenore introduced Mrs. Conahue, who reintroduced herself, but Old Bashee wasn't interested. The screen door slapped shut behind them, and they followed the witch down a warped corridor. The walls were sagging, the floor twisted, and from the ceiling, odd hunks of wood swung about, dangling on lengths of horsehair twine. Wreaths of chili peppers, dried and decaying, hung from every door handle, and the kitchen table was mounted with a globular candle centerpiece of melted wax.

Three plates were already waiting, three plates of calabash.

"So your son's a fairy?" Old Bashee deduced, as my mother laid the heels on the table. "Ain't no shame in it. More than a few in these woods."

"No shame?" my mother asked, utterly flabbergasted. "The cotillion is tomorrow, and if ever our family's to find any good footing, we'll need to wed our way into social grace! But how can I count on a marriage when all my dreams depend on sixty acres and a boy running around in...*in heels!*"

"Good footin', you say?" Old Bashee squinted, her scarred face thick with wrinkles, her lips pursed with a wry smile. "Then good footin' your child will have."

Taking the shoes, she walked over to the hearth, where three fat logs sent up a roaring fire. Muddling about the room, Old Bashee tossed oddities into the flames. A jasmine flower, a handful of turmeric, cayenne, a dash of exploding alcohol; then she rolled up her sleeve, her arm tortured with even more scars.

Thrusting her hand into the blaze, she held the shoes in the fire. My mother gasped, but Old Bashee never flinched. Sparks curled around her fingers, smoke poured about her wrist, and her knuckles blackened with soot. Removing her fist, she tossed the shoes on the table. They were hot, but completely unscathed.

"What did you do?" Lenore asked, as Old Bashee pulled up a chair, reached under her dress, and unscrewed her wooden leg.

"If this don't gain your child good footin'," she said, dropping her prosthetic foot on the table, "nothin' in this world ever will."

❖

The next morning, I woke up with nauseating, gut-wrenching fear in my stomach. I could smell Lenore cooking downstairs. My mother's grating voice, directing salt and pepper, played upon my mind. I knew they knew. I knew I'd been found out, and I couldn't face them.

Nervously, I opened my secret compartment, and there were the shoes again, their glossy straps a smile in the morning light.

More confused than ever, I headed downstairs. Mother hugged me, tighter than she had in years. Lenore dished out eggs.

"Now, you take it easy today," Mother said, touching my shoulder as I sat at the table. "The cotillion's tonight and I don't want you to overwork yourself. You do sweat when you overwork yourself, so I'll have Lenore draw a bath this afternoon. I have some pomade for your hair, and shave, darlin', you look like a hobo."

I spent that day trying to fix our old tractor in the barn. It hadn't worked in years, but a small part of me hoped to get it running. I knew a vague bit about mechanics, but the core of me wanted to run away altogether, away from my mother and all her audacious expectations. She would never understand, and I would never have the faculties to explain it to her.

Lying under the old machine, coated in oil and rust, I fantasized about the party, my vision now complete with heels. Of course I was going to wear Pa's tux, and of course I was going to dance with some sweet, wallflower girl equally shy as me. But in my dreams I saw boys plucking up the nerve to ask me, of all people, to dance.

Throughout the day, either Mother or Lenore brought me small treats, being especially nice, though I didn't know why.

That evening, Lenore drew a bath, and I was granted a little privacy. With a hand mirror and a straight razor, I shaved my face, but the contours of my chin betrayed me. In my head, I didn't look like that. In my head, my features softened, and I smiled more readily.

Looking down, I blinked at my legs. Curious, I began to shave my calves, nicking myself at the awkward junction of the knee, but I kept going. Toweling off, I escaped to my room, where my father's tux lay waiting.

It was getting close to sunset, but an urge stole my attention. Even if I never lived my fantasy, I wanted to know what it looked like, if only to put the whole, surreal affair behind me.

Closing my door, I unpacked my velvet dress and slipped it over my shoulders. Turning left, then right, I admired the contours of myself with a quiet surprise. Every time I slipped on that scandalous number, I was shocked by how well it shaped my hips. A pleasant excitement took me, nervous, but glad.

Extending my neck, I looked at myself and tried to fix my short crop of hair. I wasn't the most masculine boy about town, but I certainly wasn't a girl. Contemplating the effects of rouge, and desiring mascara I didn't have, I bit my lip, puckering so as to redden my mouth—an old trick I'd learned from the girls in Sunday school.

Behind me, the red shoes sat on my pillow. For the first time I tried them on. They pinched a little at the toes, but the heel fit snugly, and I balanced, having never actually worn a woman's shoe. Gaining height, I laughed, my legs seemingly longer and shapelier than before. I was still lacking my mousquetaire gloves. I was still lacking stockings, long hair, makeup, and a whole feminine outline, but it was enough.

In my mirror, I saw myself as my suitors would, and I curtsied in response to an unvoiced invitation. Alone in my room I waltzed with no one, dancing to a silent song. Wobbling a little to gain my footing, I stepped back and forth, and turned in a circle, tapping heel to toe with a little flourish I felt rather proud of—attempting to mimic the swing-dance girls I'd seen in New Orleans.

"Are you ready, James?" Mother called up the stairs, as I spun unseen in my room.

"Just a minute," I called back, but when I tried to stop, my feet kept going. Twirling and tapping, I whirled about, swinging out in wider and wider circles until I bumped into the bed. My legs were possessed, and when I tried to lie down, I merely bobbed upright. Terrified, and too ashamed to scream for help, I tried to unbuckle my shoes, but they moved too quickly, and with one sashay I was through the door.

Ma, aghast, stared at her red velvet son as I tangoed straight into her, knocking her back down the stairs. She screamed at me to stop, Lenore waved at me with a rolling pin, and with my arms tucked in I tore through the porch screen, fox-trotting straight into the field.

I danced as though I had an invisible partner, bending and throwing my body as if pushed by some unfelt hand. Arms open, I spun forward, whirling round and round through the field, cicadas screaming in the sunset. Unstoppable, un-trip-able, I danced in the dusk, moving as I had never moved before, overcome by passion, and power, and grace.

From the long grass, I burst onto the road. An automobile swerved. Pedestrians turned their heads, and I buried my face in my hands. Everyone was looking, but I couldn't stop. Sweeping one leg forward and following with the other, I gave a high kick in the town square, dipped in the arms of no one, and aimed straight for the cotillion.

The mayor's manor was a lavish estate in the center of town, with a long green lawn decorated for the occasion with lamps, its gazebo a stage of musicians playing softly for the arriving guests. Leaping over the fence, I landed on the garden path, arms alight, poised anticipation personified.

Men and women, parents and chaperones, eyed me with pensive caution. My preacher recognized me instantly, and I pulled my hands against my chest. For a moment, I rested. The band had stopped playing. Everything stilled.

Then my left foot tapped.

Spellbound, the drummer began to tap along, the rhythm infecting the clarinet, the trumpet, and the bass, as a joyous, wailing jazz accompanied my crisscrossing steps to the house. Startled, the mayor appeared, drawn to the commotion, and I dipped him—I dipped the mayor, my hand on his blue sash—and I laughed, my horror stolen by the humor of it. The sax kicked in, the mayor and I burst upon the hall, and the band followed us inside.

Furious, Mayor Everglass shoved me away, and for the first time I fell, landing in the middle of the room, legs akimbo, grass in my hair. The horns relaxed; only the drummer's cymbal tapped expectantly on his marching-band drum.

All around me, looking down at a mess in a soft, velvet dress, I saw boys and girls from my congregation mixed with highbrow strangers gathered from all over the state. Panting, I tried to catch my breath, but my calves were twitching, and I knew it wasn't over.

Beneath me, my legs swiveled. I rose to my knees, my badly shaved gams sliding one after the other, before I sprang, music detonating behind me. The trumpets warred with the sax, the clarinet piped between them, and the jazz was on my side. The kids around me began to smile. Cued with the band, my steps timed perfectly, they figured I had to be some kind of bizarre entertainment. The girls blushed, the boys laughed, and I spun in a wide arc, lost on how to feel. I was terrified, but I couldn't stop, and the more I trembled within, the faster I danced. And at the same time, I felt freer than I ever had in my life.

Across the room, I saw the mayor's daughter, resplendent in her gown, and beside her I saw a mousy young man standing awkwardly in a suit two times too large. Unlike the other boys, mocking me like a clown, he watched with rapt fascination. His whole stance was stiff, but he didn't blink. His blue eyes looked more scared than the rest, as if he were found out, and he was.

Following a sensual, New Orleans samba, all carnival flair and exaggeration, I swept toward him, eyes fixed. To my left, the boys jeered each other. To my right, the girls fell quiet, some shocked, some amazed, some softened by the drama of it. Nervously, the blue-eyed boy presented his hand, and I took it, though the power came from my shoes.

Whether or not he could dance was entirely irrelevant to magic. Together, we could do anything. Hand in hand, stepping and crossing our feet, we never stalled, or stifled, or tripped, or slipped, landing every step to strike out again. Trading hands, we became a flurrying flamenco. I stamped my heels, and stamped them again, he slid a hand around my waist, and the mayor ran at the sax player, screaming at the band to stop.

From the flamenco, we transformed into tango, and from the tango we launched into swing, he throwing me high into the air before sliding me between his legs. Wild, unlike anything anyone had ever seen, we caught each other's expressions. We were both grinning with surprise.

The music quickened, he spun me under his arm, and away I went, through the back door to the kitchen, to the yard, and out into the town. I heard people calling behind me, but I couldn't stop. Sliding through Snellville, tap-dancing all the way, I launched into a field, thrashing through a curtain of kudzu. My ankles were blistering, my toes screamed, and my joy collapsed into fear. I was never going to stop. I was going to dance and dance until I died on my feet.

Springboarding from one fallen log to the next, I landed with ballet refinement, but the thicket grew dense, and the branches slashed at my clothes. My dress tore, my weak stitchwork snapping apart. Thorns sliced at my shoulders and cut at my ankles, and I screamed, terrified as I danced into the swamp. The ground turned soft. My feet sank in the mire, yet still I spun like a top, my motions slowed but never stopping.

I cried again, and a voice called behind me.

Looking back, I saw my blue-eyed dancing partner. Throwing off his jacket, he waded after me, grabbing my hand. As he pulled, I slipped, sinking up to my neck. Something held me down, something fought at my legs. My foot wrenched in the bog; there was a pop, and an air bubble splattered mud across my face. The boy hauled me out, and when I looked down I wriggled my toes.

The shoes were gone.

"Are you okay?" he asked, his suit drenched, my dress a mudslide.

"I don't know," I stuttered, looking back at the swamp.

"That was amazing," he burst aloud, still excited from our waltz. "I've never danced like that! You're…you're amazing, I mean, where did you learn to do the thing—with the turn and the dip? Do you remember?"

"I just…had it in me, I guess," I said, feeling exhausted, doe-eyed, and lost.

"The whole town musta seen us! I don't think two boys ever stole a cotillion before."

"The…*whole* town?" I murmured, half wishing he'd let me drown.

"And did you see the girls back there?"

"The…*girls?*"

"Yeah," he grinned, "they were stumped—but there weren't a single girl back there who didn't want to move like you. I guarantee. You were like a dream."

Falling silent, my hands in moss, my legs tired, I listened to the cicadas.

"My name's Sam, by the way," he said, laying his formerly clean jacket over my shoulders.

"James," I answered, as he slowly helped me up.

"Careful now," he said, "it's slippery. Have you got your footing?"

"Yeah." I smiled. "I think so."

Barbara Davies (barbaradavies.co.uk) lives in the English Cotswolds and has been published by Bedazzled Ink. Her short fiction has appeared in *The Lorelei Signal*, *Lacuna*, *Tales of the Talisman*, and *Neo-Opsis*, among other ezines and magazines.

This story is based on "The Princess and the Frog."

THE PRINCESS AND THE FROG
BARBARA DAVIES

Princess Margery watched the last silk-clad servant in Tokju's retinue disappear into the distance. "Good riddance to bad rubbish."

She would not miss the exotically dressed ambassador one bit. Nor would anyone else in her father's kingdom, come to that. Not that that would bother Tokju. As far as she could make out, he had spent his month-long visit alienating everyone unfortunate enough to have dealings with him. King or commoner, he despised all alike, and he had found everything animal, mineral, or vegetable lacking in comparison with its counterpart in the Empire Beyond the Sea. As for the suite of apartments allocated to him for the duration and luxuriantly furnished to his specifications, he pronounced it "barely adequate."

"Stupid old fart," she muttered, using the phrase Bruna had coined for him.

A memory surfaced of that day last week when Tokju had come upon her unawares. She was lounging under a walnut tree in the palace garden, engaged in her favorite pastime: kissing Bruna. From his exclamation of revulsion, such things weren't allowed in the Empire Beyond the Sea. But calling the daughter of the king and her girlfriend "disgusting perverts" could hardly be deemed diplomatic.

Bruna had laughed. "Ignore him, Marg. If he can't appreciate love, that's his loss. He'll be gone soon, and besides," her eyes had crinkled at the corners as she lowered her voice, "it gives me an excuse to cook up some prank to play on him."

Fearful of endangering the negotiations then under way, Margery had taken her girlfriend's advice. But the treaty between their two kingdoms on which her father and his advisers had worked so hard remained unsigned. Now she wondered whether Tokju's insult had been calculated to cause a diplomatic incident.

But that didn't bring her any closer to solving the mystery of Bruna's whereabouts, and she was feeling neglected. Perhaps the chamberlain had sent his niece on an errand. Grumbling under her breath, Margery went in search of her.

❖

"Bruna?" said Prince Oliver, when a worried Margery approached him later that evening. "She was lurking near Tokju's apartments the last time I saw her." He looked up from the game of draughts he was playing with an attendant, a sly grin curling his lips. "You don't suppose she went *with* him, do you?"

She gave her brother a cross look. "Don't talk rot." It was an odd coincidence, though, now that she came to think of it. She went cold. "Suppose the ambassador has kidnapped her."

"A chamberlain's niece?" Oliver's eyebrows rose. "What leverage would that give him?"

"He might have done it just to spite me." She saw his puzzlement and went on, cheeks warming. "He saw us together and made it very clear he disapproved."

With a triumphant grunt, Oliver swept three of the attendant's pieces off the board. "From what I can tell, Tokju disapproves of *everything*."

But Margery was no longer listening. She had turned on her heel and was marching toward the apartments the ambassador had occupied. If Bruna had been hoping to play some silly prank on him, she might still be there—trapped in a cupboard perhaps.

Sounds of activity met her as she turned into the corridor leading to the guest wing, and two housemaids hurried past her, clutching baskets of dirty bed linen. A ladder came into view on which a groom was perched, removing one of the heavy brocade wall hangings. More servants were taking up the expensive carpets and sweeping the floors.

The steward supervising the operation saw Margery and hurried over. "May I help you, Your Royal Highness?"

"Have you seen Bruna?"

"The chamberlain's niece? Alas, no."

"I saw her in the kitchen earlier," called out one of the men taking up the carpets. "She was rummaging through the scraps intended for the pigs—"

The steward frowned him to silence and went on as if he hadn't spoken. "Bruna has a fondness for archery, doesn't she, ma'am? Perhaps she is practicing at the butts—"

A shriek interrupted him and he turned to address the housemaid who was its source. "Really, Lily! Whatever you have come across surely cannot merit such a..." His eyes widened, and Margery followed the direction of his gaze.

"It's only a frog," said the man who had spoken of kitchen scraps, this time addressing the room at large. "Ain't you ever seen a frog before?"

"Not one like that," said Margery. For a start it was a bright, virulent yellow, and its toes were long and thin, and tipped with fleshy pads.

"Tokju must have left it behind," said the steward, gathering his wits.

"Figures," muttered the groom from his ladder. "Only he could have a pet that ugly."

One of the maids, braver than the others, took off her apron and prepared to catch the creature. "I wouldn't," said Margery, remembering something she had read once. "Skin that color usually means it's poisonous."

"Poisonous?" The maid came to a halt.

"Just leave it," suggested someone else. "The palace cats will finish it off quickly enough."

Vice versa, more likely, thought Margery. "We can't have something poisonous wandering around the palace," she said. "Someone fetch the menagerie keeper. He'll know what to do."

❖

"It's undoubtedly covered with a poisonous exudation," said the menagerie keeper rather pompously, before directing two of his assistants to catch it with the aid of butterfly nets. But the frog had other ideas, and an hour later, the nets were still empty and it was in hiding, though no one knew where. With a sigh, Margery left them to it and returned to her own chamber.

While her maid undressed and readied her for bed, her thoughts returned to the missing Bruna and her sense of disquiet grew. Bruna should have returned by now. There had been no sign of her in Tokju's rooms. But if not there, then where—

Movement caught her eye: a flash of yellow on the windowsill. She swung round, just as her maid caught sight of the frog too and gasped.

"Don't touch it."

The maid threw her a glance. "I don't intend to, ma'am. Nasty slimy thing." She frowned. "What's it doing here?"

An excellent question, thought Margery. Had it followed her to her room? She was on the second floor. Could tree frogs climb walls as well as trees? No matter. It was here now. And she couldn't risk sleeping in a chamber with a poisonous creature on the loose. If it were to emerge while she lay dreaming, smear its poison on her cheek...

"Shoo!" Clapping her hands together, she took a step toward it. The frog remained unmoved, regarding her with those strange, bulging eyes.

Something pale blue flew across the room, missing the frog by a hair's breadth and landing with a thud: one of Margery's favorite silk slippers. If it got yellow slime on it, the slipper would be ruined. She turned to remonstrate with the maid, but before she could say anything, the frog hopped under her bed.

"I'm sorry, ma'am. I—"

Margery waved the maid to silence. "Never mind. Send word to the menagerie keeper I want it caught. By noon tomorrow."

"Yes, ma'am." The maid curtsied and prepared to leave.

"In the meantime, I'm afraid you're going to have to make other sleeping arrangements." The maid blinked at her in confusion. "Because tonight," she went on, "I'm sleeping in *your* bed."

❖

The palace clock chimed midday. "I'm afraid we're going to have to empty your chamber of all furniture, Your Royal Highness," said the menagerie keeper.

"*All* of it?" Margery's brows drew together. "Even the bed?"

The frog had led him and his assistants a merry dance, but really! The four-poster bed? It was massive and would require dismantling by a carpenter and then reassembling. Being deprived of its comfort for a single night had been a trial. The maid's bed was hard and lumpy, and, if that hadn't been enough, the maid's loud snoring from the truckle bed in the corner had kept waking her. If she had to spend another night like the last one...

Unobtrusively, Margery stretched the stiffness from her shoulders. If Bruna had been here, she would have been laughing like a drain. *Oh, Bruna.* Sadness washed over her. *Where are you?*

"I fear so," said the menagerie keeper. "If we're to have any chance of catching the damned—" He blushed. "I do beg your pardon, ma'am. We must deprive the creature of all possible hiding places."

"Is there no other way?" This was getting out of hand.

Calculation entered his gaze. "If you were to permit us to kill it...The fumes from some toxic substance, perhaps..."

Her eyebrows rose. "You propose filling my bedchamber with toxic fumes? And all this just to kill some hapless exotic pet abandoned by its owner?"

"Some hapless *poisonous* exotic pet," he corrected. Then he sighed. "But when you put it like that, ma'am. Perhaps we *have* been going about this all wrong. Rather than chasing the frog, perhaps we should be enticing it."

It occurred to Margery that she had yet to see the creature take

• 185 •

refreshment of any kind. It must be feeling hungry by now. "What do tree frogs eat?"

"I have no idea. But ordinary frogs eat crickets and worms and the like. And drink water," he added.

"Then bring me some of those," she said. "And a large cage."

❖

It was typical, thought Margery, that as soon as the menagerie keeper and his men departed, the frog should emerge from hiding. It squatted like a statue and regarded her.

If I were to dive and make a grab for it... She remembered the poison on its skin. *Not without gloves.*

It hopped a pace toward her, then stopped and regarded her once more.

Margery frowned. It didn't *seem* aggressive. And if it had once been a pet...Was it lonely? Missing its master? Had Tokju, for all his disregard for anyone besides himself, petted and pampered it, and perhaps even whispered fond nonsense in its virulent yellow ears?

"Why me?" she asked. It had followed her from the guest wing, after all.

The frog's loud croak, the first from it she had heard, startled her. Coincidence, or was it trying to communicate?

"Ahem," said someone from her open doorway. The frog hopped out of sight.

Hands on hips, Margery glared at the intruder. It was one of the menagerie keeper's assistants, and he shifted uncomfortably under her gaze. "Begging your pardon, Your Royal Highness, but I was told to bring this to you and ask if it will do."

This turned out to be the large golden birdcage he was carrying. Its bars were too narrow for the frog to get through. If she could entice it inside...

"Thank you. It will. That will be all."

He set the cage down, bowed, and retreated. When his hurried footsteps had faded into the distance, the frog's head peeked out from under the bed.

"It's all right," said Margery.

The frog emerged into the open. Evidently it trusted her. She felt as honored as she did whenever one of the palace's wild cats chose to sit on her lap and be stroked. Suddenly the idea of catching and caging it was distasteful. It couldn't help its color or the fact its skin was poisonous. And it hadn't actually tried to hurt anyone.

"Perhaps I should make you *my* pet. Would you like that?"

Another loud croak made the hairs on the back of her neck stand up. She could almost swear it understood what she was saying. *Nonsense. It's your tone of voice. It can tell you mean it no harm, that's all.*

"Very well." Crouching, she held the frog's gaze. The expression in its eyes was unfathomable yet also faintly familiar. "In that case I must give you a name. Hmm. How about Froggy?" The frog didn't react, so she straightened up. "Perhaps not. And I must find you something to eat." Where had those crickets and worms got to? She strode across to the bell pull and gave it a hefty tug.

❖

The frog dipped a padded toe in its water bowl and smeared it across the tiles.

Margery wrinkled her nose. "If you do that with your food as well, we're going to have words."

The live earthworms and crickets provided by the menagerie keeper had proved a problem. Though the frog was able to retrieve most from the dark corners of her chamber—its long sticky tongue flicking out and then retracting with its prey—some had escaped and even made it into neighboring chambers. Prince Oliver had complained of finding a worm on his shaving brush. And from her maid's sullen expression, she was growing tired of finding them in her room too. As a result, though the frog preferred live food, it was now being fed an unsavory-looking mess of mashed, dead crickets and earthworms, provided fresh every day.

Water splashed, as once more a toe daubed a tile. Puzzled, she watched the wet line evaporate. "Is this a trick Tokju taught you?" The frog let out a croak and tried again—this time drawing a curve. Margery's eyes widened. "Are you trying to write something?" But as before, the water evaporated before she could make sense of it.

She crossed to her writing desk, retrieved the inkwell and some paper, and set them in front of the frog. But its padded finger was far thicker than a pen, making the inkwell useless. She poured ink into a saucer, set it down, and waited, slightly apprehensive. This was going to get messy.

"Your Royal Highness?" A page was standing in her doorway, clutching a letter. He gave her and the frog a curious look.

"Yes?"

He proffered the letter. An ornate red wax seal held it closed, she noticed, as she got up and took it from him. She didn't recognize the flamboyant handwriting in which her name was written. "Who sent this?"

"The chancellor. He said to tell you they found it in the ambassador's rooms this morning, when they were clearing out a chest of drawers. It was right at the bottom," he added.

"The ambassador's rooms?" Her eyebrows rose. "You mean Tokju?"

"Yes, ma'am."

"In which case there can be no reply. Thank you," she added.

Only distantly aware of the page's departure, and of the faint scrape of an inky toe across the paper, she opened the letter and read its contents.

> *Princess Margery,*
> *I have arranged things so that by the time this letter is uncovered I will be well on my way back to my own land.*
> *This "old fart," as you and your girlfriend so "amusingly" referred to me, does not take kindly to being*

The Princess and the Frog

on the receiving end of insults and pranks. Indeed, you would have been wise to treat me with much greater respect and prudence. For I have at my disposal an armory of curses.

By now you will have discovered the poisonous yellow frog. I do hope you haven't eliminated it as a pest, but I cannot be held responsible for the actions of others. Have you recognized her yet? Yes, it is your friend, transformed.

I am not heartless. There is a way to break the curse and restore your friend to her annoying, perverted self once more. You have but to kiss her on the lips. What's that? The frog is poisonous, so such a kiss must surely prove fatal? I'm afraid you are correct. Nevertheless, that is the only way to break the curse. "Amusing," isn't it?

The choice is yours, Princess. Choose wisely.

Tokju

It must be a hoax. Someone playing on her dislike of Tokju and her anxiety about Bruna's absence to provide amusement. Her brother perhaps. But as she reread the letter, over and over, she knew it couldn't be Oliver's handiwork, and a sense of rising panic replaced her anger.

A rasping croak roused her from her paralysis, and she turned to regard the frog. It hadn't got very far with its attempts to write, but it had managed a large letter *B* followed by the beginnings of an *r*. The sight of it brought the truth thudding home, and her knees buckled.

"Bruna!" she cried.

❖

"Kissing the frog is out of the question," said the king, frowning as he regarded the yellow frog now sitting on the table in his privy chamber.

"But, Father," said Margery. "What other choice is there? We can't leave Bruna like this and we can't lose any time. If she stays in frog form, there must be a risk of her becoming more and more like one and—"

"If it *is* her," interrupted Prince Oliver, who wasn't one of the king's advisors but had barged his way into the hastily convened meeting, "we still don't know that letter isn't a complete pack of lies."

"It isn't." She brandished the frog's inky scrawl.

"Coincidence."

Margery glared at her brother. "Then provide her with more paper and ink and ask her to write something."

"Hush, child," said the queen, who like Oliver had insisted on being present. "You came here for our advice. Let us give it."

Margery bit her lip and subsided.

"That *is* Tokju's seal," said the Keeper of the Privy Seal.

"And my niece *is* missing and this strange frog has appeared in her place," said the chamberlain quietly. No one would meet his gaze, so Margery slipped her hand in his, and felt him squeeze it.

The king grunted. "Even if Tokju wrote the letter, there's no guarantee everything it says is true. I've never heard of a curse like this."

"I have," said the chancellor. Once he was sure of everyone's attention, he continued, "My second cousin is ambassador to the Khen Empire. Last year, apparently, Khen's treasurer went missing after a…a fracas involving Tokju."

"Did the emperor's moneybox go missing too?" asked Oliver.

The chancellor took the sarcastic question at face value. "No. They found a strange bloodhound in the treasurer's bedchamber, believed from its odd behavior that it was rabid, and destroyed it." He saw their expressions, and added, "The treasurer was well known to have an aversion to dogs."

Margery grimaced. It sounded like just the kind of "joke" that would appeal to the vindictive ambassador. She balled her hands into fists. If he was so dangerous, why had they permitted him to come here? Were they so afraid of offending the ruler of the Empire Beyond the Sea?

Oliver's brows knit. "All right," he allowed. "But even if Tokju *did* curse Bruna, there's no guarantee kissing the frog would undo it. It may be a trick to get Margery to kill herself."

"I don't think it's a trick," she said.

He held her gaze. "Are you willing to wager your life on that?"

"The fact remains," said the king, after a moment, "the frog is poisonous. And according to the court physician, there is no known antidote to its venom. It must not be kissed…by anyone." He threw his chamberlain a look of apology. "As the frog is Bruna, it will not, of course, be destroyed. And Margery will see that it's well cared for, won't you, my dear?"

"But, Father!" she protested.

"Thank you, sire," said the chamberlain. Disappointed by his reaction, she withdrew her hand, prompting a sad, defeated glance.

Before Margery could object further, her mother shushed her. "Your father is right, Margery. There is nothing to be done. And in any case, Bruna would not want you to give up your *life* for her, would she?"

At the queen's words, the frog let out a loud croak that made everyone jump and hide embarrassed smiles.

Margery brooded. She had been so concerned with getting Bruna returned to human form, she hadn't considered that. Were she in Bruna's place, she wouldn't want to be the cause of her death. And to live on without her and know she was the cause of that absence… Stumped, she chewed her lip and consoled herself by imagining Tokju suffering a long, painful death.

❖

The days passed and Margery grew used to seeing the vivid yellow frog that was Bruna emerge from its gilded cage, now minus a door, and hop around the bedchamber. Its sticky tongue zapped any cockroach or spider foolish enough to stray within reach. As the menagerie keeper kept it well supplied with crickets and worms, there was no need for it to supplement its diet in this way, so it must be due to frog instincts that Bruna either would not, or more worryingly could not, resist.

She missed her girlfriend. Not just for her kisses, which had sent delightful shivers through her, but for the way they could share their thoughts and feelings, light or dark, on any subject under the sun. The difference in their stations had never mattered, so why should a change of appearance? But conversing with the frog was tortuous, though it was able to form its inky letters faster now, and most of the time they were reduced to regarding one another in silent sadness.

At the King and Queen's behest, the menagerie keeper had sent word to a trader who had dealings with the Empire Beyond the Sea, requesting him to acquire some of the food a yellow tree frog would encounter in its natural habitat. Margery had mixed feelings about that, for wasn't it an admission that Bruna's condition might be permanent? Usually she was able to thrust that unbearable thought to one side. Not today, though. Seeing Bruna eating one of the largest spiders Margery had ever seen made her feel ill.

"This can't go on." At her exclamation, the crunching noises stopped, and the frog turned to regard her, two spider's legs sticking out of its mouth. *I must do something.*

The thick gauntlets provided by the menagerie keeper were lying next to the cage. Giving herself no time to think—if she did, her usual paralysis would grip her—Margery pulled on the gloves and advanced on Bruna.

The frog let out a croak of alarm and hopped sideways—not fast enough. Margery swooped and took it in a firm, two-handed grip.

Heart pounding, and with a murmured, "Forgive me, Bruna," she raised the frog to her lips and kissed it.

❖

When awareness returned, Margery found a familiar pair of brown eyes gazing down at her. *Am I dreaming?* She closed her eyelids and opened them again. Bruna was still there, standing next to the four-poster bed in which Margery lay, and which from the hangings was Margery's own.

Bruna turned and spoke to someone out of Margery's field of vision. "Tell the king and queen their daughter's awake."

She felt exhausted and bruised, as if she had been in a wrestling match with an opponent much larger and stronger than her. "Have I been ill?" The words came out in a froglike croak, as her parched tongue cleaved to the roof of her mouth.

"Very. At one point, we feared you might die." Bruna held a goblet to Margery's lips. "Drink this. It'll help."

The cool, clear water brought welcome refreshment, and relief of another kind flooded through her. *It must have been a fever dream.* "I had the most ridiculous dream," she said, smiling. "I thought Tokju cursed you and turned you into a frog."

"He did." The king's voice. Seconds later he had taken Bruna's place.

Her thoughts still sluggish, Margery blinked up at him. "Did he?"

He nodded. "It was rash of you to risk your life like that. The poison almost killed you."

"Almost?" Margery frowned. "Did the physician find some antidote at the last minute?"

Her father shook his head, expression grim. "You were fortunate."

"I don't understand."

"Bruna will tell you everything. I have a meeting to attend." His stern gaze softened. "Foolish child." He bent his head and kissed her, his beard prickling her cheek. "I'm glad you are well. Your mother will be along to see you shortly."

He vanished and Bruna reappeared and took Margery's hand in hers. "The menagerie keeper thinks it was the food I ate."

"What?"

"My diet. What Tokju didn't know, or if he did, didn't care about—a miscalculation on his part—is that a tree frog's poison comes largely from the things it eats. And as I had been eating crickets and worms and spiders—" She paled and held a hand to her mouth. "Forgive me, just the memory of it makes me feel a little nauseous."

"So you had become less deadly?" prompted Margery.

Bruna nodded. "Which is why, when you kissed me, you didn't die. Though you came close." She shuddered at the memory. "Tokju's letter went up in flames when you broke the curse, by the way. So we no longer have any evidence to bring against him."

"Damn the man."

"Your father won't permit him to come here again, though, so the Empire Beyond the Sea will have to choose another ambassador."

"Good," said Margery, with feeling.

Silence fell. From the sounds in the corridor outside, the queen would be here any minute.

"I'm so sorry, Marg," said Bruna. "If he hadn't caught me hiding the dye-filled eggshell in his luggage—"

"Is that what you were doing?" Margery rolled her eyes. "You and your practical jokes."

"Tokju had it coming. Besides, I only meant to ruin some of those fancy robes of his. How was I to know he'd curse me for it?" Bruna's indignation was fleeting, though, and her eyes began to dance and her cheeks to dimple in the most delightful way. "Anyway, all's well that ends well. But I wish we could have seen Tokju's face when he discovered the other eggshell."

"There were *two* of them?" said Margery. "What was in it? More dye?"

Bruna shook her head and burst out laughing. "Rotten fish guts."

Rhidian Brenig Jones has herded sheep in New Zealand, taught English in Poland, and run a bar on the Costa del Sol. Now settled back home in Wales, he leads an adult literacy program and writes whenever he can snatch a spare hour. He lives with his husband, Michael, and two arthritic Labradors.

This story is based on "The Snow Queen."

The Snow King
Rhidian Brenig Jones

Once, at high summer, two boys were born. Their mothers were affectionate friends and had arranged things very satisfactorily indeed, for their babies arrived within three days of each other. It often happened that if Annalena was busy hanging out the washing, Eila would take both babies to her breast, and if Eila was busy making her cheese, why, Annalena would quickly pluck her squalling boy from his wooden cradle and suckle him with her own son. The boys grew, and if there were two mothers to deliver slaps to naughty backsides, there were also two to wipe away childish tears or press honey cakes into eager little paws. They grew quickly, sturdy and straight and handsome and, hearing their laughter, the villagers believed that something of the July day of their birth had entered the boys' souls, for they were sweet-natured and sunny and loving. So they were and so they remained as the years passed, and if Dara grew a little taller, then Remi had the bluer eyes and the softer mouth.

Such a soft mouth. Dara knew it well, for as their boyhood passed, so their childlike love for each other deepened into the passionate love of young men. More than friends, closer than brothers, their souls were one, merged and mingled almost from birth, and now their bodies, too, united. Indeed, at times, when one was locked in the other and their breath came fast and one cried into the other's mouth when his hot seed spilled, neither could be sure where he ended and his beloved began. Seeing their love, the village mothers sighed, saddened that such fine seed would never swell their daughters' bellies, but there were many other lads with strong backs and stout limbs and so they held their peace.

When Dara and Remi were twenty, winter came hard and early, holding the land in an iron grip. The trees in the great forest that encircled the village creaked under a weight of snow that broke their branches, and icicles hung like daggers from every eave. Monstrous yellow clouds piled above the hills, withholding another fall of snow until it suited them to drop it on the shivering village. One day, the boys buttoned themselves into their warmest coats, jammed on their fur hats, and set out to bring home a Yule log, because the time of the mid-winter feast was fast approaching. Remi swung the ax as they wound between the trees, slashing at snow to warm his muscles; of the two, he had the best eye for a good tree and for where to cut. Dara walked at his side, flicking a rope at Remi's legs for the pure annoyance of it.

"You do that one more time and you'll be sorry."

"Why? What're you going to do?"

"You'll see...*Dara!*" Remi made a grab but Dara danced away, snapping and feinting, laughing out loud as Remi lost his footing and fell sideways into a deep drift. Still laughing, he reached out an arm and hauled his lover to his feet and dusted him down.

"You're lucky I didn't chop my foot off," Remi complained, struggling for a little in Dara's arms.

Dara kissed his mouth. "Think I wouldn't love you if you lost a foot?"

"Would you?"

"Yes." He slid his hand into Remi's coat. "Might not love you if you lost *this*, though."

"It's all you love me for, isn't it?" Remi asked, pushing into his palm.

"Mmm."

"Don't get it out, it'll freeze solid."

"I'd better not, then, had I?" Dara tilted his head and kissed him again, walking him backward toward an enormous pine. "I'll just do it like this. Nice and warm under your coat."

The deep silence of the forest held, broken only by Remi's moans and Dara's fast breathing as he stroked and caressed, feeling the hot flesh grow even harder as it readied to release. But suddenly, startling Remi, he stopped and jerked his mouth away from Remi's chilly cheek.

"What? What is it?"

"I'm not sure." Dara looked around. Nothing. There was nothing there, nothing but silence and the lowering sky and the countless trees, immense under their glittering palls of snow. He returned his mouth to Remi's puzzled face and his hand to his cock, but his eyes darted suspiciously from tree to tree. "For a moment, I thought..."

"Don't think. Just do it, make me—oh, oh, yes, like that."

But when, moments later, Remi cried out and his hot seed spurted onto the snow, Dara's flesh was crawling. Something had been watching them, he was sure of it. Dark eyes. Black eyes. Black eyes...wanting.

Even for two strong young men, the weight of the log made the return journey difficult going and needles of snow had begun to hiss through the gaps in the trees. They bent their shoulders to the wind and hauled and sweated, cursing as the log threatened to upend as it bumped and jammed on hidden hummocks. Hauling at the front, Dara turned as he felt Remi drop his end.

"What's the matter?" He slithered back to where Remi stood, bent at the waist, rocking, his hands covering his face.

"My eye, there's something in my eye."

"Let me see, move your hand, let me see."

"No, leave it—no, Dara!"

Dara stepped away and watched Remi slowly drop his hands and blink away tears.

"It's gone."

"What was it?"

"It felt like ice, ice stabbing my eye."

"Come on, let's get home." Dara picked up the rope and glanced at the sky. "It's going to come down hard tonight."

❖

Warm and snug under a goose-feather quilt, Dara ran his toes up and down Remi's calf. "My turn," he murmured, kissing his shoulder, "in case you'd forgotten."

But to Dara's astonishment, Remi shrugged away. "Not tonight."

"Is your eye still hurting? Want me to kiss it better?"

"Don't, Dara. Leave me alone. I'm tired."

The two had slept together since they were toddlers, fretful and whiny if kept in their own beds. Under the eaves of one cottage or the other, skinny legs entwined, they had planned great quests, how they would ride out to explore the mysterious north lands where the ice-dragons dreamed, curled on their hoards of diamonds. Smaller adventures, too, plots closer to home. Dara to distract Eila from her cooking fire, Remi to snatch hot currant bread from the griddle, and both to race away, laughing at her angry yells. Year in, year out, close in each other's arms, they slept. Nearing manhood, they explored the mysterious places of their bodies, their lusty loving bringing pleasure beyond imagining. But this night, for the first time, Remi pushed Dara away.

It was the beginning of a dreadful change. As if a cloud had covered the sun of his soul, Remi became morose, prone to black and spiteful moods. The villagers stared, aghast, when he followed poor, crippled Ada along the lane, lurching and hopping in jeering mockery of her lameness. He heard only the false notes from his little brother's flute and took care to point them out, sneering at the boy when he blushed and hung his head. Until then a tender and passionate lover, he curled his lip, flicking Dara's seed off his hand in disgust rather than licking it up, as he had always loved to do. People avoided him, dreading the cruel remarks that left them red and furious, unable to think of a clever answer. Even Dara recoiled from the lash of his tongue and watched him, hurt and wondering.

One night, Dara woke from an uneasy sleep. He was cold and turned over, wanting Remi's warmth, although he didn't dare tumble joyously on him as he used to do, kiss him until both were breathless, their cocks hard and aching. But Remi wasn't there. Dara pushed off the covers. Moonlight filled the room and it was very cold. Pulling a blanket around his shoulders, he got up and quietly made his way down the stairs, wincing at each squeak of the treads, not wanting to disturb Remi's family. Icy air swirled around his ankles; the door of the cottage stood ajar. He looked out into the dark and his heart stopped in his chest. Remi walked across the yard.

A man stood on the snow, tall, black-haired, black-bearded, and naked but for a long ermine cloak thrown carelessly over one shoulder. His pearly skin glowed but his eyes were dark, hidden in shadow. He wore a great crown of jagged icicles that blazed blue in the starlight and there were snowflakes in his hair. As Dara took a step, the man glanced carelessly at him and instantly Dara's feet were trapped in ice and he could move no farther.

"Remi!"

But Remi seemed to be beyond hearing. He continued to walk away across the snowy ground, and as he approached, the tall figure threw back his cloak. With every ounce of his strength, Dara struggled to move but he was frozen to the spot. As he watched and screamed his lover's name, Remi lifted his face for a kiss, his eyes closing in ecstasy and his hand closing, too, around the figure's erect cock. The long kiss deepened and Remi was lifted in powerful arms, held tightly against the broad chest. Another brief glance released Dara and he took a few staggering steps before falling to his knees. But Remi was gone. As if a candle had been snuffed out, the two had vanished, leaving no trace but Remi's footprints, already filling with snow.

❖

Days passed in fruitless searching. Each evening the men of the village returned downcast and half-frozen, shaking their heads at the waiting women. On the fifth evening, the village headman gripped Dara's shoulder. "He's gone, boy. Nothing more to be done. Get away home, now."

A fist squeezed Dara's heart. Home? There was no home without Remi. As he stood, staring blindly at the ground, old Selina beckoned him from the door of her cottage.

He sat near the fire, steaming as he thawed, and she watched him as he blew and sipped at a bowl of broth. He said, "You know what they think, that he's gone mad and run off. When he…changed, it was the start of his mind going. And they tell me I was dreaming but I wasn't, Old Mother. I know what I saw."

She stirred the fire and firelight danced on her face, brown and wrinkled as a walnut. "That day, the day he began to change, the day you went for the log. Tell me what happened. Leave nothing out."

Listlessly, he told her.

"Is that all of it?" Seeing him shift uncomfortably on the stool, she flapped her hand. "Ach, I'm not interested in that. I know what you two would have got up to in the forest." Her wise old tortoise eyes narrowed. "Think, Dara, *think*."

Frowning with effort, he said, "We saw a hare. Remi fell into a drift. We ate some bread and raisins. He got snow in his eye—"

"What? Snow in his eye?"

"Yes, well, ice. He said it felt like ice. Why?"

"Pass me my shawl, no, not that one, the brown one." She drew it closely around her shoulders and hunched forward. "Listen to me now. Are you listening? Once, long ago, a troll made a toy to amuse its master. This toy was a mirror, but it was no ordinary mirror. It only reflected what was bad and ugly in the world, and everything it showed was hateful. Now, trolls are angry and quarrelsome creatures and they fought over who should give this marvelous gift to their master. As they fought, the mirror fell and it broke into a million pieces, some as small as grains of sand. These pieces were carried away by the north wind and even now they blow about the world, working their mischief. They enter men's eyes and work their way to their hearts and freeze them. These men become like the mirror, cold, hateful."

The broth was finished. Carefully, Dara laid the bowl on the table. The old woman was confused, but then, she was more than ninety. As respectfully as he could, he said, "Old Mother, there are no such things as trolls."

"Is that what you think? But you have met their master."

"Their master?"

"Yes. The one who took Remi. The Snow King."

Dara stared at her.

"It wasn't snow in Remi's eye but a piece of the mirror. Remi is handsome, Dara, and the Snow King chooses handsome young men to be his companions. But they must be made *cold*. When Remi is cold enough, all warmth gone, the Snow King will enter him and fill him with his icy seed. And then..."

"He will be dead..."

"As good as. Lost to you forever."

Dara got to his feet. "I'll find him. I'll find him, old woman, and bring him back. Tell me where I must go."

"You'll never find him—"

"Tell me where to go!"

She sighed and sucked her gums and looked into the fire. "North."

❖

Twilight was falling fast as Dara left the track and pushed through a tangle of undergrowth into the forest. He needed to find shelter for the night, and if the snow was as deep under the trees, the cutting wind was less. There would be a hollow trunk somewhere and if he was lucky, it would be dry and full of blown leaves. He staggered a little as a bramble clawed him, because he was famished and weakened by days of hard travel. At first, his pack full to bursting with bread and juicy sausage, his pocket full of rabbit snares, he had made good time, striding strongly mile after mile along snowy roads, but his food was long gone. This far north, there were no longer kindly villagers to press hunks of black bread into his hand, a few withered apples, and for two days he had caught no rabbits. He leaned against a silver birch and unshouldered his pack. *I will die*, he thought, *if I don't get something to eat. I'll rest for a while until my legs stop shaking and then I'll see if I can find a few berries, or a tree mushroom.* Memories of his mother's hot meat pies tormented him, and the thought of Annalena's sweet nut cakes hurt his growling stomach, but he shook them away and reached again for his pack. As he straightened, he thought he saw a light between the trees. At first he thought it might be a will-o'-the-wisp but the light was steady, not dancing. Hunger forgotten, he wound his way between gnarled oaks, becoming more curious as the light grew stronger. Suddenly, he stopped, staring in bemusement. There, in a wide clearing, it was a bright summer day. There was a cottage and a young man stood at its door. A simple blue garment was tied loosely around his hips, and ears of wheat threaded through the yellow curls that tumbled around his handsome face.

"Welcome," he said, smiling. His voice was rich and mellow and his greeting seemed to Dara the most wonderful thing he had ever heard.

Dara stumbled forward and was bathed in golden light. Fine grasses and clover were soft under his sore feet. Flowers grew in profusion around the walls of the cottage, peonies, poppies and roses, yellow hollyhocks and white foxgloves, fluttering with butterflies. Sun glinted off a deep pool, dotted with water lilies, and the air was warm and full of the scents of summer. "What is this place?" he murmured, staring in wonderment.

"Why, this is my home. This is where you may rest for a little while. My name is Mehefin, and you are Dara, I think. You must eat and rest, but first take off your wet clothes and let the sun warm your skin."

As he took the outstretched hand, it seemed to Dara that warmth spread through him, filling his belly, thawing his frozen feet and numb legs. The heat spread to his cock and it rose, swelling under his breeches. He blushed, but the young man passed gentle fingers over his cheek.

"Ah, Dara, I know what you feel. Don't be ashamed, life is returning to you. You're young and strong and alive. But if you prefer, I'll leave you. Undress. Lie in the sunshine. Sleep."

His clothes in a sodden heap, Dara stretched out on a patch of clover. Heat caressed his back. The sweet scent under his cheek and the thrum of bees lulled him. His confusion and wonderment slipped away and he slept.

❖

"Good afternoon. Did you sleep well?"

A soft bed. Softer pillows. A thin coverlet of white wool across his legs. Dara blinked at golden motes of pollen swirling in shafts of sunshine. Tendrils of some tender vine crept through the window and trembled in a gentle breeze. Mehefin was sitting on the edge of the bed.

"Yes, I thank you. But, please…who are you? What is this place? How can it be summer here?"

Instead of answering, he indicated a platter at his side. There was a crisp loaf of barley bread, a wheel of cheese, and dishes of butter and honeycomb. "Eat slowly, a little at a time."

Dara needed no second urging. He had never been so hungry in his life, but he remembered his manners and offered the platter to the beautiful young man, who regarded him calmly, and smilingly shook his head. Once his first savage hunger was satisfied, Dara lay back against the pillows. He realized with a shock of surprise that his body was clean, the dirt and grime of his journey washed away before he was put to bed. Again he asked, "Who are you?"

"I am Mehefin."

"Are you magic? Is this place magic?"

"Magic?" He cut a slice of honeycomb. "Open." He slid the dripping morsel into Dara's mouth and thoughtfully licked his fingers, one by one. "Yes, for you I'd be magic, I suppose. But I'm as much a part of this lovely earth as you." Seeing Dara's brow crease, he patted his knee. "Let's say for now I am magic. And you've seen other magic, I think."

Remi. A wave of guilty horror washed through Dara. Lying here in idleness, filling his belly, while his beloved Remi— "I must go. I must leave now. I thank you but I must go now."

"Wait. Shh, now, wait."

In his panic, he had thrown off the coverlet and was bare under Mehefin's gaze. Unaccountably, despite his frantic anxiety, he stiffened slightly.

Mehefin raised serene blue eyes from his cock. "You've done well to come this far. But your love and your passion for Remi will be as nothing when set against the Snow King. Midwinter, and he in his kingdom? He's at his most powerful, Dara."

"How did you know? How do you know all this? *Who are you?*"

Mehefin raised his arms in a salute to the sun. "I am the summer, he is the winter. We are the same, but opposites. I've known you and Remi since you were born, for you were born at my time, July children. I've watched you grow, Dara. I know all that has happened. I know all that will happen if you don't have my help."

"You'll help me?"

"As far as I can. I can't draw too near his icy kingdom, for this is his time, not mine. But just as chill winds blow sometimes in June, so January days can feel a little sunshine. You may take a little summer into mid-winter. Take something of me into the frozen kingdom to help thaw your Remi's heart."

"Something of you?"

"Yes. My seed."

A great wash of color rose in Dara's cheeks.

"Given and willingly taken. Yours and mine, mingled. Carried inside you, this would be a powerful charm against the cold. Will you let me help you in this way?"

Do with you what I've only done with Remi? It would be a betrayal of our love and he would surely despise me for it. But then, without it, there will be no Remi. He took a deep breath. "Yes." He lay back against the pillows. "Please. Yes."

"I am weakest at mid-winter, but some little magics remain." Mehefin reached to his hair and pulled out an ear of wheat. "When you find Remi, bring him out of the palace, out onto the lake. Hold this and call for me and I'll hear." With a deft movement, Mehefin unfastened his garment. Tall, his body as supple and strong as a new shoot surging from the earth, he looked down at Dara, his eyes darkening and his cock rising as Dara swallowed hard and bravely opened his legs. "It needn't be a torment for you. Take me and enjoy me." He lay alongside Dara and gathered him in his arms, and strength flowed from him along with each deep kiss. Dara gave a little moan of delight, and desire for Mehefin brought his cock up, hard and eager. Dipping his finger into the dish of honeycomb, Mehefin touched it between Dara's legs, where it became sweet oil that opened him and softened the guarding ring of muscle. "Now, sweetheart." He kissed Dara's brow in blessing and entered him in one smooth, swift glide. The bliss of it made Dara cry out in astonished joy and he clutched Mehefin tightly and buried his face against his throat.

Steadily Mehefin thrust, sending pleasure to every part of Dara's body, and soon Dara felt his climax grow. He groaned and stiffened but when the climax racked him, there was no gush of seed. As if he had been brought back to the start again, the pleasure grew and Mehefin murmured and held him until he cried out a second time. But still, there was no seed. He raised his face for Mehefin's glorious kiss, wondering if he would die from the pleasure of his cock, but just as his climax took him for the third time, he felt the scalding burst of seed, thick and abundant inside him, and his own seed flooded his belly. The last thing he heard before he sank into an immensity of blue was Mehefin's urgent whispering. "Bring him to me. I will wait."

❖

Dara found himself standing at the edge of a lake, a vast expanse of rippled ice that stretched as far as the eye could see. In the center of the lake, the water had fountained far into the sky and frozen to form the walls and towers and pinnacles of a palace of ice that glittered gorgeously under a pale sky. A knifing wind skittered fine drifts of snow along the surface of the lake, but Dara was warm. His clothes were dry and even his broken boots were mended. He sent a thought of passionate thanks to kindly Mehefin and he seemed to feel a faint answering glow deep in his belly. Little magics, but enough. Enough to bring him here. Enough to give him the strength he needed to bring Remi out of the cold. He set his shoulders and took a first step onto the ice.

The palace loomed above him, colorless, but the ice flickering blue and lilac and gray as clouds scudded across the sun. He passed under a portcullis hung with icicles like spears and shuddered at the thought of one dropping to slice through him. A courtyard opened, ringed with several arched doorways. All was empty, all was silent. Nothing moved in that desolation of ice except his breath, rising like smoke in the frigid air. He walked through the tallest of the archways, through chamber after chamber, each larger than the last. Ahead of him, light streamed through a window carved into the shape of a snowflake and fell on a low dais. Silent and unmoving on his throne of granite and iron, the Snow King watched Dara approach. Pale as marble, his lips bloodless, a coronet of woven ice on his dark hair, Remi stood naked at the side of the throne.

"*Remi! Oh, Remi!*" Dara's heart gave a great leap of joy and he made to run forward, but a lazy lift of the Snow King's finger manacled his ankles in ice. "Oh, Remi."

A glacier grinding on rock, the Snow King's voice echoed in the chamber. "Why, what have we here? An unexpected visitor."

Dara's legs shook and his mouth was dry with fear but he gathered all his courage. "Please. I have come for Remi."

The Snow King sniffed the air. "I can smell it on you, his seed festering in you, the stench of the summer fool. You come here, stinking of him, and ask for…Remi? Is that his name? Summer, summer…time of rot and steaming decay, plague and pestilence breeding in sewers. Rats and flies and maggots. Look around you. Here it is cold, pure and white and clean. Cold preserves, keeps all things young and unchanging. But you want to take him back to *summer*."

Dumbfounded by the malice in his voice, Dara could only stand, trembling, and will Remi to look at him. "I love him."

"You love him." The Snow King stroked his beard and Dara caught a glimpse of sharp teeth between the full lips. "Were you loving him when you lay with Mehefin and took his rancid seed into you? Let us say that you do. But does he love you? Shall we see? Touch him. Put your hands on him."

A glance released Dara's feet and he stumbled forward, up the broad steps that led to the dais. Remi turned his gaze on him and looked him up and down.

"Remi, beloved." Dara touched the curve of his shoulder and the skin was cold, like a dead thing. There was no flicker of response on Remi's beautiful face.

"How disappointing for you. Perhaps you're not touching him as he likes. Like this." The Snow King reached out and laid his hand flat on Remi's belly, and the moan of pleasure that Remi gave then made the hairs stand up at the back of Dara's neck.

"Dear one, we have a guest. Time enough to play later. Oh, come, come," he drawled, seeing Dara's stricken expression, "no need for such sniveling." He leaned back and spread his legs. The black hair at his groin was spangled with frost above his magnificent cock and Dara felt a stab of terror at the thought of it piercing Remi, leaving him torn and bleeding. "All is not lost. Let's play a game, a wager. He is cold but not yet cold enough for me to enjoy. A chance remains for you to win him back. A small chance, I grant you, but a chance, because I keep my promises, unlike Mehefin." The Snow King's hateful mocking grin faded and the cruelty of his nature was revealed in his stare. "You love him, he loves you. So you say. It should be easy, then, for him to say your name. Just say your name. If he does, you may take him. If he does not...you will remain here, and when he is utterly cold, you will hold him for me as I enter him. Winter seed. Yes. His seed will be...exquisite."

Dara turned in anguish to Remi and took hold of his hand. "You remember me, beloved? Yes, yes you do."

As if he was speaking from a great distance, Remi said. "I remember...someone pawing at me. There was sweat dripping on my back, and I was dirty, all sticky with seed. Someone was mewling and whining in my ear, always wanting to touch me. I could never rest."

"Remi, no, it wasn't like that! We loved, Remi, because we love each other—Remi, please, *please* look at me. Remi, say my name!"

But Remi gave a little frown and turned a blank face to the Snow King.

Mehefin had lied. There was no strength in him to fight the power of the cold. He was carrying the seed of the summer in his belly but it was no charm, it would work no magic. It was nothing but proof of his foolishness and Mehefin's treacherous lust. A howl broke from his throat and he threw his arms around Remi and held him with all his strength. He began to cry, hot tears running down his cheeks and falling onto Remi's indifferent back.

"You lose the wager," said the Snow King. "Release him."

"Please, I beg you, just—"

"Release him or I will freeze you both where you stand!"

Dara knew despair then, the destruction of all his hope. "Then freeze us. Without Remi, I am dead anyway. Let us die together."

"Dara?"

His head whipped up. Remi was studying his own hand. He touched his chest and his palm came away wet with Dara's tears.

"Dara."

"Oh!" He pulled Remi back into his arms and kissed him wildly, his hair, his cheeks, his mouth. He tore off his coat and wrapped it around him. Quickly, quickly out! Out of the palace, away from the Snow King's grim and baleful stare. Dara picked Remi up and carried his shivering weight through chamber after chamber until they staggered under the portcullis, out onto the lake.

"Dara, I can't. Let me down."

"Yes, you can! Hold on to me!" Dara felt in a pocket of his coat and his fingers closed on an ear of wheat. Raising his face to the sky, to the hazy moon and the first dim stars, he called out with every ounce of his strength. And Mehefin heard.

❖

"Give him to me."

Dara fell to his knees and let Remi slip down on to the soft clover lawn. "Is he dead? Is he dead?" In his agony, Dara bit at his knuckles. "Use your magic! Make him well!"

Mehefin passed his hands lightly over Remi's chest. "He's near death."

"What must we do? What can I do?"

"Dara, listen to me. Your tears freed him from the ice. Only your tears could have done this. But now...he is very cold. He is cold inside, Dara, and no magic of mine will warm him. You must do it. You must love him. Fill him with your seed and mine. The charm against the cold, do you remember? Pour your warmth and your strength and your life into him."

"Yes!" Dara pulled off his clothes and threw them aside. He stretched out over Remi and kissed his pale lips and pushed his limp cock between Remi's legs. Mehefin made a sign in the air and suddenly Dara was hard, hard and moving easily in sweet oil, fragrant with the scent of lilacs. So cold inside, but this was his beloved Remi, so he moved with ardor, and kissed again, whispering into his mouth. Remi gave a gasp and his eyes fluttered open. Slowly, slowly, he raised his legs and wrapped them around Dara's thrusting hips. With a shout of triumph, Dara felt his seed gush and he held still, locked in Remi, so that all of the hot flow stayed inside. Remi shuddered once and his own seed came, a flood on his belly, thick and warm. Exquisite.

Mehefin was sitting on his heels, smiling down at them. "The year is on the turn. The thaw will come soon and your way home will be easier. Until then, stay. Rest, build your strength. Love each other. Enjoy each other. But now I must visit my beehives." In one lithe spring, the Summer King rose to his feet. He threw a little bunch of daisies on them that clung to their damp skin.

Remi raised himself on one arm. Blushing a little, he said shyly, "Thank you."

"You are welcome."

❖

Dara and Remi lived a long and happy life. They were never apart again, not even for a day. At times, at dead of winter, when the north wind blew, Remi was troubled by bad dreams and cried out, but then Dara held him and comforted him until he drifted back to sleep, safe and warm in his lover's arms.

Victoria Oldham (victoria-oldham.co.uk) is a full-time lesbian-fiction editor and erotica writer. She lives in England with her partner and is working on a doctorate in creative writing. Her work can be found in various anthologies, including *Women of the Dark Streets*, *She Shifters*, and *Girls Who Bite*.

This story is based on "Little Red Riding Hood."

Riding Red
Victoria Oldham

A twig snapped behind her and Red spun, her pulse racing.
She walked the packed dirt path all the time, but over the last few weeks, she felt like she was being watched. Which was absurd, since plenty of people walked the narrow forest path to get to Grandmother's House at night, and folks were always watching one another. But today she was the only one there, since it was too early for the patrons to start arriving. Late-afternoon shadows blanketed the forest, dappled sunlight creating artful designs on the dirt. She gripped the black leather bag with her change of clothes for the evening shift more tightly, glad for its heft in her hand.

A flash of black, a glint of silver in her periphery…she turned, but it was gone, vanished among the pines. She pulled the hood of her red leather jacket closer to her face and hurried. There hadn't been anything larger than a fox in the forest for decades, but that didn't mean there wasn't something big out there now. She hurried, straining to hear anything unusual. When she made it into the clearing she breathed a sigh of relief. She opened the door to Grandmother's House, the ironically named bondage club of which she was part owner. Set deep in the forest away from prying eyes and neighbors, it had a solid clientele and she worked hard to make sure it was safe. The creepy feeling in the woods diminished as she breathed in the familiar scent of cleaning products and leather.

"Hey, Red. Glad you could make it."

She grinned at her business partner, Goldi. "Just because you practically live here doesn't mean I have to."

Goldi stretched and gave her a wicked grin. "At least I get

all my needs taken care of in one place, and I don't have to go to anyone's home to get my rocks off." She pushed her boobs up in her top and wiggled her eyebrows.

Their banter continued as they got the club ready to open. They made a habit of checking every piece of bondage furniture to make sure it wasn't damaged. It wouldn't do to have someone strapped down and get a splinter or be cut by a loose screw. The bar was stocked and they were relaxing when the first guests began to arrive. Within hours the club was bouncing. Women in every state of dress filled the room, pressed shoulder to shoulder in the main bar area, dancing to the heavy bass. On the main stage a couple was giving a demonstration of intricate suspension bondage. All the play rooms were in full use too.

The door opened, letting in some of the full moon's light. For an instant a woman was silhouetted against the night, a featureless dark shadow, still and imposing. The door closed and Red shook her head at the sudden tremor of anticipation in her stomach. She saw plenty of women here, and few ever struck her fancy. The really butch ones that made her wet were few and far between, and when they did come along, they were too often posers who demanded submission simply because they thought it was their right, not because they'd earned it.

The hairs on the back of her neck rose and a shiver slithered down her spine, making her cold in the hot-red leather that was her trademark. She looked around, but no one seemed to be watching her or trying to get her attention. Just as she was about to turn away she thought she caught a glimpse of unnaturally green eyes, but her attention was diverted by someone asking for another bottle of whip cleaner, and she quickly forgot about it.

The night finished as it always did. Couples and groups finished playing in the early hours of the morning after last call. They stumbled out into the forest to take the long path back to the distant car park. Red shook her head when a group of Dommes herded a group of bottoms out the door on their hands and knees, leather paddles and riding crops driving the women on their knees into the night. She loved the power exchange, the giving and taking of sex by people who knew exactly what they wanted and needed. When they'd first opened the club, she had always found a willing play partner at the end of the night to take the edge off, but over time it became a job like any other...well, not exactly like any other, but a job, nonetheless, and many nights she was too tired for play time of her own. The thought of the woman in silhouette occurred to her and she hugged herself. She scanned the forest around the clearing, but the sound of women's laughter was far off and the club area was empty now. She went back in, finished sorting out the money, and waved to Goldi, who was making use of the empty main stage with a particularly beautiful blond woman whose bottom was already striped from the thin rattan cane in Goldi's hand. Goldi waved and turned back to the upturned bottom in front of her. She ran her free hand over it before raising the cane again. It sliced through the air with a hiss and then cracked against the welted ass.

Red sighed, suddenly feeling more alone than she had in a long time. She shrugged on her coat and headed out into the night, remembering the feel of a strong hand on her back as someone painted stripes of loving discipline along her skin. It had been too long.

Once on the forest path, she breathed deeply and stopped to look at the stars. This far away from the city, it felt like she could reach out and touch them, just gather them up in her palms like so much hot glitter. The full moon gave off enough light so the path was clear and bright. An eerie howl shattered the night and goose bumps covered her flesh. Nothing that sounded like that should be in these woods. She turned to go back to the club, figuring she could wait until Goldi was done and they could walk to their cars together. Hell, she would sleep on one of the spanking benches if she needed to. But walking through the forest alone wasn't going to happen.

Before she took two steps, someone stepped out of the trees and onto the path in front of her, backlit by the moon. She knew it was the same woman she'd seen silhouetted in the bar. She was tall, at least six feet, and broad shouldered. Black leather pants hugged muscular legs, and the white T-shirt pulled taut over her ripped arms and flat stomach. But more than anything, it was her eyes that made Red stumble backward. They were an earthy green, like new grass on a spring day. And they were focused intently on Red as she approached, slowly, like an animal stalking its prey.

Red took a few steps back, then turned and started to run. But before she could think to scream, the woman was behind her, on her, her arms wrapped tightly around Red's waist as she lifted her from the ground and carried her off the path and into the forest. Red kicked and squirmed, but the woman was insanely strong.

"Put me down, you oaf."

The woman laughed and the sound sent a thrill to Red's core. It was deep, husky, sexy. The woman set her down in front of a massive pine, using her grip on Red's waist to turn her and pin her against it with her own hard body. Red kept her hands on the woman's shoulders, but she wasn't sure if it was to push her away or keep her in place. Something about her was dark, dangerous, and called to that place in Red that needed pain's promises. Would she stop if Red said no? Did she want her to? She felt the hard body against her and thought of the rattan cane slicing through the air at the club. Saying no wasn't an option. She wanted what this woman was offering.

The woman's hands slid down Red's arms to her hands and pulled her arms over her head. She held both wrists in one massive hand, and with the other she dragged sharp nails over Red's exposed stomach. When Red hissed with pleasure, the woman's strange eyes darkened.

"I want you, little Red. I want to do things to you."

The stranger's breath was hot in her ear, and suddenly Red couldn't think of anything she wanted more than "things" done to her.

"We can go back to the club," Red said, arching her back to make contact with the hard body pressed against her, the feel of her pinned wrists making her wet. The bark of the tree dug into her skin, the hands holding her as hard as the tree at her back. Her body was on fire with need.

That strange, eerie wail sounded through the night again, and the woman jerked away, her eyes narrowed as she looked into the forest. It didn't come again, though, and she pushed her thigh between Red's legs and kissed her roughly, her tongue seeking immediate entrance. She pulled away and her breathing was ragged, her chest heaving as though it took effort to control herself. The look on her face was inscrutable, though her jaw was clenched tightly and Red could feel the bowstring tension in the arms pinning her to the tree. The unearthly cry shattered the night, and the woman swore. She let go of Red's wrists and backed away.

"Not tonight, little Red. But I'll be back for you." And with that she turned and loped off into the forest, silently swallowed up by the shifting shadows of the night.

Red slid down the tree, baffled, turned on, and irritated all at once. *What the hell just happened?*

❖

Another week went by, and Red grew more convinced that she had imagined the whole damn thing that moonlit night. Grandmother's House continued to be packed every night, but her mysterious hot stranger hadn't made another appearance. She had given up, chalking it up to just another weird thing that club owners sometimes had to deal with. But the experience had left her aching, hot and desperate for a session of rough, sweaty sex. Being around women pushing past taboos and shattering boundaries every night of the week didn't help.

She made the rounds, making sure no one had been forgotten and left tied up somewhere. Goldi looked up from between the legs of a woman bound spread-eagle in one of the play rooms, thick black rope attached to her wrists and ankles. "Want to play?" She wiggled her fingers and held up a bottle of lube.

Red considered it for a moment. She had played with Goldi plenty over the years, and they both enjoyed it, although they never had a real connection. The bound woman was attractive, but Red decided she didn't feel like being a second tonight. "Thanks, but no. Enjoy."

Red locked up and headed to her car. She hadn't heard that

freaky animal call since the night of her strange encounter, and the feeling of being watched had disappeared. She sighed. She could still feel the stranger's hands on her wrists, the feel of her strong body, the smell of leather...and something she couldn't place. Something musky, warm.

She was at the densest part of the path, just about to cross the little stone bridge, when she felt it. That same feeling. She stopped and closed her eyes, and when arms slid around her from behind, she leaned back against the body she'd been fantasizing about. Leather, musk, strength. The combination was heady and her knees went weak with desire.

"Have you thought about me, little Red?" The woman's mouth was against her neck, her teeth grazing the sensitive skin under her ear.

"I thought I'd dreamed you." She felt stupid for saying it, but when the woman's hands slid up her stomach to cup her breasts, all thought fled.

"You couldn't dream up something like me." Her teeth were sharp, her hands insistent as they worked their way under Red's leather halter top. "I've thought of nothing but you. How I want to get inside you and hear you come."

Red moaned as the woman pinched her nipples, making them rock hard. "Yes. God, yes. Should we go back—"

"No. I want you here, in the open." She walked them forward, her hands never leaving Red's breasts. Red looked down and saw that the woman was barefoot, and her feet were firmly planted in the soft dirt at the edge of the bridge. The woman pressed her against the little bridge wall, bending her forward over it and pressing her hips against Red's ass.

Red pressed back. The woman was packing, hard evidence of what was in store. She moaned, ready, and lifted her arms to allow the woman to pull her top off. The cool night air caressed her hot skin and she shivered. Sharp nails slid from her shoulders to the top of her ass, thin lines of fire left in their wake. For a split second she thought about the fact that she was naked, out in the open. Anyone could see them, could see her, being taken. Somehow it was completely different from the public scenes she'd been involved in at the club. Here, under the stars, she was more vulnerable than she'd ever been when tied up in front of a group.

"You're so beautiful, Red. So fucking hot. I've wanted you for so long."

She cried out when the woman twisted her nipples, pulling and pinching them hard. "Please. Fuck, take me." The woman grew still, her hands holding tightly to Red's naked waist.

"Say it again." Her mouth was hot in the hollow between her neck and shoulder, and Red needed it, wanted so much more.

"Please fuck me," she whispered.

It was all the invitation the woman needed. She cupped Red's breasts, and her teeth sank into Red's neck. She bit hard and endorphins took over Red's mind. The stranger let go of Red's breasts but kept her mouth in place, biting, sucking, driving Red insane with desire. She quickly unzipped Red's leather pants and peeled them down, her hands sliding over Red's heated flesh until they stopped to cup her wet center.

She placed her hand on the base of Red's back to hold her still and knelt behind her. She yanked Red's boots and pants off, then pulled the black thong aside so she could run her tongue over her wetness. Red held on to the wall, feeling more dirty bent over a wall in the forest than she ever had in her own club. When the woman pushed her fingers deep inside her, she let herself go. The woman fucked her quickly and deeply from behind, covering her back with bites as she pressed hard against her, owning Red's body with powerful strokes. Just when Red thought she was going to come, when her thighs were shaking and she couldn't hold off any longer, the woman pulled out and spun her around. She lifted Red to sit on the wall and dropped to her knees in front of her. Pressing her legs wide, those strange green eyes on Red's face, she pushed her tongue into Red's cleft, licking a hot line to her clit before going back down for more. She devoured her, and Red watched as she closed her eyes and seemed to lick every drop of wetness from her. She kept Red on the edge, circling her clit, pushing inside her, only to pull away when Red got close. Red held on to the wall, her fingernails breaking against the stone, the water from the creek a few feet below gurgling past.

    She stood and kissed Red deeply, her tongue hot and demanding. Red tasted herself in the heat of the woman's mouth and drank it in, sucking it from her. When Red heard a zipper rasping down, she pulled back to see the large fleshed-colored dildo in the woman's big hand, her expression a challenge. Red slid to her knees on the hard stone, clasped her hands behind her back in a classic submissive pose, and licked the length of the dildo. The woman's head fell back, and she gripped Red's hair as she fucked her mouth, deep and slow. Red took her time, licking and sucking, wrapping her lips around the head and taking it deep in her mouth while she held the base firmly and pressed it against the woman's body. She looked up and met the woman's lust-filled gaze and sucked hard, allowing her eyes to flutter closed. There was something about sucking a butch's cock, taking that basic piece of kit and making her crazy with it. The woman fucked her mouth harder, faster, her grip in Red's hair tight as she pumped her hips.

    The woman yanked her up by her hair and the pain caused a rush of pleasure, making her dizzy, bringing with it a haze of need so intense all she could see was the woman in front of her. She sat on the wall and Red lowered herself onto the woman's butch-cock. It filled her and she sighed happily. The woman wrapped her arms tightly around her. "Ride me, Red. Ride me the way you want to."

    Red did as she was told, rising and falling, the woman's strong embrace giving her leverage and keeping her secure as she followed orders.

    A shaft of moonlight cut through the trees and fell on the woman's face. Red was riding hard, rising and falling, and the woman's intense gaze was locked on her face. At that moment, in the moonlight, Red saw what she hadn't before. The unearthly eyes, the sharp incisors, the feral look of a predator. The woman she was riding wasn't just a woman. She was something else, something more. And whatever that was called out to Red, not as something to be feared, but as something to be cherished and explored. Something to say yes to.

She felt her orgasm building, the fear and danger of the situation an aphrodisiac.

"Come, baby. Let go. Give yourself to me."

She couldn't have stopped if she wanted to. The pleasure was too intense, the woman's embrace so strong and sure, the desire to please too much a part of her. She rocked on the cock and cried out, arching in the stranger's arms, the feeling of her nipple caught between those sharp teeth sending her even higher.

She collapsed against the woman, who held her close, almost protectively.

"So beautiful, Red. So fucking perfect. My little Red," she murmured against Red's hair, brushing her lips over her head.

"I don't even know your name," Red mumbled against the woman's shoulder, exhausted and satiated.

"Chris. Chris Lupine."

Red raised her head. "Lupine? That's unusual. Doesn't that mean..."

"Wolf."

Red shivered at the look of hunger in Chris's eyes, an expression that did look very wolfish.

"Well, my wolf, how else can I please you?"

Chris's eyes darkened and her smile revealed those strangely sharp teeth.

"Believe me, I'm going to show you. Repeatedly." She lifted Red from her lap and they both moaned as the dildo slid from Red's tight, wet pussy. Chris set her on her feet and tucked the dildo away. "But not tonight." She leaned down and kissed her softly, with such tenderness it brought tears to Red's eyes. "You're mine now, Red. Forever. And I'll come for you, always. I want to devour you, eat you up and make you mine in every way."

Red braced herself against Chris's body, reveling in her dark, hot kisses.

"But not tonight." She backed away, her grin wicked, and disappeared into the forest as silently as she'd come out of it, a wet dream come to life, only to fade with the dawn.

Fletcher and Bass are happily civilized living in Britain. This is their first joint story and they hope it won't be their last.

This story is based on "Sleeping Beauty" and "Snow White."

Bad Girls
Jane Fletcher and Joey Bass

Never had the castle ballroom witnessed such a joyous event. The music was divine. The food was sumptuous. Never had such a good-looking group of guests been assembled. But none could match the beauty of the two brides, nor the handsome gallantry of their princes.

The two newlywed couples led the dancing, as onlookers could not agree who was the more beautiful: Snow White or the newly awoken Princess Aurora. Although a hundred years' beauty sleep surely had given Aurora an unfair advantage. The two princes were tall, firm jawed, and athletic.

The sounds of music and laughter reverberated through the stone walls of the castle, permeating down to the small cold cell in the dungeon.

"Stuck up little Goodie Two-shoes. She's so sugar sweet if you ate her you'd get tooth decay. Prince bloody Charming won't look so handsome when his teeth drop out." The ex-queen paused in her rant, speculating whether the prince ever would eat her stepdaughter. "Never mind, they're not that creative. I bet they'll only do it doggie-style."

"Assuming the prince can ever stop looking at his own reflection long enough."

The ex-queen spun around. "Who's there?" She had not heard the cell of her door open.

The dungeon was dark, but slowly a light blossomed in the corner of her cell, resolving into the shape of a woman.

"Who are you?" the ex-queen asked.

"Someone just as pissed off as you." The figure was now clearly visible. A woman, no longer young but handsome with fine strong features and steely gray eyes. The softest part of her face would have been her lips were they not currently pursed tightly together. "I'm the other aggrieved party. Malcara. And that little brat Princess Aurora was supposed to die, not sleep. Those damn do-gooding fairies just spoil all of my fun."

"Like those dwarfs. I'd like to shove those pickaxes right up their Hi-Ho!"

"Oh, tell me about it. I've had the same thought about those twinkly magic wands. Smarmy little bimbos in their pink tutus. Is that any way for a fully grown fairy to dress?"

"But what are you doing here?" the ex-queen asked, having finished their initial introductions and bonding over their mutual distaste for princesses.

"I wanted to gate-crash the party again, but the ass-kissing bitches and royal farts have put up wards around the ballroom. I hit one at full bippity-boppity and BOOM. I got bounced out to here." Malcara looked around and grimaced. "The dungeons?"

"Yes. They dumped me in here so they can go on their honeymoon, but they're talking about a trial."

"This is no place to put a good-looking woman like you, but I think I can do something about the décor." Malcara snapped her fingers.

The stone walls of the cell shimmered and then took on the aspect of wood paneling. The temperature rose. A thick colorful carpet materialized on the floor, then a table and two-comfy looking chairs. Malcara tilted her head to the side, observing her work, then as an afterthought wiggled her fingers. Candles appeared, along with a bottle of wine and two glasses.

"My, that is handy," the ex-queen said, smiling.

Malcara motioned for her to take a seat. "Be my guest."

Once they were seated, they lifted their full glasses and the ex-queen made a toast. "May both princesses gain two hundred pounds overnight."

"May their tits sag down to their knees."

"And may all their children marry minstrels."

Malcara laughed. "I knew from the moment I saw you that I liked you."

As the bottle emptied, the bonding continued. The conversation ranged from their hatred of presumptuous spoiled royalty, to the crass stereotyping of stepmothers, to the inane stupidity of believing in happily-ever-after, and a few good recipes for poison apples.

"You know, you've had a really raw deal of it," Malcara said as she emptied the last of the wine into their glasses. "No one ever tries to see it from your side. They never even give you a name, do they? You're just the 'evil queen.' Talk about stereotyping." She frowned. "What is your name?"

"Brangomar."

"Tough luck there. I tried to change my name to something more magnificent and malevolent, but some little rat had gone and copyrighted it. May I call you Bran? You can call me Mal."

"Why do people like us never get the pretty little names?"

"Would you want one?"

Bran's eyes narrowed as she thought of the possibilities. "Not really. But someone as attractive as you should really have something better than Malcara."

The fairy blushed faintly. "Do you really think I'm attractive?"

"Oh, yes." Bran had been thinking this more and more strongly as the conversation progressed, and she was sure it wasn't purely due to the wine.

Mal flicked the empty bottle, magically refilling it, and poured them each a fresh glass. Her deliberate actions and her pensive expression suggested she was buying herself a few seconds. She raised her eyes to meet Bran's.

"Being bounced out of the spell like that must have knocked me out," Mal said. "Your voice woke me, but it was so sexy and your scent so alluring that I thought I was dreaming." Cautiously Mal reached across the table to take Bran's hand. "And upon seeing your face, I'm still not sure that I am awake."

The breath caught in Bran's throat. "I...I think I feel the same."

The table between them vanished. Magic can be so useful. Their arms wrapped around each other. Their lips met in a passionate kiss.

Sometime later they broke apart, both breathing heavily.

"I want you," Mal said.

"I want you too, but not here."

"Done!" Mal snapped her fingers.

The dungeon cell with its snazzy new décor vanished. Bran found herself in the most opulent bedchamber she had ever seen, and as an ex-queen she had seen some astonishingly baroque bedchambers. "Where are we, Mal?"

"A little place I like to call home."

Again Mal's arms wrapped around her and they kissed, but this time Bran felt Mal's fingers untying the back of her bodice.

Mal leaned back and stared deep into Bran's eyes. "I want to be wicked with you."

About the Editors

Radclyffe has written over forty-five romance and romantic intrigue novels, dozens of short stories, and, writing as L.L. Raand, has authored a paranormal romance series, The Midnight Hunters. She is an eight-time Lambda Literary Award finalist in romance, mystery, and erotica—winning in both romance (*Distant Shores, Silent Thunder*) and erotica (*Erotic Interludes 2: Stolen Moments* edited with Stacia Seaman and *In Deep Waters 2: Cruising the Strip* written with Karin Kallmaker). A member of the Saints and Sinners Literary Hall of Fame, she is also an RWA/FF&P Prism Award winner for *Secrets in the Stone*, an RWA FTHRW Lories and RWA HODRW winner for *Firestorm*, an RWA Bean Pot winner for *Crossroads*, and an RWA Laurel Wreath winner for *Blood Hunt*. In 2014 she was awarded the Dr. James Duggins Outstanding Mid-Career Novelist Award by the Lambda Literary Foundation. She is also the president of Bold Strokes Books, one of the world's largest independent LGBTQ publishing companies. Find her at facebook.com/Radclyffe.BSB, follow her on Twitter @RadclyffeBSB, and visit her website at Radfic.com.

Stacia Seaman has edited numerous award-winning titles, and with co-editor Radclyffe won a Lambda Literary Award for *Erotic Interludes 2: Stolen Moments*; an Independent Publishers Awards silver medal and a Golden Crown Literary Award for *Erotic Interludes 4: Extreme Passions*; an Independent Publishers Awards gold medal and a Golden Crown Literary award for *Erotic Interludes 5: Road Games*; the 2010 RWA Rainbow Award of Excellence in the Short/Novella category for *Romantic Interludes 2: Secrets*, and a Golden Crown Literary Award for *Women of the Dark Streets: Lesbian Paranormal*.

Books Available From Bold Strokes Books

Venus in Love by Tina Michele. Morgan Blake can't afford any distractions and Ainsley Dencourt can't afford to lose control—but the beauty of life and art usually lies in the unpredictable strokes of the artist's brush. (978-1-62639-220-5)

Rules of Revenge by AJ Quinn. When a lethal operative on a collision course with her past agrees to help a CIA analyst on a critical assignment, the encounter proves explosive in ways neither woman anticipated. (978-1-62639-221-2)

The Romance Vote by Ali Vali. Chili Alexander is a sought-after campaign consultant who isn't prepared when her boss's daughter, Samantha Pellegrin, comes to work at the firm and shakes up Chili's life from the first day. (978-1-62639-222-9)

The Muse by Meghan O'Brien. Erotica author Kate McMannis struggles with writer's block until a gorgeous muse entices her into a world of fantasy sex and inadvertent romance. (978-1-62639-223-6)

Advance by Gun Brooke. Admiral Dael Caydoc's mission to find a new homeworld for the Oconodian people is hazardous, but working with the infuriating Commander Aniwyn "Spinner" Seclan endangers her heart and soul. (978-1-62639-224-3)

UnCatholic Conduct by Stevie Mikayne. Jil Kidd goes undercover to investigate fraud at St. Marguerite's Catholic School, but life gets complicated when her student is killed—and she begins to fall for her prime target. (978-1-62639-304-2)

Season's Meetings by Amy Dunne. Catherine Birch reluctantly ventures on the festive road trip from hell with beautiful stranger Holly Daniels only to discover the road to true love has its own obstacles to maneuver. (978-1-62639-227-4)

Myth and Magic: Queer Fairy Tales, edited by Radclyffe and Stacia Seaman. Myth, magic, and monsters—the stuff of childhood dreams (or nightmares) and adult fantasies. (978-1-62639-225-0)

Blackthorn by Simon Hawk. Rian Blackthorn, Master of the Hall of Swords, vowed he would not give in to the advances of Prince Corin, but he finds himself dueling with more than swords as Corin pursues him with determined passion. (978-1-62639-226-7)

Courtship by Carsen Taite. Love and Justice—a lethal mix or a perfect match? (978-1-62639-210-6)

Against Doctor's Orders by Radclyffe. Corporate financier Presley Worth wants to shut down Argyle Community Hospital, but Dr. Harper Rivers will fight her every step of the way, if she can also fight their growing attraction. (978-1-62639-211-3)

A Spark of Heavenly Fire by Kathleen Knowles. Kerry and Beth are building their life together, but unexpected circumstances could destroy their happiness. (978-1-62639-212-0)

Never Too Late by Julie Blair. When Dr. Jamie Hammond is forced to hire a new office manager, she's shocked to come face-to-face with Carla Grant and memories from her past. (978-1-62639-213-7)

Widow by Martha Miller. Judge Bertha Brannon must solve the murder of her lover, a policewoman she thought she'd grow old with. As more bodies pile up, the murdered start coming for her. (978-1-62639-214-4)

Twisted Echoes by Sheri Lewis Wohl. What's a woman to do when she realizes the voices in her head are real? (978-1-62639-215-1)

Criminal Gold by Ann Aptaker. Through a dangerous night in New York in 1949, Cantor Gold, dapper dyke-about-town, smuggler of fine art, is forced by a crime lord to be his instrument of vengeance. (978-1-62639-216-8)

Café Eisenhower by Richard Natale. A grieving young man who travels to Eastern Europe to claim an inheritance finds friendship, romance, and betrayal, as well as a moving document relating a secret lifelong love affair. (978-1-62639-217-5)

Balls & Chain by Eric Andrews-Katz. In protest of the marriage equality bill, the son of Florida's governor has been kidnapped. Agent Buck 98 is back, and the alligators aren't the only things biting. (978-1-62639-218-2)

Because of You by Julie Cannon. What would you do for the woman you were forced to leave behind? (978-1-62639-199-4)

The Job by Jove Belle. Sera always dreamed that she would one day reunite with Tor. She just didn't think it would involve terrorists, firearms, and hostages. (978-1-62639-200-7)